Art of Death

Art of Death

A Mindful Detective book

Laurence Anholt

CONSTABLE

CONSTABLE

First published in Great Britain in 2019 by Constable

1 3 5 7 9 10 8 6 4 2

A CIP catalogue record for this book
is available from the British Library.

ISBN: 978-1-47213-000-6

Typeset and designed by Initial Typesetting Services, Edinburgh
Printed and bound in Great Britain by Clays Ltd, Elcograf S.p.A.

Papers used by Constable are from well-managed forests
and other responsible sources.

MIX
Paper from
responsible sources
FSC® C104740

Constable
An imprint of
Little, Brown Book Group
Carmelite House
50 Victoria Embankment
London EC4Y 0DZ

An Hachette UK Company
www.hachette.co.uk

www.littlebrown.co.uk

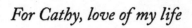

For Cathy, love of my life

Chapter 1

The Happening

On a golden evening in July, two hundred art lovers assembled at an über-hip gallery in Somerset.

Flicking the locks on expensive cars, they meandered through the swaying grasses of the gardens towards a fibreglass pavilion shaped like a giant womb on stilts.

Amongst the chosen ones were critics, London art dealers, stars of music and TV, and friends of the artist.

In the noisy interior of the pavilion, cheeks were kissed, selfies taken, glasses sparkled and bare shoulders gleamed as ponytailed waiters hovered with canapés and champagne. A bewildered group of local dignitaries huddled near the vaginal doorway.

All around the hemispherical walls, grainy film flickered. The cultured throng needed no reminder that the silent footage of a naked and shockingly beautiful young artist – head flung back in ecstasy, entangled in the limbs of her lover – comprised scenes from her infamous student work, *Preconception*.

It wasn't just the film that crackled with electricity; the notorious performance artist, Kristal Havfruen, had been absent from the art scene for many years. A feeling of anticipation permeated the air. If Kristal had chosen tonight to re-emerge, she would do so explosively.

There were rumours of another happening.

Havfruen fans enthused loudly: the woman was a life force ... an artist with the imagination of Frida Kahlo and the theatricality of Marina Abramović. In the shadows, a few sceptics grumbled about a career defined by appropriation. Havfruen was an artist who divided opinion.

'Well, is she here or isn't she?' asked a heavily bearded man in a skirt.

'Of course she's here,' replied his companion. 'After all, Kristal *is* the art!'

At 7.45 precisely, the hubbub in the pavilion was silenced by the silvery tinkle of a spoon on a champagne flute. All eyes turned towards an angular man in a tartan suit with an ironic pencil moustache on his slightly sweaty upper lip.

'Ladies and gentlemen, welcome to the Meat Hook Gallery. For those who don't know me, my name is Saul Spencer. It has been my immense honour to curate this seminal retrospective show. I am sure you are as excited as I am to view the life work of Kristal Havfruen, brought together in one place at long last. I have heard much speculation about whether Kristal will be joining us tonight ... I could tease you a little longer, or tell you that the artist is indeed in the house. In fact, Kristal has spent nearly a month overseeing the breathtaking show we are about to enjoy.

'The exhibition has been laid out in chronological order, and I am thrilled to announce that Kristal has created a major new work exclusively for Meat Hook, which will be revealed in the master gallery as the climax to our evening. This work has been a closely guarded secret, which even I have not been allowed to see. So, a thrilling night lies ahead. If you would kindly follow me, we will make our way to the galleries. Do please take the time to enjoy the gardens, which are looking absolutely splendid tonight, and take care as we pass the ponds.'

Like children following the Pied Piper, the guests fell in behind Spencer's gaunt frame, filing out of the womb, along the gravelled paths towards the galleries. A single dragonfly hovered over the water. Pashminas were tightened against a slight nip in the air, as the last rays of sunshine cast Giacometti shadows across the lawns.

And now they entered the splendid Meat Hook Gallery, an elegant marriage of Elizabethan farm buildings and postmodern glass and steel.

Over their heads a banner proclaimed:

KRISTAL HAVFRUEN – A LIFE

Beside the door, a smaller notice cautioned:

Some exhibits may be unsuitable for minors.
Discretion is advised.

In the first room they were greeted by another film projected across an entire wall. This piece was the sequel to the footage in the pavilion, and although the movie had that slightly yellowing quality that came with age, it still managed to elicit intakes of breath from the guests. This was Kristal's infamous degree show from Falmouth School of Art. It showed a dramatically spotlit mattress on the stage of a densely crowded theatre. On the mattress, a young Kristal Havfruen was struggling in the last stages of labour. With one final convulsion, her ivory body heaved, and a wailing baby slid and tumbled into the world. The first sound that met his tiny ears was applause.

Whatever people thought of Havfruen, no one came close for sheer chutzpah. And of course, the extraordinary thing was that the baby was here ... right here amongst them tonight: Kristal Havfruen's son, Art.

Now aged twenty-four, Art was a successful advertising executive. He had been spotted earlier, dressed in a fashionably crumpled suit and long pointy boots. But where was he now?

At that precise moment, Art was locked in a cubicle in the Meat Hook's unisex toilets, busily hoovering lines of snowy CK1, his current drug of choice – cocaine mixed with a low dose of ketamine.

When he was done, he wiped his nostrils with the back of a frail hand and washed his face at the pig-trough sink. Then, fortified by the sweetly balanced double punch of marching powder and equine tranquilliser, Art Havfruen glided back into the galleries, feeling his groin stir at the sight of the willowy art aficionados around him.

The guests had crowded into a high-ceilinged room, formerly a cowshed, dominated by an early sculptural work. The piece was a full-sized Day-glo tree, festooned with what appeared to be multicoloured apples, but which on closer examination proved to be immaculately rendered resin foetuses. A printed card explained that the work was entitled *Forbidden*

Fruit and that the somewhat withered snake-like entity in a formaldehyde-filled tank amongst the roots was the umbilical cord of Havfruen's newborn child.

Not surprising then that Art Havfruen felt a tad paranoid and queasy as he levitated into a cobbled yard for air. It was a strange and heavy burden to be not just the subject of so many of his mother's famous pieces, but the work itself.

In the courtyard, he was met by another vision of his mother: a gargantuan squatting superwoman named *Pissing Kristal*. The hyper-real effigy showed the artist in her trademark short lacy white dress and oversized cherry-red Dr Marten boots, and it had been ingeniously engineered to emit a never-ending gurgling stream of water.

The Meat Hook guards, who sat discreetly on stools throughout the show, overheard the mumbled observations of the guests – shock, fascination, and mutterings of plagiarism or derivation from artists such as Damien Hirst, Ron Mueck and Yayoi Kusama.

It was no secret that Havfruen did not make the works herself; instead she engaged the services of skilled technicians in workshops and foundries all around the West Country. As she had famously declared to a sceptical Channel 4 arts correspondent: 'Anyone can make, but few dare to dream.'

In the luminous galleries, a group of the artist's family and friends from the early days had reunited for the evening. The years had wrinkled, stooped and whitened, in some cases quite shockingly. Marlene Moss, the former head of painting at Falmouth School of Art, was now as frail as a bird in her wheelchair; pushed in turn by her devoted former students, whom she often described as her children. Notable amongst her protégés was Kristal's husband, Callum Oak, a talented artist in his own right, though far more conventional than his wife. The likeness to their son, Art, was plain to see; Callum was a handsome, curly-haired man, still boyish in his forties. Another former student and lifelong friend of the Havfruen-Oak family was Oliver Sweetman, an ever-smiling ginger giant, who had, by virtue of his ubiquitous presence over the years, become Kristal's assistant and photographer.

The guests proceeded into the older galleries, ancient piggeries, barns and slaughterhouses that had been transformed into airy whitewashed spaces where the eponymous meat hooks still hung. These rooms were crammed with works from Havfruen's middle period. Here were shining tanks in which shockingly lifelike figures floated or dived through amniotic liquid. The model and star of these aquatic tableaus was, in every case, the narcissistic figure of Kristal herself, creepily small or alarmingly large, always in a short lacy white dress and red boots.

Along a corridor, a row of screens showed interviews from arts programmes and archive footage of the artist at work in her studios. Kristal was mesmerising to watch, so assertively articulate that it was easy to forget that English was her second language. But the strange thing about her was that she never smiled. Yes, those green eyes sparkled, but the deliberately smudged lips remained tightly drawn over pearly teeth.

It was a little after 8.30 when the tartan-suited curator, Saul Spencer, paused by the industrial hammered doors of the master gallery. The light here was an insipid yellow, giving him the sinister appearance of a master of ceremonies at a freak show as he waited patiently for the last stragglers to arrive. Then he drew himself on tiptoe and whispered theatrically:

'Ladies and gentlemen, beyond these portals we will discover ... what? Who knows? I certainly do not. Even those who have disparaged Kristal will acknowledge how she plays with our emotions. She is indeed a sculptor of sensations. I have no doubt that something unforgettable awaits. Are you ready, ladies and gentlemen? Then throw wide the gates!'

Behind him, uniformed attendants slid back the well-oiled doors, and Saul Spencer led the feverish crowd into the final room.

The master gallery was a vast, cathedral-like space, high-ceilinged and stone-walled. The art lovers peered about in the semi-darkness. There was only one work here. One dark object positioned carefully on a podium in the dead centre of the room. It was a rectangular glass tank, no bigger than a small fridge.

The onlookers formed a reverential circle. The only sound was a slight sniffing from Art Havfruen, and the trundle of wheels as Marlene Moss was rolled across the flagstones.

And then, in an ear-splitting instant, the silence exploded into the deafening blasts of Beethoven's Choral Symphony. As one, the guests leapt an inch off the floor, but before they could recover, half a dozen laser-bright spotlights converged on the tank.

Above the booming music came the laughs, gasps, cries and sighs of the uneasy audience.

On the sealed lid of the tank sat a gleaming pair of red Dr Marten boots.

Inside the tank floated an ethereal vision of beauty – a shock-ingly realistic model of Kristal Havfruen, suspended delicately in a foetal position. Her green eyes were open wide. Long fingers trailed. Her knees were raised like an Inca mummy, and her slim body was draped in white lace that billowed like a christening gown as she drifted in the amber liquid.

The craftsmanship was astonishing, but what made the piece so deeply unsettling was that, unlike anything she had created before, this image of Kristal was precisely life-sized, showing her as she was now: a forty-three-year-old woman with protuberant bones and subtle wrinkles on her lovely face. And when you looked closely, you noticed that it was not made of rigid resin or fibreglass. Instead, the skin seemed soft, the perfectly crafted limbs waved like delicate tendrils. Her blonde hair flowed and rippled in a shimmering halo.

Some at the back could not see, and they pushed towards the phosphorescent tank.

'Astonishingly lifelike,' muttered a woman.

'Incredibly so,' someone agreed.

'Every pore. Every detail.'

'The crow's feet around the eyes.'

'And is that . . . a trickle of blood from the side of the neck? Do you see?'

And now, as the guests gazed in alarm, a few tiny bubbles burbled from those painted lips, and drifted upwards like a necklace of pearls.

In the shadows, Saul Spencer felt dread creep over him like fog. Frantically he caught the attention of one of his attendants. Raising his little finger and thumb, he mimed a phone, and at the same time mouthed a single, unmistakable word:

'Police!'

Chapter 2

The Clammy Odour of Death

When the phone vibrated in her pocket, Detective Inspector Shanti Joyce was focused on a mouse in a forest.

She had reached the part where the mouse meets the wart-nosed Gruffalo, and she was relieved to notice that her son, Paul, had finally dropped off to sleep.

'This had better be important, Benno,' she hissed, stepping onto the landing and quietly closing the bedroom door. 'I mean, life-and-death important.'

'Looks like both those things, boss.'

Shanti felt her pulse quicken. Part of her had been waiting for this call.

Downstairs in the kitchen she swallowed half a cup of tepid coffee as Benno filled her in on the goings-on at the Meat Hook Gallery. Pulling on trainers and grabbing her jacket, Shanti called to her mum, who was watching TV in the living room.

A few minutes ago, she'd been set for a couple of glasses of Merlot, a bath, an hour's junk TV and a microwave dinner with

Mum, followed by the gentle slide to sleep. But Benno's call had slapped her into wakefulness. She pulled on her seat belt and accelerated out of the quiet cul-de-sac.

The story was bizarre: the body of an artist floating in a tank of formaldehyde at her own private view.

Shanti recalled the first time she'd smelt the heady chemical – standing alongside her fellow rookies on a morgue visit during her training. The corpse was many months old, so the flesh had become rubbery and yellow, but it was the smell that haunted her: a low, invasive stench that crept beyond your nostrils to the very back of your skull, where it lingered for a long, long time. The men had recoiled at the experience, one even passing out. But not Shanti Joyce. She was made of tough stuff, and that steel core was why she'd become a DI in her early thirties.

But that was a long time ago. Before the botched case and the move to the West Country. Before the shit divorce.

Now the determination to set things right seemed to power the Saab 900 along the leafy Somerset roads towards her destination. The satnav showed the gallery just fourteen miles along the A359. She'd be there in nine minutes.

Shanti's eye was caught by the pile of detritus in the footwell – discarded sandwich wrappers, a pair of Paul's football socks, and several folders of unattended paperwork. She winced at the sight. Named Shantala by her parents, she'd been Shanti since she was a little girl, and inevitably, her colleagues back in north London had referred to her chaotic office as Shanti Town.

As she swung into the softly lit car park, she lowered the window to speak to the uniform at the gate.

'Don't let anyone leave or enter, Dunster. Not even Jesus Christ himself.'

'Yes, boss. Paramedics are on their way. What shall I do if Jesus is driving?'

'Listen, Dunster. If you'd prefer a job as a stand-up, that could be arranged.'

She parked alongside four patrol cars and a big van belonging to the HazChem team. She took in the converted farm buildings and a series of incomprehensible sculptures around the courtyard. Then she stepped into the pulsing blue night.

Sergeant Bennett, the man who'd thwarted the encounter between the mouse and the Gruffalo, approached her. Shanti liked Benno. He was an older cop with teenage daughters. One of the few male officers whose eyes didn't circumnavigate her anatomy as they spoke.

'First thoughts, Benno?'

'Weird. With a capital W. But it's doubly tricky because we have a chem spill on our hands. I've evacuated the premises and we've got a couple of hundred guests waiting outside. But until HazChem give the all clear, no one's allowed inside.'

'I need access, Benno.'

'I know that, boss. You'll have to tog up.'

He led Shanti into the Meat Hook gift shop, where a thin man with a pencil moustache was waiting. The faint smell of formaldehyde clung to his tartan suit.

'Saul Spencer,' he said, extending a tremulous hand. 'I'm the curator. This is like a nightmare. I keep thinking I'm going to wake and—'

'The thing about nightmares, Mr Spencer, is they don't smell. This place reeks like Frankenstein's workshop, so let's assume it's the real thing.'

It came out harder than she'd intended, but inside Shanti was morphing from mum to cop, and gallows humour was part of her armour. She followed Benno and Spencer between baffling artworks, and with every step the sinister stench grew stronger.

'The master gallery is through there,' said Spencer, ashen-faced. And then, clutching a paisley handkerchief to his mouth, he retched violently and fled along the corridor like a spindly spider.

A man in a blue hooded suit with fitted goggles and respirator guarded the huge metal doors.

He reached out a gloved hand and handed them each a package of protective clothing. When they were fully togged up, Shanti felt as if she had entered a world of restricted sensations in which communication was diminished and visibility began a few feet from her body.

The HazChem officer checked them both for weak spots around the gloves and tops of their boots. Finally he nodded and hauled back the metal door.

Shanti thought she had seen it all in the old job, but the spectacle made her gasp. Inside the immense room, alien figures moved slowly in the lunar gloom. On a spotlit podium beside an upturned tank, a masked officer was attempting CPR on the limp and dripping body of a woman in a white dress. A pair of red DMs lay in a spreading pool of amber liquid.

Benno tapped Shanti on the shoulder, and when she turned to face him, she saw that he was signing. Two fingers across the throat and a solemn shake of the head meant the same thing in any language – the porcelain woman was deceased.

In minutes, Shanti assumed control. Photos to be taken of the corpse. This area should be cordoned off . . . and that one too. She identified points of entry – a large double door with a ramp for forklifts and wheelchairs, which had already been thrown wide. In addition, there were two fire exits. These she examined and then opened carefully with fingertips, to increase ventilation.

This was the golden hour, in which clues could slip away like blood down a drain.

Outside, the night pulsated like a fairground as more emergency vehicles arrived. On the gravelled area and the lawn beyond, a hundred or more elegantly dressed art lovers stood blubbering and choking like paid mourners at a Roman funeral. In contrast to the selfie-taking crowds that assembled at crime scenes in London, this lot had backed as far as possible from the scene, and some were being treated by first-aiders for streaming eyes or irritable throats.

Gesturing for Benno to join her, Shanti stepped outside and pulled back her hood and respirator. The inside of her suit was like a sauna, and the cool air bathed her lungs.

'Jesus, Benno, any one of these people could be a witness. Look at them wandering all over the place. Is there somewhere we can assemble them and start getting statements?'

'The HazChem guys have given the restaurant the all-clear,' said Benno. 'Shall we put them in there?'

'OK, but obviously they can't go back through the gallery.'

'There's access round the side.'

'Right, see to it, will you, Benno? Get them seated and rustle up some coffee or something. No alcohol. Hand out blankets if they want them. I need ID and initial statements from everyone – no exceptions whatsoever. I want to hear from anyone who noticed anything funny. If anyone took photos, I want their phone. Oh yes, get them to stay off social media if you can. And send someone out to record every reg plate in the car park.'

A tall, curly-haired man huddled in a foil blanket against a wall appeared to be in a particularly bad state. His woollen suit was soaked and his shoulders heaved as several friends tried to comfort him.

'Who's this, Benno?'

'That's the widower, Callum Oak. I took a statement. He was the first person to realise it was Kristal in the tank, rather than another of her weird artworks. He tried to lever the lid but it was tightly sealed. Then he got desperate and hauled the whole thing over and eventually prised open the seal and dragged her out, along with a couple of gallons of formaldehyde. It was grim as hell because he tried to give her mouth-to-mouth; in the process he must have inhaled plenty of the stuff.'

As they spoke, the man was helped into a wheelchair and hauled backwards up some steps to an ambulance, his whole body convulsing with shock and misery. No chance of interviewing him tonight.

As Benno ushered the crowd towards the restaurant, Shanti studied their faces – some visibly distressed as they filed past, others wide-eyed with excitement. As was always the case, a few were actually complaining about the inconvenience. Towards the back of the crowd she noticed the reedy curator, Saul Spencer.

'Quick word, Mr Spencer.'

He looked at her with mournful eyes and nodded.

'I noticed some cameras in the roof of the big gallery; presumably there are more elsewhere. Are they in working order?'

'Yes, there's CCTV in every room of the building.'

'I don't want one millisecond of that footage to be lost. Is that clear?'

'Yes, I'll see to it immediately.'

'Who set up the exhibition?'

'Well, my team were involved with everything except the final work in the master gallery. Kristal demanded absolute secrecy in there.'

'That's weird, isn't it?'

'Not really. Kristal loved a bit of theatre.'

'I gather there was a light show – I mean dramatic music and spotlights. Who operated that?'

'Kristal had everything wired to a motion sensor with a time delay. It was activated as we entered the gallery.'

'OK, I'm trying to compile a list of the key players in this incident. Besides yourself, of course.'

'Am I a suspect?'

'Your word, Mr Spencer. Not mine. Tell me, who else had knowledge of this artwork?'

'Very few people. Let me think . . . There was her assistant, an old family friend named Oliver Sweetman. A big, funny fellow – he's here tonight. Then I suppose her husband, Callum Oak, knew what she was planning.'

'He's just gone off in an ambulance.'

'Yes, poor man. And that's everyone. Except Art, of course.'

'Art?'

'Art Havfruen is Kristal and Callum's son. You've heard of *A Boy Named Art*?'

'You're losing me. I'll come back to you on that. But to be clear – the only people who knew what Kristal had planned in the master gallery were her assistant, Oliver Sweetman, her son, Art Havfruen, and possibly her husband, Callum Oak.'

'That's correct.'

'But presumably someone delivered the glass tank? Tell me about that.'

'I'm sorry, I should have said. We use a specialist art courier called MasterMoves – they're well known in the art world … "Pay the Monet and watch our van Gogh".'

Shanti looked bemused.

'MasterMoves have been running back and forth between here and Kristal's studio for weeks,' continued Spencer. 'They delivered all the artworks for the show. The tank in the master gallery must have been their final delivery; I saw two guys this afternoon unloading a crate on a forklift and I guess the tank was inside. It came down that ramp and into the master gallery though those double doors. The lads from MasterMoves are very quick and efficient. But we can check all of that when we get the footage from the security cams.'

'What about the formaldehyde? When was that added to the tank?'

'Kristal didn't do it like that. The tank would have been delivered already filled to the top and tightly sealed. I know because there are several formaldehyde-filled tanks in the smaller galleries and I supervised their installation. They were all delivered pre-filled, otherwise the insurance would have been impossible.'

At the back of the shuffling crowd, a pasty-faced young man was noisily agitated.

'You can't keep me here!' he was yelling. He wore a rumpled suit and pointy boots, fair hair sculpted into spikes. He was pacing about, gesticulating as if delivering a fiery speech.

'That's the son,' Spencer whispered. 'Art Havfruen.'

'Excuse me, I'd better deal with this,' said Shanti, stepping towards the commotion. 'You need to calm down, Mr Havfruen,' she soothed, although his behaviour was becoming more erratic by the minute.

Even in the half-light, it took her only seconds to realise that the unhealthy-looking lad was as high as an Airbus, with dilated pupils and twitchy behaviour – coke or speed, probably.

Art Havfruen was suddenly in her face. 'Who the fuck do you think you are?' he spat. 'That's my mother in there and I'm being treated like a petty criminal.'

Up close, Shanti noticed white specks around his nostrils and the telltale way he ground his teeth. 'I realise this is terrible for you,' she said, 'but you need to step back and calm down, Mr Havfruen. We are trying to investigate what's happened. I'm sure you'd want that for your mother.'

He began jabbing a finger inches from her eyes. 'You've no fucking idea what I want.'

'Get your finger out of my face, Mr Havfruen.'

The finger moved, only to poke hard at her shoulder. 'You can't tell me what to do.'

The plastic suit impeded her movements, but in a single action, Shanti swung the offending digit and the attached arm behind the boy's back.

'You're hurting me, bitch!' he screamed.

'And you are wilfully obstructing a police officer in the execution of their duty.'

Maybe she had been a little too forceful, but Shanti had an extreme allergy to aggressive men. 'Sergeant Bennett, would you help Mr Havfruen to the restaurant? He can choose between coffee and handcuffs, it's all the same to me.'

'You can't do that,' whined Havfruen.

'Section 89 of the Police Act 1996 says we can,' answered Benno.

There was one last wriggle from Havfruen, an action that bunched his jacket and loosened a plastic pouch from a pocket, which tumbled to the ground.

Shanti glanced down. 'Oh, I think you've dropped something, Mr Havfruen. Let me look after this for you. I'll leave it at Lost Property.'

As Benno guided Art Havfruen firmly by the arm, Shanti crouched to examine the packet, which had spilt a fine cloud of powder onto the gravel. Tapping the torch on her phone, she touched the powder with a fingertip and brought it to her nose. The scene-of-crime team were on their way. She'd mark the packet off and get them to bag it. At least the night was dry. That was something.

The HazChem team had fired up a noisy ventilation system to expel fumes from the gallery. As she pulled on her hood, Shanti caught that smell again – the clammy odour of death.

In the distance, she heard the echoing shouts of the Boy Named Art, arguing about harassment and human rights. She knew that she was in for a long night, but she didn't care. Besides the sleeping eight-year-old in Yeovil, she cared about only two things: getting this investigation right, and rebuilding the reputation of DI Shanti Joyce.

Chapter 3

Beautiful Artistic Murder

By midnight, the scene in the master gallery resembled a Dada theatre production.

The main actors, Shanti and Benno, clad in white paper suits and pull-on overshoes, stood centre stage in earnest conversation beside the upturned tank.

All around them, beneath dazzling arc lamps, SOCO officers crawled like woodlice across the floor. The spillage had been mopped and flushed, and air-monitoring detectors had verified the room as non-hazardous.

The victim, Kristal Havfruen, had been pronounced dead, her dripping corpse zipped inside a body bag and wheeled away on a gurney. The guests' initial statements had all been recorded and they had been allowed to leave.

It seemed that Shanti's plea to keep the events away from social media had fallen on deaf ears. Benno informed her that the startling image of Kristal in the tank had already gone viral, with the hashtag #WhoKilledKristal. Even worse, there had been a number of journalists amongst the guests, and several major publications were now fighting over the story. One way or another, Kristal Havfruen was back in the limelight.

Kristal's son, Art, whose anger had dissolved into pitiful sobs, had been taken to the station to be questioned about possession of an as-yet-to-be-confirmed substance.

Shanti spotted Dawn Knightly, the senior forensic investigator, tapping notes into an iPad in the corner of the gallery. They had only known each other a few months and Shanti was younger by several years, but there had been an instant connection between the two somewhat world-weary female professionals.

'You an art lover, Dawn?'

Knightly, who had a plump, amiable face, was sealing the red Dr Marten boots inside a large polythene bag. 'Prefer the pub if I'm honest, but I must admit this has my full attention. A body in a tank of formaldehyde. Never seen one of those before.'

'Any initial thoughts?'

'The body seems clean apart from slight bruising to the ribcage, which you'd expect after CPR. There are no defensive marks that might have come from fighting off an assailant. But I found one unusual thing . . .'

'Oh yes?'

'There's a crude puncture wound on the side of the neck. Looks like a botched hypodermic job.'

'That's interesting. And any clues in the room?'

Knightly lifted the bag. 'These boots were placed on top of the tank – part of the artwork, so I'm told. Normally a glass tank would be ideal for prints, but there were none except where Oak grabbed it to push it over.'

'From what I've heard, this Kristal Havfruen was some kind of . . . what did you call her, Benno?'

'A performance artist, boss.'

'Right. Like a performer without the talent.'

'The great and good assembled here might disagree.'

Shanti raised an eyebrow. She'd walked around the other rooms. Seen the Day-glo tree and the umbilical cord in a tank. The floating figures and the videos that looked like borderline porn. For God's sake, who would be taken in by this stuff? It was the Emperor's new clothes, wasn't it? From what she could gather, the artist, Kristal, had spent her life making art about herself. A thought occurred to her.

'Bear with me, Dawn, but given the woman's self-obsession, how do we know she didn't top herself? Wouldn't that be like the ultimate performance?'

'It crossed my mind,' said Knightly. 'But everything points against it. For a start, that puncture wound on the neck is inconsistent with suicide. In any case, with drowning, the body's natural instinct kicks in and you start struggling like hell, especially in a small tank of neat formaldehyde.'

'Take a look,' said Benno, holding up his phone. 'She's floating easy as you please. That's why everyone thought it was a model.'

The outlandish image of the foetal woman made Shanti shudder.

'So you think she was dead before she entered the tank?'

'I'll bet my pension we discover she was drugged.'

'Big stakes, Dawn.' She reflected for a moment. 'I suppose she could have drugged herself. Maybe she helped herself to Junior's stash.'

'Forget it,' said Knightly. 'She would either be too drowsy to climb in, or too lucid to drown. No. There's more to it than that.'

'Go on ...'

She laid a gloved hand on the upturned tank.

'The widower, Callum Oak, hauled the tank onto its side, and it would have been damned heavy. Guests describe him attempting to smash the glass with a chair before clawing at the lid. In the end they had to bring tools to prise it open. Eventually she tumbled out like a baby being born. Someone filmed the whole show. But here's the thing, Shanti – that tank was sealed from the outside.'

'Do you think she might have persuaded someone else to drug her and seal her in? You know, like a final attention-grabbing performance.'

'Sounds far-fetched to me. But even if that was the case, we're still looking for a killer.'

'So what you're saying is ...'

Knightly smiled. 'You know me. I don't say anything till the fat corpse sings. But my money's on murder, Shanti. Beautiful artistic murder.'

The Saab's headlights pierced the velvety blackness of the lane. In the passenger seat, Benno shifted uncomfortably and eventually extracted a plastic stegosaurus from beneath his buttocks.

'Excuse the mess. Still haven't finished unpacking.'

'No worries, boss,' he replied unconvincingly.

She had offered the sergeant a lift because she wanted to pick his brains.

'Listen, Benno, you heard what Dawn said, didn't you?'

'Murder.'

'I trust her instincts. But do you realise what this means? Right now, we've got a killer wandering the West Country – I mean a demented killer. What kind of person would do that? Drug somebody, seal them in a tank of formaldehyde and put them up for public display? You'd have to have a mind as twisted as . . . as . . .'

'As an umbilical cord in a tank.'

'Exactly. I have to find them, Benno.'

'I'm wondering about the motive. Money? Revenge? Jealousy? Love? Why would someone want to murder Kristal Havfruen?'

'To be honest, her so-called artwork would be enough of a motive for me.'

'Do you suspect the son?'

'Snow Boy? He's definitely worth looking at. I'd like to know what kind of relationship he had with his mum, although I doubt he has the wherewithal to engineer something that elaborate.'

A black and white badger stumbled ahead of them like a chubby convict on the run. It had been four months since the move from Camden, but Shanti doubted she'd ever get used to the nights out here. The absence of street lights. The absence of people. But then she remembered various inner-city estates in the small hours of a Sunday morning, and the West Country night seemed like a warm hug.

'What about the husband, Benno?'

'Callum Oak? He was clearly grief-stricken, although of course the formaldehyde had them all weeping.'

'Where does he live?'

Benno flicked through his notebook with the light of a torch. 'Here we go. Mangrove House, just outside Sidmouth.'

'Where's that?'

Benno adopted a bad West Country accent. 'Oi'm forgettin' you're not from these parts. East Devon. 'Bout forty mile away.'

'And that's where he lived with Kristal?'

'As far as I know.'

'Then there's Saul Spencer, the curator. And that big bloke, Oliver Sweetman, who's some sort of family friend. He's a bit odd, isn't he? Never stops grinning.'

'Boss, this could be simpler than you think.'

'Why d'you say that?'

'The galleries are jammed with CCTV. We may get lucky and see the offender at work – I mean actually opening the tank and . . . you know . . .'

'Shoving her inside. Maybe. Or maybe Kristal was already in the tank when it was delivered. Listen, Benno, this is my first opportunity to prove myself to some of those dicks in the canteen, and it means a hell of a lot to have you on my side. Could you oversee the operation at the station so I can get out and about? Scour that CCTV footage. Go through initial statements for any anomalies. Check reg plates for previous offences, even a bloody parking ticket. Stick some names and faces on a board if it helps. Start roughing out a timeline. Most of all, I want you to study Art Havfruen. They've tested him, have they?'

'Yes, the lad's a walking chemistry set. We'll get a full analysis in the morning.'

Shanti began to sense the familiar internal conflict, which manifested itself like indigestion. Tomorrow was Sunday and she had promised Paul they would spend the day together. But she was on fire with adrenaline. She wouldn't sleep a wink tonight, she knew that. Endlessly questioning suspects in her head was her thing. Of course it was tough on the family, but a woman was dead, and they couldn't keep her crazy son banged up for long. In addition, there was an urgent need to visit the widower, Callum Oak, the minute he was released from hospital. Above all, an investigation needed to be tackled while it was hot. Paul would understand that – he was dead proud of his mum. Lately he'd been saying he wanted to be a detective himself one day.

It came to her that if Benno was tied up at the station, she was going to need another pair of eyes and ears. Preferably someone who knew this part of the world as well as he did. She didn't want to miss a detail, and two heads were better than one. She went through the other members of the team in her mind. She'd been shocked by how small the crew was on her arrival – a station trimmed to the bone by cuts. There was no one spare. Benno would need every available hand, and the weekend was always busy.

'Know anyone who can support me, Benno? Someone good. Not a bloody plod.'

'Hmm . . . there are a couple of smart guys in Wincanton and Crewkerne. But trust me, they're not going to lend their top boys for any length of time.'

Silence settled in the car as both cops struggled with the perennial problem – how to do their job against an ever-decreasing budget.

'There is someone . . .' said Benno, his voice hesitant.

'Go on.'

'He's another Yeovil DI . . . In fact you inherited his desk.'

Shanti had felt his ghost when she'd arrived. The immaculate desk surface, which was the complete opposite to Shanti Town.

The well-ordered files and drawers, and the obsessively aligned stationery. More than a whiff of OCD, she reckoned. She recalled the mail that turned up for a while, addressed to ... what was his name?

'Caine, wasn't it? DI Vincent Caine.'

'On second thoughts, cancel that idea, boss. I'll think of someone else.'

'Why? What's he like, Benno?'

'This is off the record. I like the guy, but most of the team couldn't get their tiny heads round him. Vince is a strange one. A little distant. Not interested in a pint after work. Prefers his own company. He enjoys a joke as much as the next person, but he would call out anything racist, or homophobic, or sexist, which some of the lads had trouble with. Spent his time reading weird books – Buddhism and mindfulness and all that. He had a great way with young people, but no family or kids of his own as far as anyone knew. Not detective material you would say ... Except ...'

'Except what, Benno?'

'Except he was bloody brilliant. Best DI I ever met, and I've known a few. He approached everything a bit left-field – slow and intuitive, not textbook at all.' He smiled. 'He had a daft nickname ...'

'Oh yeah?'

'The kids in town called him Veggie Cop.'

Shanti laughed. She had met the teenagers Benno was talking about, the ones they called the Yeovil Yoof. She wondered what name they were concocting for her – female, Asian, Londoner. There was plenty of material.

'So why did he go? This Veggie Cop.'

'Sick leave, although I've no idea why. I've never met anyone healthier. He was off for six months initially. Then you came along and stepped straight into his size ten Afghan slippers.'

'So is he up to the job?'

'That would be for you to judge. Between you and me, the Super is desperate to get him back. I warn you, though, Caine is the most reluctant cop you'll ever meet. And whatever prompted the sick leave will only have compounded that. I'll be astonished if you can persuade him.'

'Where does he live?'

'Now that's an interesting question ...'

Chapter 4

The Cop in the Cabin

The Saab dropped steeply down Lyme Regis's main street, passing fossil shops, fudge emporia, clothes boutiques and delis. Cheery bunting was strung between ancient buildings, as if the place was on permanent holiday. At the bottom of the hill, a huge swathe of sea gave the illusion of rising up like a sparkling wall. The pavements were thronged with people – sunburnt parents, kids clutching shrimping nets and spades, their faces deep in ice creams. Shanti felt a stab of jealousy. It had been years since she and Paul had taken a break. A short weekend in Brighton that his dad had ruined.

The place was rammed and it took nearly half an hour to find a space in a car park by the front. As she fumbled for change for the ticket machine, she was greeted by a large splat of guano on her windscreen and heard the demonic cackle of a gull.

She was already tired and disgruntled, and her mood darkened when she noticed a small sweet shop with racks of newspapers outside, every front page carrying that dreadful image and the same unanswered question: *WHO KILLED KRISTAL?*

It was like a rebuke. A reminder. As if she needed one.

Shanti hadn't been in to the station that morning, but Benno informed her that the media were setting up camp outside Yeovil HQ.

Instead she had driven straight over to Lyme, attempting on the way to contact Caine several times. All she got was an enigmatic and faintly annoying message:

'You've reached the voicemail of Vincent Caine. I'm currently on retreat, but if you leave a message, I'll get back to you in time . . .'

What did that even mean? For a start, what was a retreat? Second, when was 'in time'?

Shanti strode briskly along the promenade, in and out of dawdling families with buggies, and wheelchairs, and waggy-tailed dogs, following the directions she'd memorised that morning. Benno had visited a few years back, when Caine was constructing his hideaway – a wooden cabin in the wilderness, perched high on the Undercliff. You walked west along the coastal path for an hour or so, then, when you came across an old brick construction in a clearing, known as the Lost Chimney, you climbed steeply up a tiny track. It wasn't exactly a grid reference; more like a description from *Treasure Island*.

The Undercliff, according to Wikipedia, was a World Heritage Site to the west of the town. Part of the world-famous Jurassic Coast, this was the closest thing to virgin rainforest in the UK. The land was incredibly unstable and there was a constant threat of cliff falls. So why would anyone want to live there?

She felt tired and agitated. This expedition could be a massive waste of precious time. On the other hand, she desperately needed a partner on this case, and Benno, who chose his words carefully, had described Caine as the best detective he'd ever met.

So how could she persuade this reluctant cop? As she walked, she imagined herself telling him that the case was unique – bizarre beyond anything she had come across. If Caine had even half her investigator's temperament, he would be unable to resist.

In her jeans and denim jacket, Shanti began to perspire beneath the relentless sun. She peeled off the jacket and stuffed it in her shoulder bag. On the beach to her left, small children ran in and out of the lapping surf, squealing with delight. She found her eyes welling, then pushed that emotion firmly away.

She passed a bleeping games arcade, cafés and overpriced trampolines. It was just before lunch, and the pub terraces overlooking the famous Cobb were crammed with drinkers, their voices raised in pealing laughter. The vinegary aroma of fish and chips reminded her that breakfast had consisted of a packet of crisps at the wheel.

Beyond a bowling green and a boatbuilding school, the town petered out and wild countryside began. Following the wooden signs to the coastal path, she struggled up a long stairway hacked into the cliff – a depressing reminder that she wasn't as fit as she used to be – and emerged into a meadow, her T-shirt clinging. She passed dog walkers who waved cheerily in her direction. Her bra was too tight and she felt prickly. With every step, the expedition seemed more absurd – she was a DI on a fresh case, not David Bloody Attenborough.

Now the path became a leafy tunnel, which hummed and throbbed with life. To her left, the sea glittered between the leaves, and the polished track beneath her feet wound deeper into the cool forest, dappled with purple shadows.

She staggered up and down timber-faced stairways, at one point disturbing a pair of skittish deer – Jesus, did deer bite … or impale you with their antlers? – and stumbled over roots and lianas that groped at her feet like fingers. Out here, the ever-shifting ground had caused the trees to grow in stunted forms, like ancient dancers.

She hadn't taken this much exercise since her training days, and by God she'd been fit back then! Now her body punished her for her lazy habits and poor diet. She pulled her phone from her pocket in order to hear the reassuring voices of Paul and her mum, but the screen showed no bars. For a moment she longed for the mean streets of Camden, speckled with vomit, blood and chewing gum – at least you could get a signal there.

Dizzy with hunger, she was moments from aborting the mission when she entered a clearing beneath colossal beech trees. And there stood the Lost Chimney. It was just that – a tall stack of ancient bricks, which seemed as incongruous as she was in this place.

Jesus, why hadn't she brought a drink? That warm can on the passenger seat would go down a treat. To the side of the chimney she spotted the track, a steeply rising animal trail, and high above her head the flash of a window, like a winking eye amongst the trees.

As she hauled herself ever upwards, she made out a building of some kind – a timber structure, but without a single sharp edge, like an ark. Pausing to catch her breath, she noticed solar panels, a string of coloured prayer flags, wide windows, a raised wooden deck, and a turf roof where smoke drifted faintly from a flue. If this was Caine's gaff, he was less Veggie Cop, more Bilbo sodding Baggins.

She found herself wondering if this man, Vincent Caine, was as unstable as the geology on which he lived. He had been away on sick leave. Perhaps he had turned feral. Become some kind of hillbilly. She imagined fleeing in terror, buttocks peppered with buckshot, as some bearded crazy hurled abuse in her wake.

On the other hand, she had to admit that the building was strangely pleasing to the eye. Misshapen, yes, but masterfully constructed so that it appeared in perfect harmony with the leafy landscape, which pitched and heaved like an ocean.

But what was that on the roof? Shanti's heart flipped. Above an exquisitely crafted wooden porch was seated something large and alive. It was a bird, for God's sake! A bird of prey as big as a pit bull! As she drew close, it rose sluggishly, its brown wings outspread like a battered sailing ship. Then it found a thermal and circled serenely over the forest.

Her body was at its limits as she reached Caine's door, which had been built from planed planks with a twisting driftwood handle. Her cop's eye noted the absence of a lock of any kind. *Need to talk to you about that, sir* ... Composing herself, she knocked loudly, realising her fingers were swollen with dehydration. She waited. Knocked again. But answer came there none.

She tried the handle and an internal latch dropped noiselessly, the sweetly oiled door swinging wide.

She noticed a long black coat on a hook, two battered surfboards, and pairs of canvas shoes placed tidily as if at a mosque. She hesitated, then pulled off her own trainers, feeling the cool wood beneath her feet.

The interior of Caine's cabin was minimal and silent. A few scattered cushions lay around the open-plan kitchen and living room, and a raised area held some kind of shrine adorned with peculiar objects: a weeping candle, some feathers, a tiny vase of wild flowers, and a carved Buddha.

She noted some novels and hardbacks in a modest bookcase, and in the immaculate kitchen area, a small stove and slender hand-made chairs around a table. A row of mugs sat on a shelf, each printed with a jokey slogan. The one facing her had a cartoon of a Zen monk in a small car, with the words *Your karma ran over my dogma.*

The air in the room felt refined – cool, in spite of the stove, and perfumed with something like sandalwood. It made her ridiculously aware of her tangled hair and saturated clothing. She was a trespasser, yet drawn on by some invisible force.

'Hello,' she called. Then, louder, 'Hello!'

Nothing.

Ahead of her, a drape of white cotton hung over an archway, like something from those damned interiors magazines that no one ever read. In her stockinged feet, Shanti padded over and pulled it aside. A surprisingly large and airy bedroom revealed itself. White, and neat in the extreme – just a futon on the floor with cotton sheets and pillows. Her gaze was drawn through the large window, over the roof of the forest, across the gleaming sea and out to the horizon beyond. Without thinking, she let her bag tumble onto the bed.

On the far side of the room, another curtain wafted in the breeze. Between its waving tendrils, she caught sight of a man. He was stripped to the waist, sitting cross-legged on the deck, his back towards her. She noted the elegance of his posture and the dark hair that tumbled to his broad shoulders. His back and arms were tanned and sinewy as woven leather.

In one slow movement he raised a rounded mallet and tapped it three times against a brass bowl. An extraordinary vibrating song filled the room and the vernal world outside.

And then the man turned and their eyes met.

'Ah,' said a faraway voice. 'The unexpected visitor.'

Chapter 5

Murder Most Mindful

It had been the longest solitary retreat of his life. Three weeks, three days, three hours and – with exquisite serendipity – precisely three minutes when the visitor opened the door and called, 'Hello!'

It was the strangest thing: although they had never met in this lifetime, it was as if he had always known her.

The old monks who had taught him meditation used to emphasise the need to emerge slowly from retreat, with compassion and caring, as if from hibernation. You needed time to reflect on what had been attained, and to discuss the experience with dharma friends. Also, you would have eaten little during your retreat and your body would feel stiff from long hours of sitting. Most of all, you hadn't spoken to another soul.

The woman arrived at the cabin like a messenger from another star. Her agitated manner reminded him of a place he had left behind, where people existed in a frantic dream of expectation and disappointment. There had been moments in the retreat when he had woken fully from that dream, and now he needed to process that.

He rose slowly, instinctively touching fingertips to forehead in the dedication of merit. His body felt light and unsteady, and now he became aware of something else about the stranger that disconcerted him. In Thailand, the retreats had been strictly segregated so that men and women had no contact at all. There was a reason for that. As he stepped towards her, he felt a smouldering heat emanating from her body, and a subtle scent of citrus and musk . . . and woman.

'Why did you say that?' she was asking.

'What did I say?'

The words tasted foreign on his tongue. Like unfamiliar food. He would not have been surprised if another language had emerged. Or more likely birdsong.

'Something about an unexpected visitor.'

'Oh, excuse me. Last night I was reading a book of verse. The unexpected visitor is from a poem by Rumi called "The Guest House".'

'Right. I'll look out for it.'

'Rumi was a Sufi mystic.'

'Is that a career option?'

'I suppose he's saying that everyone who comes into our life has been sent for a reason – you know, to teach us something. But I think he means feelings as well as people. And of course the emotions and experiences that are most difficult can be the most enlightening.'

'OK, so what's the reason for me being here?'

The tall man walked barefoot into the bedroom and slid open a drawer.

'I'd say you're a cop. And you're short of hands.'

He took out a neatly folded white T-shirt and pulled it over his head, rolling the sleeves up over lean biceps.

'Jesus, you're right,' said Shanti. 'I am a cop. How did you know that?'

'Partly mystical intuition. Partly the handcuffs and pepper spray in your bag.'

He was laughing at her, she could tell. And that infuriated her. Nothing fazed Shanti Joyce. She'd faced up to junkies who'd kill for a hit. Mobs of pissed-up football fans. Feral kids with knives. Once she'd floored another officer who touched her arse in the canteen.

But this cabin on the Undercliff was a different world. She didn't understand the rules, and it unnerved her. She found herself babbling.

'Look, I don't normally wander into people's homes. It was Benno's idea ... coming to find you, I mean. You remember Benno? He sends his best, by the way. The thing is, I need to ask you ... No, wait a minute, I haven't even ... DI Shantala Joyce ... call me Shanti. I took over your desk at Yeovil ...'

She was holding her hand out. He took it slowly and ... Jesus! When he looked in her eyes, it was like falling down two oil wells.

Caine realised that when the words ran out, the silence was still there. Behind everything, the stillness was all around. He led her into the kitchen and invited her to sit. He poured spring water from a jug, which she gulped down as if she hadn't drunk in days. Then she shoved the glass back at him, like a child demanding more.

She needed a lot of things, he could tell, but he was in no hurry to find out what they were. All that stuff with laws and crimes and uniforms felt like a game from a distant childhood.

The visitor was Asian in origin, possibly Indian, with shoulder-length brown hair and big kind eyes. She carried the natural beauty of a young mother, and her forehead ran with sweat like beads at a temple door. Her posture was full of tension, and although they had only just met, he could tell that her head was a bustling city. It reminded him of how he used to be when he was a cop.

Outside the window, the buzzard drifted majestically over the forest canopy, like a scrap of the forest itself.

'Benno described you as a reluctant cop,' she said.

'I'm not even sure I *am* a cop.'

'So you won't be persuaded?'

'No. But I'll tell you what I will do – I'll make us something to eat and then I'll walk you back to Lyme. Are you hungry?'

'Christ, yes. Starving, actually, now you mention it.'

'What do you fancy?'

'Oh, you know, something simple. I could murder a bacon sandwich with like a ton of ketchup . . . Jesus, I'm sorry! Whatever you're having.'

He walked to the stove and placed a log inside. She watched his movements – unhurried, precise, agile. She noticed the way he wore silence like some people wore clothes. He was smiling still. Completely unfazed by the insane awkwardness of the situation.

He reached for a wok and a bottle of oil. Then, testing the blade of a long knife with his thumb, he opened a small back door and stepped barefoot onto the grass outside, where an immaculate kitchen garden was fenced against the forest animals. She heard him rooting about, cutting and gathering, and a moment later he returned, arms laden with dark leaves, soil-caked carrots, onions and an array of herbs.

'You'll have to be patient,' he said, as he cleaned and diced and fried. 'I've been in a different place. But now we are here. It's good to meet you, Shanti Joyce.'

'And you, DI Caine. So where exactly *have* you been?'

As he cooked and stirred, he told her about the retreat – what it meant to take time out. To live fully in the forest of the present moment. To be conscious of every sensation, so that the simple act of washing or eating became a sensual activity, until memories of the past and worries for the future dissolved.

Shanti thought of Benno's description – slow, intuitive, left-field. He'd neglected to mention windbag. She was itching to tell him about the case. Reluctant or not, he'd come around when he heard the juicy details.

But the man could not be rushed. It was better to play along.

'But don't you get lonely out here? Doesn't it hurt to sit on that cushion? Don't you get bored as hell?'

'All of those things. And I fail all the time. It doesn't matter, so long as there is awareness.'

'But . . . I mean, what is the *point* of it?'

Benno had told her that the boys at the nick liked to imitate Caine – the long gap before he spoke, so long you could almost fall into it. What was the phrase they'd used? A Veggie Pause. Well, he was deep in one now. Thirty seconds passed. A minute.

'Well I don't know about you,' he said eventually, 'but there were years when I lived on autopilot, completely lost in my head.

I acted impulsively, with no thought of the consequences. So the point of meditation is to stop. You find a place between effort and relaxation, and suddenly, POP! Your head clears. You wake up. You actually hear the forest. You feel the weather. You see the light. You walk along a woodland path, just minding your own business, and suddenly you are mugged by beauty.'

When he turned around, Caine was holding two plates piled with richly coloured food. He placed one carefully in front of her and an exquisite aroma filled her nostrils. She forked it hungrily into her mouth. It was bloody extraordinary. There were wild flavours and textures break-dancing all over her tongue, and it reminded her of something from long ago – the sultry child-hood summers she had spent with her grandma in Kerala, when there had been time to cook and eat and play. It made her shamefully aware of the rubbish she'd become accustomed to.

Caine chewed each mouthful many times, swallowed with great ceremony, then resumed his monologue about the retreat. If bullshitting were an Olympic event, this man was going for gold.

'The thing is, there are moments when you realise that you are not a separate entity at all. You are an integral part of the whole thing – you know, the flow and the rhythm of life. And you realise that this is enough. Just being alive on this beautiful blue-green ball revolving in space. Can you understand what I am saying?'

She had a vision of getting stuck here forever with ivy growing around her body.

'Totally,' she said, putting down her empty bowl. 'Listen, Caine, all of this is fascinating and the food was top-notch. But I'm here for a reason . . .'

'Let me guess. You want to persuade me to help solve a case.'

'Maybe. And how will I do that?'

'You'll say the case is unique.'

'Which it is.'

'You'll say it's the most bizarre and intriguing crime you've ever come across.'

'But supposing it actually is?'

'Listen. I'll tell you what's bizarre. I'll tell you what intrigues me.'

'Go on.'

'You see the way that shaft of sunlight creeps across the floor? You can actually tell the time of day by it. That's what intrigues me. I don't know if you noticed, but a moment ago, the light fell onto the half-full jug, and there were jewels of light dancing around the room . . .'

'I didn't notice that.'

'They were dancing on your face, Shanti Joyce.'

'Pardon me, did I just roll my eyeballs out loud? Listen, I don't mean to be rude, but today is day one of the biggest story to hit the West Country since . . . since . . .'

'The Tolpuddle Martyrs?'

'But instead of catching the bad guys, I'm being given a foundation course in psychobabble. I'm sorry, Benno told me you were a brilliant cop, but I might as well send my mum and my eight-year-old to catch the killer.'

'Benno is a lovely man, but he's got it wrong. I'll never make a good cop, because my heart isn't it.'

'OK. You don't want to get involved. But could you please spare, like, ten minutes to hear about the case? I mean, you used to do my job and you may have some insights.'

There was that silence again, longer and louder than noise. Finally he said, 'Of course I will, Shanti. It's nice to have a visitor. It's good to hear you talk.'

'Thank you. Right . . . so there's been a murder. A weird one. Last night a woman named Kristal Havfruen was found floating in a tank of formaldehyde at her own art exhibition.'

'Kristal Havfruen? She's dead?'

'You know her?'

'Not personally, but I know her work. Everyone does.'

'Not me, pal. I'd never even heard of her.'

'Hmm . . .'

There was a mini pause.

'Why would someone want to kill Kristal Havfruen?'

She felt something snap. 'OH MY GOD, THAT'S THE THING! That's the question I've come to ask! If I knew the answer to that, I would be eating popcorn in the cinema with my son instead of hacking through twenty miles of virgin rainforest.'

Caine flinched.

'Sorry,' she said more quietly. 'I shouldn't raise my voice. It's just that I'm damned tired. I was up most of the night. I moved house recently and I had a shit of a divorce and this case is *so* important.'

'I'm sorry to hear that,' he said gently. 'You'll have to be patient. I'm still a bit spaced out with the retreat. Let's start again, shall we?'

'Listen, Caine, I don't really have time for this. I have to go. I've got another appointment this afternoon.' She glanced at her phone. 'Jesus, is that the time?'

'I'll walk with you.'

42

'Thanks. I can find my own way. I've just remembered I work better on my own.'

'No, wait. I'll get dressed and come with you. I've been sitting too long ... I need the exercise. Talk to me on the way. Tell me the whole story.'

Chapter 6

A Karmic Killing

The snaking path through the Undercliff could only be navigated in single file. Shanti was glad of this. If she kept two or three steps behind Caine, he would be less likely to notice how she was struggling to keep up with his easy gait and the fact that she was practically boiling with frustration about coming all this way for nothing.

At one stage, she was alarmed to hear him muttering under his breath, like a prayer or an incantation. My God, she thought, perhaps he really is some kind of nutter. But then she realised that he was reciting the names of the many birds that flittered and called in the dense undergrowth.

'Blackbird, woodpecker, song thrush, and . . . wait a minute, you know what that is?'

'Another bird?'

'Listen! It's like molten silver. That's a nightingale, Shanti. Some people think he only sings at night—'

'Or she.'

'I think it's the male who sings. He's calling for a mate.'

Ninety-nine per cent of Shanti found him intensely irritating. The other one per cent found him fascinating as hell.

At the cabin, he had changed into trainers, cargo trousers and a loose hemp shirt. He had swung a canvas bag over one shoulder, into which he had slipped a well-worn notepad and pencil, a bottle of water and a couple of apples.

'Have you really had no exercise for three weeks?' she asked.

'No, I haven't been more than a few metres from the cabin. It's amazing to get out – see the way the leaves have opened now? Except for yoga and t'ai chi, I've hardly moved.'

'Of course,' she said dismally.

At one point they crossed a wooden walkway over a stream. Beside it stood a simple but beautifully constructed oak bench, where Shanti threw herself to rest.

'Look at this, Caine. How can the council justify spending money on this sort of thing when the police budget is cut to the bone?'

'It wasn't the council . . . I built this.'

'You built it? The bench? The bridge? Why would you do that?'

'Just a fun thing to do. Besides, don't you know that what you give out, you get back ten times over? It's karmic law.'

A mile along the track, her phone hit a signal and began to pop and buzz with messages and missed calls. She scanned the screen with her finger.

'Excuse me a moment, I need to get this.'

There was Benno's voice – gruff, reassuring, professional. 'Quick update, boss. Young Art is quieter today – not exactly grieving for his mum, though. You might be interested to know that the package that fell from his pocket was top-grade CK1 – coke and ketamine mix – and that's what we found in his bloodstream too. I've had him checked over by the doc. He's a heavy user, but there are no puncture marks on his skin, meaning he doesn't inject. In the meantime, I've got a small team scrutinising the CCTV footage from the Meat Hook. There's bloody tons of it, but Spencer was right, you can see a crate being delivered into the main gallery on a forklift at 15.26. It appears heavy but not massive – must have been the glass tank.'

'Top marks, Benno. And check out that delivery company.'

'MasterMoves. I've got someone on it now. Problem is, I can't keep Art much longer unless we have something to go on. Hope you managed to track down Vince. Quite a character, isn't he! Takes a while to get warmed up, but he'll surprise you before long, I guarantee it.'

Oh, Caine was surprising all right. She had tried to fit him into all kinds of stereotypes – dreamer, hippie, eccentric, psycho – but he wasn't any of those things.

'That was Benno,' she told him. 'He's got Kristal's son in custody on a drugs charge.'

'A Boy Named Art.'

'Sorry? Say that again.'

'A Boy Named Art. That's his name, isn't it? What age is he now?'

'Twenty-four. But why did you use that particular phrase – A Boy Named Art? I've heard it before.'

'You really don't know about this, do you? OK, let me give you a little background. I got quite interested in this at the time. Back in the nineties, Kristal Havfruen became notorious for a particular series of works. The tabloids couldn't get enough of it – they pretended to be shocked, but of course they relished every detail.'

'Go on.'

'Kristal was Scandinavian – Danish, I think – and she enrolled as a student at Falmouth School of Art in Cornwall. At the time, the college was pretty conventional, but after Kristal arrived it began to get a reputation for being ultra-experimental and cutting edge. As you know, she was into daring performance art, but it was two events in particular that made her name. In the first piece, she made love with another student in front of an audience.'

'OK. And in what possible way is that art?'

'That's what the papers asked at the time. But Kristal argued that it was radical feminist art, because she was in control of everything. She called it *Preconception*, which is a kind of play on words.'

'No comprende.'

'Well, I suppose it was challenging our preconceptions about what is art. It was also conceptual art about the conception of a child.'

'That's sick.'

'She stage-managed the whole event and hand-picked her lover. I seem to remember that she even employed another student as a kind of unpaid publicity assistant to control the press and organise the set and lighting. I know what you're thinking: didn't Yoko Ono do all that back in the sixties?'

'I wasn't, actually. Who was the lucky lover?'

'Another student, I think. I can't remember.'

'He wasn't called Callum Oak, by any chance?'

'Could be. Yes, Oak. I'm pretty sure that was the name.'

'That's the man I'm going to see next. He's her widower. He tried to resuscitate Kristal last night. They released him from hospital in the small hours. Benno has arranged an interview at three.'

She remained unconvinced about Caine, but his knowledge of Kristal Havfruen and her work could be invaluable. 'Listen, Caine, I know you don't want to get involved in another case. I respect that, I really do. But would you like to meet Callum Oak? It would be incredibly helpful to have you there, because I don't know the area yet, and to be honest, I know absolutely nothing about art either.'

'That's very kind of you, Shanti, but I know how these things take over your life and I'm on leave, you know.'

'I know, sick leave. Do you mind me asking what happened? Was it stress? A family thing, maybe?'

He turned sharply, silencing her mid-flow. For the first time, she became aware of something unpredictable in his gaze, as if she had stirred up dark memories.

'Could we talk about Kristal?'

'Sure. I'm sorry. It's none of my business.'

They emerged from the forest into dazzling afternoon sun-light, and now the path was wide enough to walk side by side, although Shanti found herself taking two paces for every one of Caine's. He was like somebody waking from a long sleep. But unless she was mistaken, he was becoming interested in the story.

'The thing to understand is that everything Kristal did was micro-managed for maximum impact.'

'A control freak?' she said.

'Maybe. The performance I've just mentioned, *Preconception*—'

'The sex show.'

'Well, call it what you like – the point is, it was scheduled precisely nine months before her final degree performance, *A Boy Named Art*.'

'Wait a minute. Are you saying . . .?'

'Yes, that's exactly what I'm saying. The birth took place in the college theatre in front of a large audience of journalists and TV crews from around the world. I'm amazed you've never heard of it.'

'Like I say, art's not really my thing. And that's exactly the kind of stuff that puts me off. It sounds pretentious and self-indulgent and deliberately provocative.'

'Trust me, if you see the film, you won't forget it in a hurry. There's a scene in which Kristal holds up the new baby, still connected by the umbilical cord, and tells the audience he will be named Art.'

'Jesus! That's nuts, isn't it?'

'She gave what became known as her Declaration, proclaiming that the boy would be a living work of art – that everything he ever did would be art. When he went to school, or drew a picture, or—'

'Took a shit?'

'Art. All art. When he got a job, that would be a work of art too.'

Shanti thought fondly of her own son, out somewhere with Mum.

'What kind of mother would do that? That's like abuse, isn't it?'

'For a few years the media couldn't get enough of the story. They followed the kid everywhere. But the trouble was, he was a bit boring. After a while, they lost interest. Oh, I've remembered something else . . .'

'Go on.'

'A few years ago, Kristal published an expensive coffee table book of photos of her life and work. You might want to track down a copy. It was called *The Mother of Art*. If I remember correctly, the student she employed as her studio assistant put it together. Anyway, it went down like a lead balloon. A publisher paid a fat advance, but it only sold a couple of hundred copies. That was pretty much the end of Kristal's career.'

'Until last night, when it all kicked off again.'

They had reached the meadows above the harbour, from where they could see tiny figures walking on the Cobb below, like ants along the spine of a Jurassic creature.

'Hey! You know what, Caine? I'm pretty sure that's where they filmed *The French Lieutenant's Woman*. That was one of my mum's favourite movies. Didn't Meryl Streep stand at the end looking out to sea for her lost lover?'

'Exactly right, Shanti. And Jane Austen wrote about it too. Remember the scene where Louisa Musgrove falls from the steps in *Persuasion*?'

'Must have slipped my mind. Anyway, listen, this has been really helpful. I'm parked at the far end, near the clock tower. Thanks a lot for that information and once again, I apologise for butting in on your, you know, retreat. It's a pity I can't persuade you to come aboard, but someone's got to do the meditating.'

At first she thought he was taking a breath, then she realised it was another pause. She turned away, feeling her hackles rise.

'OK,' he said eventually. 'I'll admit, I can see why you are intrigued. And presumably there's a killer out there somewhere who you desperately need to catch. But like I say, Shanti, I've changed. I have everything I need now.'

'Your leave is paid, isn't it?'

'For now.'

'Well, I'm glad you've got everything sorted.'

A thought entered her mind.

'What you've told me about this lad Art being a, you know . . .'

'Living artwork?'

'Yeah, that. Well, that would make you royally pissed off, wouldn't it? I mean, his mum, Kristal, sounds like a right prima donna. A narcissist. Well, that's not a good place for a kid, is it? Art would have grown up in her shadow and that would make anyone resentful. It's not surprising he's such a mess.'

'I see where you're going, Shanti. All I can tell you is that there is a strong Buddhist teaching about embracing uncertainty. Not filling in the gaps. There's no proof of anything, is there? I certainly have no idea who killed Kristal Havfruen, so all I can do is feel compassion for her family.'

Shanti thought of the volatile youth who had jabbed his finger at her eyes, and her own compassion felt a little thin. Then her phone vibrated again. It was Dawn Knightly. She took a few paces out of earshot.

'Dawn, how's it going?'

'Hi, Shanti.' Her voice sounded frothy with excitement. In the background, joshing voices and clinking glasses. 'Can you hear me?'

'You in a pub, Dawn?'

'It's Sunday, Shanti. And I've been working all night. I think I deserve a shandy.'

'Course you do.'

'Anyway, I'm here to tell you my pension's safe, girl. I've got something for you and it's exactly what I thought. Kristal *was* drugged. I've received the initial findings from Pathology: it's ketamine, every vet's favourite. You know the old joke? "Ketamine: just say neigh."'

'You're a bloody legend, Dawn. Have you talked to Benno?'

'He just informed me that young Art had ket in his pocket. I don't want to jump the gun, but it's not looking good for our boy.'

'Anything else, Dawn?'

'I can also confirm that the botched wound on her neck is a syringe entry to the jugular – I'm assuming that's how the drug was administered. It's hard to gauge exactly how long she'd been dead because of the delaying effect of formaldehyde on the decomposition process. Oh my God, Shanti, what kind of son kills his own mum? I'll have to watch out for my boys. By the way, I hear you paid a visit to Vincent Caine?'

'Jesus, is there a news shortage in this part of the world?'

'What do you make of him?'

'Why does everyone ask that? He's spectacularly annoying, if you want to know.'

'But he's strangely attractive too, isn't he? He does something funny to your underwear.'

'I hadn't noticed. Look, he's not interested in police work and I'm not interested in men, in any shape or form.'

'I forgot . . . your divorce. I'm sorry.'

'My only interest is finding who killed Kristal Havfruen and sticking them away for a long time. Anyway, thanks a lot, Dawn. What are you up to now?'

'Getting pissed and going to bed, in no particular order. See you Monday.'

An unconscious smile had settled on Shanti's face as she followed Caine down the steps towards the pubs and cafés of Lyme. Dawn was right, they shouldn't jump the gun, but it would be bloody nice to think that her first big case in the new job might be straightforward. Maybe she didn't need this Veggie Cop after all. It would be way more impressive to handle it alone. She tapped out a message to Benno telling him to ask the Super for authorisation to keep Art for another night and to set up an interview with him for the following morning.

As if reading her mind, Caine spoke.

'You can't arrest Art Havfruen for murder.'

'No one's saying he's the murderer, but it's looking more than a little suspicious, don't you think? Especially with the dodgy background story you've been telling me. Think about it, Caine. Number one: Art has one hell of a motive for hating his mum. Number two: he happens to be carrying the same drug as Kristal has in her system, which is not that common round here. Big coincidence. In fact when you think about it, the whole thing is deliciously neat. She turns his birth into art. In return, he turns her death into art. I like that. I like it a lot.'

They had joined the noisy holidaymakers and locals along the seafront. From all directions, people acknowledged Caine.

'Hey, Vince. Been away?'

'How you doing, Vince?'

'Hello, Mr Caine, we've missed you.'

And Caine returned each greeting with a smile, a handshake, a high-five, a cheek kiss, a fist bump, a shoulder squeeze. For a man who'd just emerged from many days of silence, he seemed remarkably at home amongst people.

'You asked my opinion, Shanti,' he said once they'd moved on, 'so I'm advising you that it's way too early to jump to conclusions. It's your case, but I detect a whiff of injustice, which is my least favourite smell. I don't want to go into it, but I know what it's like to have a challenging relationship with a parent, so I feel for this lad.'

As they entered the car park, she felt his dark eyes turn towards her. Dawn was right – he was certainly an unusual-looking man. She climbed into the scalding seat and wound down the window.

'Listen, Caine, you know that stuff you were telling me about people being sent into our lives to teach us something?'

'Rumi.'

'Whatever. Well, supposing it works both ways? Supposing you've been sent into my life for a reason?'

'I'm listening.'

'Let me level with you. My last investigation in London went south. It damaged my reputation as a cop and it knocked my self-confidence big-time. That's how I ended up in the West Country. It wasn't a demotion exactly . . .'

'But that's what it felt like.'

'I guess so, yeah. I mean, I did it for my kid too – you know, fresh air, school chums without blades in their satchels. But I've been waiting for a big one to come along so I can set the record straight. And this is that case, I know it is. Let me be clear: I can handle it alone, but you have knowledge – you know about Kristal and you know the area too. So maybe we're *destined* to work together. Isn't that how you'd put it? Listen to the universe, Caine.'

There was a pause. A long pause. Shanti counted the seconds. One, two, three, four, five, six, seven . . .

Then Vincent Caine walked slowly around to the passenger door and slipped in at her side.

Chapter 7

The Weeping Widower

As Shanti steered the faithful Saab between the winding hedges of the A3052 coast road from Lyme Regis to Sidmouth, Caine pressed her for every detail. Who had she talked to on the previous night? What was their behaviour? Who besides Kristal had access to the master gallery where the foetal corpse was found?

He listened intently to her answers and scribbled continuously in the worn notebook. When Shanti glanced at the pages, she was surprised to see not a list of bullet points, but a flowery mind-map of doodles, memos, annotated bubbles and diagrams.

As they peeled off the coast road and along a rough single-track lane, she felt her excitement grow. This was the house that Kristal Havfruen had shared with her husband, Callum Oak, for more than fifteen years. From what Benno had told her, Art had spent his formative years there too.

Mangrove House was situated on an elevated site near the

golf course above Sidmouth. It was the last in a row of expensive detached properties, ranging from modern constructions in glass and steel to a retirement home in a former Georgian rectory.

The tall sunbeam gates were open, and as Shanti steered up the unkempt drive, the eastern elevation of Mangrove House rose dramatically into view.

'Art deco,' Caine told her. 'It's a beauty. Late twenties or early thirties, I should think, but it looks a bit neglected.'

The sweep of the drive allowed them to take in the crisp geometric construction, white and understated against the backdrop of the sea. The building was an elegant arrangement of balconies and patios. The only curves were in the magnificent double-height bay window overlooking the ocean. The house had been ingeniously sunk into the sloping geology, so that the large oak front door stood on the second floor at the back.

There were no cars outside and when they stepped onto the courtyard and Caine pushed the Bakelite doorbell, all they heard was the half-hearted bark of dogs inside.

'Shit!' said Shanti. 'I bust a gut to get here for three p.m. Where the hell is Oak? I'll have to call Benno . . .'

'Slow down, Shanti. Listen, I'm not saying I am going to get involved, but you may as well know how I work. The guys at Yeovil never quite got it, but I act from here, not here.' He tapped a finger to the centre of his chest, then to his forehead. 'You may think this is weird, but I believe in going with things the way they are. I try to learn from what life offers, not constantly wishing it were different. Serendipity, if you like. It really works.'

'OK, I understand all those words individually, but together they make no sense at all.'

'Well, right now we have a perfect example. It seems like there's no one home . . .'

'Which means I've wasted my afternoon as well as my morning.'

'Which means that we have an opportunity. An opportunity to look around and get a feel of the place.'

'Well, I wasn't going to leave this second.'

'That's good. I'm not trying to teach you your job—'

'Please don't, Caine. I'm a bloody experienced cop, and don't forget, I'm the DI here. You're on sick leave, remember? You've been a little poorly.'

'See, that's another example of serendipity.'

'What is?'

'That you and I find ourselves working together. Maybe we have complementary skills. Like yin and yang.'

'Like balls and testicles, Caine. Look, I needed an assistant and you needed to get outside and do something with your leisure time.'

He was smiling.

They set off down the side of the building to a paved terrace, where a canvas cover lay half submerged in a stagnant swimming pool. Around the poolside stood elegant thirties deckchairs, a tattered parasol and a table on its side, all mildewed and faded by the sun. It was as if a slow-motion hurricane had passed that way.

'Watch where you walk,' warned Shanti. The ground was littered with dog excrement.

At the far end of the once manicured gardens they found an enclosed area surrounded by iron railings that reminded Shanti of the gated communal gardens in the wealthy parts of NW1.

After a bit of rummaging in the undergrowth, she discovered a rusting gate. It took a few hefty kicks to open it enough to squeeze into the secret space within.

They found themselves in an abandoned sculpture garden, with broken benches, drought-stricken potted plants, a row of animal graves and a parade of carved stone figures with animal heads.

'These are interesting,' said Caine. 'Bloomsbury with an Egyptian influence. Maybe they came with the house.'

'Yeah, that was my theory,' said Shanti drily.

There were other sculptures too, and even Shanti could spot the Havfruens – images of Kristal in a variety of sizes and states of undress.

The centrepiece of the garden sat on a circular concrete plinth overgrown with laurels. An embossed plaque read: *Preconception2 Kristal Havfruen*. It was a shockingly graphic depiction of naked lovers in a contorted carnal embrace. The piece had been skilfully cast in polished steel, which had once gleamed like a mirror but was now dulled. Birds had built nests in orifices, and thrusting body parts were encircled by ivy.

'I think someone has been looking at Jeff Koons,' said Caine. 'It's heavily influenced by *Made in Heaven*.'

'Jesus, Caine. Do you come with an interpreter?'

'It's a bit sad really,' he observed as they stepped into the sunlight. 'The whole place seems like a reflection of her declining career.'

'You're obviously not a tabloid reader, otherwise you'd know that Kristal is currently staging a major comeback tour.'

At the far end of the garden, Shanti found a flight of steps dropping steeply to the beach. Then she joined Caine, who was skirting the perimeter of the house. The windows were large, but subdivided by countless flaking frames. Peering into a huge living room, they saw an overweight Labrador and an arthritic spaniel wallowing on a worn rug, intermittently barking and thumping their tails in a puzzled sort of way. Above a conical steel woodburner hung a large mirror. Every wall was lined with overpopulated bookshelves.

On the western side of the building, they scrambled up a weed-lined driveway to a pair of French doors. Now they found themselves peeping into Kristal's colossal light-filled studios.

'Holy moly!' gasped Shanti. Staring back at her was a dismembered legion of hyper-real Kristals – blonde, naked and disturbingly fleshy. And lolling casually on every surface were feet, arms, blonde wigs and heads.

Caine was crouching, examining the ground at his feet. 'There's been a small vehicle here recently – a forklift maybe. Probably the couriers collecting the glass tank.'

Then he paused and raised his head, as if hearing something beyond Shanti's range.

'He's here,' he said.

Still she heard nothing. But Caine was already returning the way they had come, and by the time the tired-looking silver Volvo lumbered through the gates, the two DIs were resting nonchalantly by the front door.

Callum Oak's face fell when he saw them. Not that it wasn't already collapsed into a mask of melting despair. He staggered from the car as if he'd been beaten by a mob. He wore paint-splattered work boots and old-fashioned tobacco corduroys with burgundy braces over a collarless grandad shirt. His gentle features were topped with a mop of slightly greying curly hair. One of those men who would appear boyish to the day he died.

'Mr Oak, we met last night. I'm DI Shantala Joyce and this is my colleague, Vincent Caine.'

Caine grasped both of Oak's hands firmly with his own and stared manfully into his eyes. 'I'm sorry for your loss, sir. My heart goes out to you.' Both men were tall, but Oak was a willow while Caine was a cane.

It was the right thing to say. Oak relaxed and sighed mournfully.

'I forgot you were coming. I went to Yeovil to visit my son, who is still in custody. Then I stopped in Branscombe to go to church.'

'To church?'

'Yes, it's Sunday, Inspector Joyce. Is that so strange? In fact it seemed more necessary than usual today.'

'Of course.'

'Well you'd better come in, but I warn you, I spent several hours in hospital after that horrific night, so I'm *tired*! And I'm not functioning well. Can you please explain why you're holding Art at this catastrophic time? We need to be together, can't you understand that?'

'I'm sorry, Mr Oak,' said Shanti. 'But I can't go into details at this juncture.'

'All his generation take recreational drugs. Couldn't you let it go at a time like this?'

Clutching his chest and panting for breath, Oak unlocked the front door. As he let Shanti and Caine inside, the two dogs swayed and lumbered towards him.

'Oh my poor boys, I forgot to feed you! What will you think of me?'

Shanti and Caine stepped into a magnificent entrance hall with a staircase like a tower of grand pianos. The walls were peppered with artworks in every conceivable style. But as with the exterior of the house, the place had a musty, neglected air, as if the owners had run out of money. Or love.

They followed Oak into an unexpectedly small and untidy kitchen, where he began tending to his dogs. There was a foul smell in the air.

'Oh, poor boys. Had an accident, did you? Forgot to take you out, didn't I? Everything has rather gone to pieces since Mummy ...'

'Let me get you something, sir,' said Caine. 'Tea, I mean. Or something stronger.'

'You're most kind. It's all over there. Biscuits somewhere, I should think. And yes, splash something in, for heaven's sake.' Oak slid a whisky bottle towards him.

Shanti watched in astonishment as Caine began preparing a tray, even stooping discreetly to clear up the dog mess with a paper towel.

'While we're waiting for tea, why don't we sit down, Mr Oak?' she said.

Hunched and unsteady, Oak led her into the big drawing room, which looked out on dizzying vistas towards the horizon. By the time Caine joined them with a tray crammed with a teapot, milk, chipped art deco crockery and a slightly dry ginger cake, the widower was convulsing with grief on a huge Scandinavian sofa, while the dogs anxiously wagged their tails – stiff and stumpy respectively. Shanti was standing awkwardly at his side, attempting to say comforting things.

'Oh dear God!' he wailed. 'What a night! What a day!

Whatever will I do without her?' He clasped a hand over his mouth as if he were afraid he would choke his heart out. 'Lord knows she wasn't easy, but . . . but we've been together more than half our lives.'

Shanti busied herself with the teapot.

'Would you like to talk about her?' asked Caine.

'What is there to say? You've seen the work – she was an insufferable genius. Fiercely intelligent and . . . and . . .'

'And what, sir?'

'One shouldn't speak ill of the d . . . of the departed. But Kristal could be cruel. She used to argue that a great artist should be ruthless – like Picasso or Gauguin or Mozart. She chided me, said I'd never amount to anything with my own work because I was too emotional. Perhaps she was right. I mean, who is interested in paintings by Callum Oak?'

'I am, sir,' said Caine. 'I'd love to see your work.' As he spoke, he massaged the scabrous ears of the Labrador, who appeared to be on the verge of orgasm.

Christ, thought Shanti. The man's a bloody snake charmer!

'Well, that's nice of you. I appreciate it. I have a little studio above the garage. Maybe we could wander over when we've finished here?'

'Thank you, Mr Oak.'

'Call me Callum.'

Another hand grip.

Shanti cut a piece of stale cake. The fat Labrador was far too close, sniffing at the plate and slobbering on her jeans. The old hound smelt too. She shoved it away, pretending to pat it.

'Well, go on and ask away,' said Oak. 'Whatever you need to know. I'll do my best. I've got nothing to hide. God alone knows why someone would do that to poor Kristal. She could rub people up the wrong way, that's true. But to . . . to . . . *murder* her, in that brutal, appalling way! It's beyond comprehension.'

'I don't mean to seem insensitive,' said Shanti, 'but there's one possibility I'd like to rule out. Do you think it's conceivable that your wife planned all this herself?'

'I don't follow.'

'I mean could she have persuaded someone to drug her, in order to stage the ultimate final work?'

Oak stared at her, eyes bulging, lower lip trembling. 'Good God, no! What an unspeakable idea. In any case, Kristal lived for adulation and acclaim. Being dead would not have interested her one jot.'

'I take your point,' said Shanti. 'I had to ask.'

Oak sighed and settled back into the settee.

'So could you tell us how Kristal and Art got along?'

The question was a winter draught in the room. Callum Oak got up and let the dogs out through the French doors. Shanti watched the spaniel squatting on the gravel outside and prayed it wouldn't be allowed back in.

Oak returned and looked at the cops with the moist eyes of a seal.

'I . . . I don't know how much you know about our . . . er . . . history.'

'A little. I've heard about *A Boy Named Art*.'

'Right. An unusual start for any child. What you need to understand is that Kristal and I are . . . were . . . very *different* individuals. I come from a pretty conventional middle-class family – my father was a senior clergyman, a bishop, in fact. I've always been a very private person. But as I said, Kristal adored the limelight. Like it or not, Art and I were drawn into it all, but it was particularly challenging for him, especially as an only child.'

'Did they argue?'

'Yes. I can't deny it. Like cat and dog. Kristal wasn't what you'd call maternal. It was me alone who cared for Art as a baby and throughout his childhood. Kristal liked to get her own way, and Art was spirited like any young man. But he was fond of his mother in his own way, he really was. Eventually he found his vocation in the world of advertising and he's done remarkably well – if you count fast cars and glamour models as success. It was easier when he got his own apartment in London, and later a weekend place not far from here. But one thing I will say is that he always looked after us. Kristal wasn't the least interested in money. Her stepfather was a wealthy man and she assumed that the stuff would simply fall from the trees like … like … foetuses. Well, things haven't been particularly easy in recent years, but Art used his connections to help. Did you know, for instance, that he instigated Kristal's big retrospective at the Meat Hook? He and the curator, Saul Spencer, are old friends, and Art really twisted Saul's arm.'

'How did he do that, Callum?'

'It was Art's idea that his mother would create a major new work for the master gallery – a secret work that would intrigue the media. Kristal got terribly excited about it. All the old passion returned. She sat up half the night working like a demon, and she and Art managed to convince Spencer. As usual, I was kept out of Kristal's plans, but the three of them had endless meetings about the show.'

'So Art was in on the secret. He knew what Kristal was planning – the tank and everything?'

65

'Oh dear, I'm making it sound like he was more involved than he actually was. Sadly, Art never lived up to his name – I mean, he was never very interested in art. He knew all about the show because he initiated it, but as far as I'm aware, he didn't know exactly what Kristal had planned for the final room.'

'Might there be plans or drawings in Kristal's studio? I'm not sure how it works.'

'Perhaps. We can have a look. You must understand that the dogs and I were strictly forbidden to go in there. Kristal had a cruel joke that one of us was flatulent, but she could never work out who it was. As I said, I have my own modest work space over the garage and I'm perfectly content up there. I'll fetch Kristal's studio keys. But I need to know when they will be released to me.'

'When will what be released, Callum?'

'My family, for God's sake! My son and ... and the b-b-b-body of my wife! I need to make the necessary arrangements, don't you understand? Kristal was, unfortunately, never a Christian, but it came to me in church this morning that this, at least, is my call. I talked it through with the vicar and she is more than willing. I think Branscombe has the most beautiful church-yard in the West Country.'

Oak dissolved into tears and immediately Caine bounded to the sofa and began hugging him – actually hugging him. In all her fifteen years in the job, Shanti had never seen another cop hug someone. A polite English squeeze of the shoulder maybe, but what was taking place in front of her was a full-on man-on-man empathy session. Foreheads pressed together. Gripped arms entwined. Of course she felt sorry for Oak, but it was essential to stay detached. She hadn't yet worked out what Caine was, but she at least was a professional. In any case, she hadn't eliminated the grieving widower as a suspect.

But as Caine had made clear, he had his own way of doing things, and astonishingly, his methods seemed to work. Oak shuddered and sobbed in Caine's arms, and when he finally calmed a little, he began to talk, detailing his life with Kristal, from the first very public coupling, which had begun their relationship, to the equally public death, which had terminated it. There were mentions of other protagonists in their lives: Marlene Moss, his old teacher at Falmouth, had been at the show, as well as Oak's student flatmate – and later Kristal's photographer and assistant – Oliver Sweetman, who had still worked for Kristal on an occasional basis, though compromised by some sort of head injury.

Although there was nothing in his monologue that struck Shanti as particularly suspicious, she had heard many emotional outpourings from people who turned out to be pathologically lying psychopaths. Some of the most convincing ones had studied drama at school. Her ex-husband had been an excellent example of someone who was economical with the truth.

She made a mental note to seek out Marlene Moss, Oliver Sweetman, the curator Saul Spencer – anyone, for that matter, who could help raise the enigmatic artist from the cloudy fluid and into the spotlight.

'One final question, Mr Oak,' she said. 'Can you remember where you were in the hours leading up to the show?'

Oak looked at her with hollow eyes. 'I remember exactly. I went to church in Branscombe—'

'Sorry, I think you're getting confused. You went to church this morning, but the show opened yesterday, Saturday.'

'I'm not confused at all. Yesterday was St Mary Magdalene's

day. I always go to church on a holy day of obligation. After the service I had a crab sandwich and a half-pint of Branoc at the Fountain Head. Then I came home and walked the dogs on the beach, then worked in my studio until five forty-five. After that I got shaved and changed so I could be at the Meat Hook by seven.'

'Who else was at home?'

'Oh, I've no idea. I saw Kristal at breakfast time running around like a headless chicken. To be honest, the dogs and I learnt to keep out of the way when she was in one of her creative frenzies. She could be very snappy indeed.'

'Did Art visit Mangrove House yesterday ... or Oliver Sweetman?'

'Honestly, I don't know. I'm in a world of my own when I'm painting. In any case, my studio has roof lights but almost no windows.'

'Is there anyone who could corroborate your movements?'

Shanti noticed Caine studying Oak.

'Well, the vicar and congregants at Branscombe; and the landlord of the Fountain Head. After that, I was alone in my studio.'

'But you walked on the beach. Did you meet anyone there?'

'No. You hardly ever see people down there.'

'Is it a private beach?'

'Not private, but it's almost inaccessible except from the steps at the foot of our garden. I suppose I didn't see anyone until I arrived at the Meat Hook, which was already busy. Then I met Marlene and Ollie Sweetman and many others.'

'But to be clear, you don't know where Art was in the hours before the private view?'

'You'll have to ask him. But if you think he was in the master gallery, submerging his mother in a tank of formaldehyde, then you're seriously mistaken.'

As they got up, Shanti turned to Oak. 'I'd like to take a quick look at Kristal's studio.'

'If you must. I haven't been in there for years.'

He led them to the far side of the house and up a short flight of stairs, where he fumbled with keys in the lock until the studio door swung open. Something spectral rose out of the room and swept across the vast floor to where they stood. It was a blanket of doom – the dull, deadly smell of formaldehyde.

The room had probably been a grand dining room when the house was built, with the French doors they had seen from the outside and a huge multi-paned bay window. The main studio was an expansive split-level workspace. A flight of steps led up to a platform like a minstrel's gallery overhead. In contrast to the rest of the house, the place was clinically clean and precise – more operating theatre than artist's studio. A long trestle table was piled neatly with dozens of sketchbooks, while the walls up to the raised gallery were hung with photographs of Kristal posing with celebrities and dignitaries in front of her artworks. As she studied the photos, Shanti noticed that, whether as a gazelle-like student or a beautiful forty-year-old, the artist's demeanour never changed: blonde hair tied back carelessly with a band; a garish smear of lipstick that might have been applied in an earthquake; a starkly short lace mini dress; and those red DM boots that Knightly had bagged and tagged. The only variation to the carefully branded red and white style was when Kristal was naked. And that was plenty of the time.

The shrine to herself was not limited to photos. There were dozens of framed newspaper articles and cuttings. Alongside fawning pieces from broadsheets were prurient tabloid hatchet jobs. Good or bad, publicity seemed all the same to Kristal Havfruen. So long as people were talking about her.

The deeply unsettling thing about the place was that Shanti found herself wandering amongst a dumbstruck crowd – the ampu-tee army of hyper-real Kristal Havfruens; chillingly large or weirdly small, naked or dressed in red-booted laciness. They lay and flew and posed in melodramatic stances. Long-legged. Slender-waisted. Pert-breasted. Green-eyed. Smudge-lipped imperiousness.

'I have an important question, Mr Oak – do you have any idea if your wife originally intended to put a model of herself in the tank?' asked Shanti.

'Yes, it's quite possible,' replied Oak, his voice a husky croak.

'Then where is that model? The one that was swapped for her body? There are many Kristals here, but none are life-size and none precisely resemble the figure in the tank.'

'Look, I have absolutely no idea. As I explained, Kristal didn't discuss her work with me. She said it was beyond my compre-hension.'

Shanti approached one of the humanoids – an alarmingly larger-than-life naked Kristal with hands clasped in prayer. She touched its face and a chill ran through her. The skin was waxy and stiffly yielding. Like an hour-dead corpse.

It had been a hard day's night, and Shanti trailed behind the two men up the main stairway. When they reached the front door, she was dismayed to hear Caine say, 'We won't keep you much longer, Mr Oak, but you said we might have a quick look at your own studio?'

Oak led them silently past the silver Volvo on the unkempt

cobbled yard, surrounded by outbuildings and overgrown laurels. A rusting spiral staircase led to a creosoted structure above a double garage. Oak had been correct – there were no windows overlooking the yard. The small door was not locked, and he ushered them into a low-ceilinged space beneath the gables, which smelled sweetly of turpentine and linseed oil. The sloping ceilings had been fitted with Velux windows, but the overhanging laurels blocked all but a greenish gloam.

As their eyes adjusted, Shanti and Caine made out a crustaceous cavern oozing with paint, like a mud-splattered trench at Passchendaele.

'Well, this is where I exorcise my demons,' said Oak in a matter-of-fact tone.

Congealed brushes bristled in pots amidst a barnacled forest of petrified easels. And all around, on shelves and chairs and easels, stood Oak's thickly painted canvases, a riot of chaotic brushstrokes and sombre colours.

The work was as impenetrable as Kristal's, but to Shanti it was equally deranged.

As she stepped closer to the paintings, she noticed words or hieroglyphics scratched angrily into the coagulated surfaces with a nail or a knife. With an inward shudder, she realised they were biblical quotations.

He wasted his seed upon the ground.

Return to your mistress and submit to ill treatment at her hands.

The sun will be darkened, and the moon will not give its light; the stars will fall from the sky; and the heavenly bodies will be shaken.

Surely a bloody husband art thou to me.

In the car, Caine seemed reinvigorated. It was as if the detective

71

work had rekindled a hidden fire. Shanti, on the other hand, felt utterly drained.

'I'll tell you what, Caine, this case has put me off art for life. What the fuck was going on in Oak's man cave? And there's me telling Paul off for leaving his socks on the floor.'

'Yeah, that work was intriguing . . . a mass of contradictions. I sensed a struggle between the figurative and the conceptual. The paintings were full of softness and space, and then it was as if he had attacked them with those angry words.'

'You know what? I hear the Meat Hook Gallery are looking for someone to write the bullshit in their catalogues. You could do that.'

'The lesson is to avoid making presumptions about people. I had Oak down as a meek, downtrodden husband, but those images were aggressive, weren't they?'

'All I know is my mum wouldn't want one above the TV. But I must admit, you were good. All that lovey stuff made him open up. Maybe better than I could have done. So listen, DI Vincent Caine, although you are possibly – definitely – the most unlikely cop of all time, there's a job for you if you want it.'

'Ah, wait a minute, Shanti. I'm still not convinced about this.'

'Come on, you had fun today, you know you did.'

'I enjoyed your company, that's true. But what I'm trying to explain is that I'm not cut out for police work. There's too much pain and suffering.'

'Listen, Caine, tell me this is none of my business, but your paid sick leave won't go on forever. How will you manage then?'

'I live simply. And people are very kind.'

'But you can't just take. We all have to give something back.'

'That's true.'

'And what you give out, you get back ten times over. Karmic law, see.'

'That's very good, Shanti.'

'Listen, you said it yourself, we make a great team. Yin and yang. I'll buy the coffees, how's that?'

'I don't drink coffee.'

'Carrot juice. Beetroot smoothies. Fairy tears. Whatever you want.'

'Tea is good. Half a spoon of honey.'

They were rolling down Broad Street in Lyme Regis, where the late-afternoon sun picked out every colour on the overhead bunting, creating a kaleidoscope of dancing lights.

'Well, if you come to the station tomorrow, there'll be as much tea as you can drink.'

His face fell. 'The station?'

'I need someone to help me grill Art – you know, good cop, bad cop. Take your pick.'

'There's no reason for Art to be in custody, Shanti. He's just lost his mother and his father needs him at his side.'

'But you see, this is my problem: unless you can help to eliminate him from inquiries, I'm going to be under massive pressure to make an arrest. You've got to look at the facts. Art argued with his mother. He likes his ket. Hell, he even helped arrange the show, and he knew about the glass tank! I'm sorry, but it's not looking good for A Boy Named Art.'

Shanti steered the Saab around the clock tower at the bottom of the hill and came to a halt. But Caine did not climb out. A pause was developing. A long one.

'You know what, Shanti? We're more alike than you think.'

'I don't think so, Caine.'

'I mean, we are both obsessed with the same question.'

'What question?'

Outside the sweet shop, the ancient owner was dismantling the display, gathering up sunhats, buckets and fishing nets. Caine pointed to the board beside the newspaper rack. There, in bold capitals, was the infernal question that had greeted Shanti at the beginning of this long, strange day:

WHO KILLED KRISTAL?

'You really, really want to know, don't you, Shanti? Well, I can't deny it. So do I.'

A grin blossomed on Shanti's face. 'So you're in?'

Vincent Caine unclipped his seat belt and swung open the door. She leaned over and grabbed his arm.

'Wait a minute, Caine! How do I contact you? We need to be in touch, and carrier pigeons are unreliable.'

He wrote something in his notepad. Tore off a corner of the page and handed her an elegantly written name and telephone number.

'Zeb? What the fuck is Zeb?'

'Zeb's a Syrian guy I know. He's a local youth leader and also a keen mountain-biker. Let's just say I did his family a favour a few years ago and Zeb feels the need to repay me. He's my messenger boy. You call him, night or day, and he will pedal to the cabin with a message. His best time is around fifteen minutes door to door. Is that OK?'

'I've got a better idea. Why don't *you* get a bike?'

'I do have a bike, but I only use it in town. I took it along the Undercliff once, but the forest objected.'

He climbed out of the car, waved once and walked away. Shanti watched his lean silhouette against the dazzling sea.

And the sun created the weird illusion that Vincent Caine was shimmering and dissolving, like a nomad at an oasis.

Chapter 8

Love You to Death

Yeovil police station was an ugly building, where ugly things happened. As Caine walked towards the main doors, his body yearned to be elsewhere – somewhere with less concrete and more compassion.

Spotting the media scrum by the front steps, he slipped around the side, where a congregation of his old buddies stood vaping and smoking at a fire exit.

'Bloody hell! Who have we here?'

'Veggie Cop!'

'Been busy, Vince?'

'Busy growing his hair.'

'How's the lentil health?'

'Still got your finger on the pulse?'

'I always knew being vegetarian was a missed steak.'

Caine could take it. He could give it too if he wanted. But he did not want. It was at times like this that he knew that he had changed – only the ego felt threatened. Without ego, there was no threat.

He smiled warmly, squeezed a few palms and stepped inside the building. 'Soya later,' someone called.

Benno spotted him and they exchanged greetings. Caine missed the man's fatherly ways. His innate sense of integrity. The ability to generate respect without ever raising his voice. In the steaming forests of Thailand, he had met other men like Benno.

As he wandered along the corridors to what used to be his office, Caine was a wild fox who had strayed indoors. The fluorescent lights, the polystyrene ceiling tiles, the cold colours of the walls were anathema to him now.

Stepping into his old office was like stepping into the past. But things had changed. The place was messy but alive. Every surface was piled with papers. There were children's paintings on the wall. A tub of Lego on a rug on the floor. Some big-leafed plants near a low settee. When Shanti Joyce smiled at him, he remembered why he was here.

She was wiping two reasonably clean mugs with a reasonably clean tea towel. 'Weird to be back?' she said through the steam of the kettle.

'Weird's my thing,' said Caine. 'This your boy?' He lifted a photograph from the desk.

'His name's Paul.'

'He'll break a few hearts some day.'

The beaming boy had his mother's big soft eyes and an apple face that was all his own.

'He's a good kid. Spends too much time staring at screens. And he pines for his dad. Zeb got the message to you, then?'

'Thanks for sending Dunster with the car.'

'Thought you'd enjoy the intellectual banter. Hey, listen …

77

I'm sorry if I was scratchy yesterday. Don't take it personally – I hate all men equally.'

He looked to see if she was joking, but she had already moved on. 'OK, quick briefing. Our boy's in Interview Room 2 with his lawyer – some stuck-up cow from Kensington. Locals lawyers aren't good enough for the living artwork.'

'You've really taken against him, haven't you?'

'Everyone's a suspect to me, Caine. Including you. But I've noticed that he spills out all kinds of stuff when he's angry. Like I say, good cop, bad cop. You dry his tears and I'll give him a light grilling. Gas mark 7.'

She handed him a mug, a teaspoon and a jar of honey.

'Sorry, I couldn't afford organic. But what's a few pesticides between friends?'

She picked up her laptop and tapped a finger knowingly on its side. 'You wait till you see what I've got on here . . .'

'Show me.'

'That would spoil the surprise. Let's just say it's a little movie, which Art Havfruen will be keen *not* to see. I can't wait to see his face.'

They carried their mugs, notes and the laptop along a mile of corridors, where every door opened memories for Caine: of hookers, hustlers, boozers, paedos, crackheads, arsonists, domestics. The hopeless. The abused. The lost. Those who had started life with a poor hand of cards. If Caine knew one thing, it was that everyone had a backstory. And pain was passed on like a baton.

Interview Room 2 had been designed by an architect who considered light, colour, space and love to be superfluous details. Windowless. Airless. Flickeringly fluorescent. Fitted out with mirrors and spycams and lists of rules where pictures should be.

Shaking hands with the lawyer (rigid) and the boy (angry), Caine took a seat at the scratched Formica table and searched for the resources that had got him through these situations before. The lawyer, a haughty woman with a scoop of vanilla hair, was instructing the dishevelled green-eyed youth that he had no obligation to say anything at all. But Caine guessed her advice was wasted. Art Havfruen could not help spilling words, and even when he was not speaking, his twitchy body language was as easy to read as a mime artist. Right now, despite a night in a cell and the obscene nature of his mother's death, the young man was bristling with indignation.

Shanti pushed a few buttons on the recording device and, pulling up a plastic chair beside Caine, began to recite the formalities: place, date, time and names of those present.

'Art Havfruen, I'm DI Shantala Joyce . . .'

'I know who you fucking are.'

'. . . and with me is DI Vincent Caine. I'm sure you're anxious to get away so I'll come straight to the point – on the night of the twenty-second of July, you were arrested at the Meat Hook Gallery in Bruton, Somerset, in possession of three point seven grams of CK1, cocaine–ketamine mix.'

'At this point I would like to state that my client does not deny the charge and remind you that he has cooperated in every way possible,' interjected the lawyer.

'In fact your client resisted arrest and assaulted an officer,' said Shanti. 'How I look at that depends on how we get along today.'

'How we get along today depends on how much bullshit I get from you—'

'Art,' said Caine softly. 'Listen, mate. This is a devastating time for you. We get that. We want exactly the same as you – to find the person who did this to Kristal and get you home as soon as possible. DI Joyce and I met your dad yesterday. He's a lovely man and he's missing you . . .'

The boy looked up at this sincere man with the long hair and kind dark eyes, and for a moment there was something like a connection.

'Unfortunately, it's not just the possession,' said Shanti. 'Can I draw your attention to Item 1a in the file in front of you?'

The lawyer opened the file and studied the first page, sealed inside a plastic sleeve.

'You're looking at the preliminary findings of an autopsy on Art's mother, Kristal Havfruen. If you scan to the middle of the list . . . just here . . . you'll notice the presence of an unusual substance in the bloodstream.'

Art's already pale face emptied of colour. 'This is a stitch-up!' he roared, rising to his feet and kicking the chair violently. 'You put that there! My mother never touched ket . . . she wouldn't even know what it was!'

'Sit down, Mr Havfruen. Your mother drowned in a tank of formaldehyde, but she was drugged before she was placed inside it. Drugged with an extremely large quantity of the very same narcotic we found in your possession and in your bloodstream.'

'Shows how much you know – there's a difference between CK1 and ket.'

'But the latter is found in the former, I believe. I know you don't inject drugs, Art, but do you own a hypodermic syringe?'

'Fuck off!' he scoffed.

'Do you have anything to say about why your mother had so much ketamine in her system?'

'Cos you put it there, bitch! Because you and your scummy mates needed to give the press some answers, and as usual, Art Havfruen is the story they're looking for. They're exploiting you and you're too dumb to see it.'

Caine saw Shanti momentarily rise to the bait. He got up, took Art's arm and guided him gently back to his seat.

Shanti said, 'Art Havfruen, I'm going to remind you to keep calm and avoid personal abuse. Is that perfectly clear? Now let me move on to my next question – where were you during the day of the private view? That is, Saturday the twenty-second of July.'

Art flinched visibly.

'You don't need to comment,' whispered the lawyer.

'We're on your side,' soothed Caine.

'All right, I'll tell you. I've ... I've got a weekend place in Charmouth. You probably know that anyway. I was chilling. Minding my own fucking business. Watching Barcelona beat Arsenal.'

'Can anyone corroborate that?'

'What, that Barcelona beat Arsenal?' Art leaned in to the lawyer and whispered in her ear. The lawyer responded on his behalf.

'Mr Havfruen has nothing more to add. He was watching TV at home.'

Shanti sat back. Breathed out heavily and folded her arms.

Now it was Caine's turn.

'Your mum was an extraordinary woman, Art. She seemed to affect people in a lot of ways. Some people loved her work and others ... not so much. But I have a question that I keep thinking about. What was it like to be the son of Kristal Havfruen?

What's it like to be A Boy Named Art?' His warm voice thawed the chill in the room.

Art shrugged. 'Dunno. What's it like to be anything? It's all I've ever known. Seemed normal, I suppose.' He wiped his nose with his fist like a hurt child. 'When I was a kid, I wished I was just her son, you know, instead of her fucking career.'

'I can understand that. And how did that make you feel?'

Art sighed and shook his head. Was this a police interview or a counselling session? Caine's gentle questioning seemed to have thrown him.

'I fucking . . . I felt . . . confused!' The lawyer tapped his arm, trying to catch his attention, but Art shook her off. 'I worshipped her when I was a kid. I was sort of in love with her, I suppose, the way every kid is in love with their mum. But she never, *ever* gave anything back, and that made me . . . *angry!*' he said, eyes glassing, teeth grinding.

'Did you hate her?' asked Shanti.

'See, she's at it again. Planting words in my mouth and planting evidence where she fucking wants it. Look,' he said, 'I know what you want to find – some fucked-up drug user who killed his mother because he wasn't breastfed or cuddled as a child. I've done the therapy. Yeah, Kristal wasn't perfect. But she was a fucking genius, and maybe geniuses can't help the way they are. I did my best to look after her. Dad, too. And I didn't . . . I DID NOT fucking kill her.'

'So who do you think did it, Art?' whispered Caine.

Art subsided in his chair. 'That's your job, mate. That's what you're paid to do. You figure it out.'

Caine remained steady. 'OK, you're doing well. Really helpful. But I want you to think back, over the years or in recent weeks – is there anyone who might have wanted your mother dead?'

'Listen, Mum pissed people off. That's what she did. She was a professional pisser-offer. She pissed people off in Denmark. She pissed people off in Falmouth and she pissed people off for her whole career. But no . . . I can't think of anyone who would go that far.'

'I have an important question for you, Art,' said Shanti. 'Did you argue with your mother at the gallery before the show?'

'Fuck, I don't know. Probably. We always argued. But no . . . wait a minute, I never saw her at the gallery. In fact I only saw her once that day, and she was floating in a tank.'

'You're sure about that?'

'Hundred per cent.'

'OK. Well, I'd like to show you something, if you don't mind,' said Shanti, flipping open the laptop and angling it so everyone could see.

'What's this?'

'Just wait a second . . . Right, this is CCTV footage. We're at the Meat Hook Gallery on the day of the private view. A man and a woman come into the master gallery at 18.30. The time's at the top of the screen. They're arguing, aren't they, Art? Isn't that what you'd say?'

'I dunno, the camera's too high.'

'But that's you, isn't it? The camera's pointing at your face.'

Squirming in his plastic chair, Art Havfruen had turned a whiter shade of pale.

'You're dancing about quite a bit, and although there's no sound, I'd say you were yelling. Like you yelled at me later that evening.'

'Fuck you, bitch.'

'Also, you're shoving that woman, and shaking her by the shoulders in a very aggressive manner. Who is that woman, Art? Who are you arguing with?'

'My client has no further comment. The quality of the film is poor. The lighting in the gallery is bad, and in any case the image of the woman is mainly a back view. You know perfectly well this would be inadmissible as evidence in court.'

'Inadmissible? Do you agree that we are watching Mr Havfruen – who has just categorically denied meeting his mother at the gallery – having a violent confrontation with a petite woman with very distinctive blonde hair, a short lacy white dress and a pair of red Dr Marten boots? Is that what we can all see?'

'It's not what you think,' muttered Art Havfruen.

'And watch this bit carefully. This is where she runs outside. There are those boots. She stumbles on the doorstep and almost crawls away. She's terrified of you, Art.'

'So what did you think of my little film show?' asked Shanti as they returned to her office. 'It's a knockout, isn't it? Did you see how he responded?'

'It's definitely significant,' agreed Caine. 'But I still don't think he did it.'

'Significant? This is nuclear, Caine! What do you mean, he didn't do it? Am I the only one with functioning eyesight? Did you not see that aggressive argument with Kristal? It's as clear as day.'

'I agree, it doesn't look good. But Callum Oak told us they argued all the time, so maybe Art forgot about that incident. We don't see him murdering her, Shanti. And I don't know if you noticed—'

'Of course I bloody noticed. You're talking about the tank in the background that appears to have a figure inside.'

'Which means that Kristal was still alive at six thirty. If Art murdered her – in fact, whoever murdered her – we would see that dummy being hauled out of the tank and Kristal's body being placed inside.'

'I know that, Caine. I admit, it is unbelievably weird. Like Harry bloody Houdini.'

Now they were in the office, where Shanti stretched herself behind the desk in a proprietorial way. Caine carefully moved a pile of papers and toys, pulled off his shoes and sat cross-legged on the low sofa. Shanti turned the laptop towards him.

'Look, I'll whizz through the whole afternoon in the master gallery. Right ... at 15.26, the forklift brings in the tank. Here are the two guys from MasterMoves, who lower it carefully onto the podium. They unscrew the plywood packing, which they take away when they leave. They're in and out of the gallery in seven minutes flat. At 18.30 we see the heated argument between Art and Kristal, and as you noticed, the tank remains completely untouched behind them. Eventually Kristal runs outside, stumbling on the doorstep, as if she's terrified of Art's raging.

'Then Art leaves and nothing happens until 19.00 – I'll slow it down here – when the big guy, Oliver Sweetman, comes in and places the boots carefully on top of the tank, gives the glass a quick polish, then steps outside. If you look carefully, you can see he's smiling the whole time, which is either a bit creepy or it means he's completely blameless. After that, the camera picks up no movement whatsoever until the curator, Saul Spencer, leads the guests into the gallery at 20.38, followed by utter bedlam as Callum Oak pulls the tank onto its side and eventually levers it open, and the body tumbles out along with a few gallons of formaldehyde. It's absolutely baffling.'

'Did you say that Benno has talked to the couriers from MasterMoves?' asked Caine.

'Yes, he's convinced they're sound. Hang on, here's their website ...'

Shanti opened a very professional-looking site. Alongside a photo of a small team beside a couple of vans was another of their punning slogans: *MasterMoves. We step on Degas. You have nothing Toulouse.*

'I don't get it,' said Shanti.

'These are the names of ... Oh, never mind!'

'According to Benno, the MasterMoves guys had been back and forth for weeks, delivering weird things in glass tanks from Kristal's studio to the Meat Hook. It wasn't their job to check what was inside. Besides, the gallery had very low lighting when they unpacked the crate.'

'You're suggesting they wouldn't have known whether the tank contained a replica or an actual body?'

'That's what they say. And Benno is convinced they weren't hiding anything. MasterMoves is a squeaky-clean family business. But anyway, we've already established that it was a dummy they delivered, because we see Art arguing with Kristal at 18.30, and she's very much alive.'

'That's certainly the way it appears.'

'Well, Caine, you can say what you like, but if you ask me, Art Havfruen isn't behaving like someone who's just lost his mother.'

'Everyone grieves in their own way, Shanti. I've come across this before. Listen, here's a boy who was raised by emotionally immature parents, so his feelings are a bit ... stunted. To be honest, I've never come across anyone with such conflicted opinions about a parent – he said he was in love with her, didn't he?'

'Yeah. He said that every kid is in love with their mum. Were you in love with your mum, Caine?'

'Not like that, Dr Freud.'

'And tell me this, why was he so shifty about his movements before the show? He told us he was in his weekend gaff in Charmouth, but he sure didn't want to talk about it.'

'It's true, the question threw him. But he could be feeling guilty about any number of illicit activities.'

Shanti bit a nail. 'Look, I admit I have literally no idea how someone drugged Kristal and swapped her with a silicone replica without any of it showing up on the cameras. It's like a damned ghost story or something. But I will find out, Caine – that's what I do. I'm like Shantala sodding Holmes. If you want to tag along and see how it's done, that's fine. In the meantime, Art Havfruen has one hell of a lot of explaining to do. The Super wants him rearrested. The station is under massive pressure from HQ. Did you see that pack of newshounds out front?'

'I saw them.'

'If I get asked one more time, "Who killed Kristal?" I swear I will commit murder myself.'

'Then surely it makes sense to get it right? Listen, Shanti. You're under a lot of strain, I know that. But you told me that your last case went south, so if you charge the wrong person, it may be the end of your career. I advise you to slow down. Really. Art isn't going anywhere. I think we should release him right now. He's no harm to anyone.'

'You're telling me to slow down. But if Art is innocent, that means there's still a killer at large.'

'That's true, but my instinct tells me that this was very personal indeed. I mean, the thing was specifically designed to target Kristal and no one else.'

'But it's so frustrating, because I can see that Art is hiding stuff. If he isn't guilty, why is he being so obstructive? I just don't get it. But yeah, the custody clock has run out. I have to charge him or let him go. And in spite of the CCTV footage, and the drugs, and all his lies, I don't have enough to nail him.'

'Exactly. Get Benno to instruct him to remain in the West Country for the time being – either with his dad at Mangrove House, or at his pad in Charmouth. I'm sure he can work from home for a few days.'

'So what do you suggest now, oh Wise One? Shall we meditate?'

'We could do worse. I think we need to listen to what Art was telling us. He said that Kristal has been pissing people off for years. We need to go back.'

'Go back where?'

'Back to where it all began.'

Chapter 9

The Deadly Siren

If you've never been to the Cornish town of Falmouth, you might imagine that a giant toddler has tipped her building blocks down the hillside, where they have tumbled higgledy-piggledy to the water below. Indeed, some of those granite buildings appear to have settled in the harbour itself, where they perch on rocks and piers amongst the groaning umbilical cords of the boats. There are mysterious alleyways, leg-aching stairways and unexpected palm trees. Above it all is the murderous screaming of gulls.

On the phone, Marlene Moss had welcomed their visit enthusiastically. 'I'm not sure if I can contribute anything of value, but I don't get many visitors these days, so it would be lovely to see you.' She had gone on to give detailed directions to her cottage. 'It's quite a climb!' she had warned, and ended by conveying her profound shock and sadness at Kristal's death.

With another hour to kill before their appointment, Shanti and Caine found themselves on an elevated street called

Woodlane. A sign by a pair of iron gates informed them that this was Falmouth School of Art, the college where Moss had been head of painting, and Kristal, Callum Oak and Oliver Sweetman had spent their student days.

They strolled down a gently meandering drive beside soft lawns and elephantine plants, where a number of self-assured students with topiary hairstyles talked and relaxed in the sub-tropical gardens. No one paid the slightest attention to the two DIs as they wandered past glass studios and noisy workshops. One building was particularly impressive – a sharp-edged theatre complex of steel and glass, in which expensive film and computer equipment could be seen. A plaque explained that this was the Havfruen Building, the construction of which had been made possible by a generous donation from the Rasmussen Foundation of Copenhagen. Beside the plaque someone had left a bunch of red and white roses, wilting in their cellophane.

In a less manicured part of the campus they came across the slightly tired fine art studios – modest timber-clad buildings in which a few students chatted or worked half-heartedly at paint-splattered easels.

'Do you notice the difference?' asked Caine.

'The difference between what?'

'Maybe I'm imagining it, but it's almost as if the traditional arts have been left behind in favour of performance and video. I wonder if that's Kristal's legacy?'

'All I know is I wish someone had paid me to lie around sunbathing when I was that age,' sighed Shanti.

Walking out of the art school and into the town, they found themselves dawdling along cobbled streets with hot pasties in hand – vegetarian and chicken respectively. Despite the urgency of the case, Shanti almost found herself enjoying the sunshine and, although she would not have admitted it, the presence of the tall man at her side.

She was brought out of her reverie by a headline in the local paper outside a newsagent:

WHO KILLED KRISTAL?
STILL NO ARREST IN HAVFRUEN CASE

'Oh Jesus. As if I needed reminding,' she muttered.

But she was talking to herself. Caine had left her side and was crouching beside a sleeping bag in a doorway, from which an old man reached out a pathetic Styrofoam cup. Caine unquestioningly rooted in his pocket and dropped in a generous handful of coins.

Was it a uniquely male thing, to wander off in the middle of conversations? And now Caine and the old man appeared to be deep in a conversation of their own.

'Hey, Caine, are you with me or your new buddy?' she called.

He squeezed the man's hand then briskly caught up with her. 'Sorry,' he said.

'We're cops, not social workers,' she reminded him.

'As I always say, what you give out—'

'Yeah, I know what you always say. And what did you get back? A copy of the *Big Issue*?'

'I got some information. That old boy has lived in Falmouth all his life. His wife died and he fell on hard times—'

'That's deeply tragic, Caine. But how is it helpful?'

'He knew all about Kristal Havfruen. He says everyone in the town knew about her. As a student, she rented a place called Rock Cottage. Apparently you get to it down one of these alleyways ... that one, I think. It's a bit of a weird place by all accounts. You want to look?'

She checked the time and nodded, and in a moment they were heading down a slippery alleyway beside a bare-breasted ship's figurehead, where cats prowled and huge gulls fought over upturned bins. It was a gloomy place, and it stank. At the bottom of the slope, oily water lapped at their feet.

'Oh, I can see it,' said Caine pointing out into the water. 'Look, Rock Cottage.'

'Sorry? Kristal lived on a boat?'

'No, look carefully ... see that black rock out there? There's a building on it.'

There was indeed a minuscule fisherman's cottage on a rock far out in the water, but it was well camouflaged. The building appeared to be constructed of the same black stone as the tiny island itself, and it was similarly caked with barnacles and guano.

'You're telling me that's where she lived as a student? But ... I mean, how the hell did she get there?'

'When the tide's low, there's a causeway,' said a voice behind them. 'Otherwise you row it.'

They turned to see a pear-shaped man in dungarees and wellingtons. The front of his wide belly was smeared with blood and silvery fish scales. In one hand he held a bone-handled knife, in the other a bucket of writhing crabs.

'Didn't mean to give you a fright, but Rock Cottage is my place. I rented it to her back in the nineties. You talking about Kristal, are you?'

'We were,' said Shanti. 'How well did you know her?'

'Not well. Her stepdad paid the rent into my bank account, so I never had no problems. Mr Ras-something ...'

'Rasmussen?'

'That's the fella. But no one forgot Kristal once they'd met her, and I'm proper sad to hear the news. She was a right looker, I'll tell you that. Little white skirt. Shiny red boots. Turned every head in town. I live up there,' he said nodding upwards to an overhanging window on a ramshackle building. 'So I could keep an eye on my tenants. You stand on a chair in the back bedroom, you can see everything. Many times I watched her crossing the water, with her blonde hair shimmering in the moonlight. As if she were walking on water, it were.'

'Did she live alone?'

'Press, are you?'

'Not press . . .' Shanti took out her warrant card and flashed it at the man, who nodded sagely.

'Mind you, I'm not allowed to rent the place no more 'cos of health an' safety. So all I have is the crabbing.'

Caine read him like a book. He pulled out his wallet. 'How much for all the crabs?'

'Twenty.'

'Ten?'

'Done.'

The man handed over the bucket and stuffed the note in a fishy pocket. Shanti watched his gruff countenance change to an affable smile.

'Kristal lived alone, but she had plenty of visitors. Two lads in particular seemed very taken with her. Art students they were, so Lord knows what they got up to.'

'Did you know their names, these lads?'

'No, but I've a good memory for faces. One tall and good-looking with a curly top, the other a giant of a fella with a face like a John Dory an' a mop of orange hair. Back an' forth they were, over the causeway. I remember one night in particular – I happened to have my binocs, so I saw it all – the ugly one came calling. Walked across the causeway as if he were terrified of falling in. Rapped on the door, and when she opened up, she barely had a strip o' clothing on her young body – I didn't know where to look. And behind her was the good-looking one. There was some raised voices and you could tell there was tension between the two lads. But it was all a game to Kristal.'

'Did you have feelings for her?'

'Course I bloody did. A clam would've had feelings for a girl like that. There was a lot of talk about what went on up at the art school – life models sitting for hours with their bits and pieces dangling while the students drew them. But that show was on another level. You know what I'm talking about – that bloody sex show. A group of my mates went to watch. She provoked people, she did. Stirred up unnatural desires. And now she's paid a price for it and I'm not saying I agree, but I have some heart for them that did it, that's all I want to say.'

The pear-shaped man turned and retreated into the shadows.

'And what the hell are you going to do with those?' said Shanti, nodding at the bucket.

In answer, Caine knelt down and tipped the container slowly into the lapping water, guiding a few stragglers on their way with gentle fingers. When they were gone, he rinsed the bucket carefully and returned it to the crabber's door.

'Jesus,' sighed Shanti.

Back on the high street, Caine said, 'I suppose the curly-haired one was Oak.'

'And the one with a face like a fish?'

'Whoever that was had their heart broken, that's for sure.'

Following Google Maps on Shanti's phone, they began to climb steeply towards the eastern end of the town. It was heavy going, and when they reached the place called Jacob's Ladder, Shanti stopped and stared in dismay.

'You have got to be bloody kidding!'

In front of them rose the longest flight of granite steps she had ever seen in her life, worn smooth by hundreds of years of footfall.

The climb was hard enough, but the infuriating thing was that Caine kept chattering as if he barely registered the Alpine feat they were enduring.

'You know what I kept thinking when that man was talking?'

'What?' gasped Shanti.

'He was like something out of Central Casting, wasn't he! But the image that came to mind was of a beautiful siren, luring sailors to their doom.'

Shanti was almost bent double, but she paused long enough to splutter, 'Typical sexist bullshit! That sort of folklore has kept women in their place for centuries. Trust me, every culture has its own way of repressing women. We're either old and past it, or young and lethal.'

'You're probably right. I'll think about that. I suppose places like this are filled with legends. You want to rest?'

'I am absolutely fine, thank you very much. You go ahead. I'm enjoying the view.'

And what a view it was, across the bay to St Mawes and the Helford River, with Pendennis Castle in the distance.

When she finally reached the summit, gulping in hungry lungfuls of air, Caine had already located Marlene Moss's tiny terraced cottage on Vernon Place. The front yard was dominated by a wheelie bin and recycling boxes, with little piles of leaves and scraps of litter.

He seemed to be having trouble with the doorbell. He pushed it long and hard, but the battery was almost flat.

The dull peal sounded like a death rattle.

Chapter 10

House of Bones

She was a birdlike woman who seemed as skeletal as the walking frame on which she hung. But she sparkled with humour and it was clear that Marlene Moss had been striking in her day – like Charlotte Rampling, Caine thought, or one of those fiercely intelligent stars of European cinema.

'You must be Ms Joyce and Mr Caine,' she said, her voice husky. 'Dead on time. Come in, come in!'

She swung the Zimmer through 180 degrees and shuffled along a narrow hallway, where Caine had to stoop beneath an arch. The place reeked of tobacco. Even in the half-light, Caine noticed the paintings. His eyes moved over exquisite watercolours, charcoal life drawings, and small portraits in oil. At the end of the hall, they reached a minuscule sitting room. Again, Caine was struck by the artworks, like dozens of little worlds on every wall. Casting his eye around the room, he saw echoes of Cornish masters like Alfred Wallis and Roger Hilton, and great oil painters like Bomberg and Auerbach. Could these be originals? If so, the decrepit Marlene Moss owned a collection of national significance.

'Welcome, welcome,' said Marlene, breaking into a rattling cough. 'It's so exciting to have you here. All the neighbours know about your visit. I've become quite a celebrity in Vernon Place. Shall we have tea?'

The old lady slumped into a high-backed chair by a fireplace and reached for a plastic tube draped over the arm. It was connected to an oxygen canister to her right, and she tucked the tube over her ear and inserted a pair of cannulas into her nostrils. She took a deep, slow breath and began to calm. On various surfaces around the room, Caine noticed ashtrays overflowing with brown stubs; the old lady had obviously chosen a slow suicide.

'You stay right where you are,' said Shanti. 'I'll make the tea.'

'That's very sweet of you,' said Marlene, still catching her breath. 'The kitchen is just through there.' She indicated a door behind her. 'You'll find everything laid out.'

Turning to Caine, she said, 'You can see that I don't get out as much as I'd like, and you'd be surprised how often people promise to call and then disappoint you.'

'Well, here we are,' said Caine.

'I have lung cancer, Mr Caine. It's entirely my own fault because I've been a smoker all my life. I know I shouldn't, but I still enjoy a cheeky one. Do you?'

She waggled an open packet at him and Caine noticed an amused intelligence in her cloudy blue eyes.

'No. No, I don't, but I don't judge you. We all make our own choices.'

'Well, my choice is to slip away with a smile on my face and

a Silk Cut in my hand. You know what they say – life's a dangerous business and you're lucky if you get out alive.'

As she rattled and fumbled with matches, Caine wandered
around admiring the artwork in the room, and in particular a
large painting over the fireplace. It was of cliffs and a raging sea,
and although the paint had been applied in bold, angular brushstrokes, the effect was incandescent and full of depth.

'Are you an art lover, Mr Caine?' asked Marlene.

'Very much so. This isn't an actual Bomberg, is it?'

'You know your painters! No, that's by one of my students.
These are all paintings by my students. I never had a family of
my own, so I think of them as my children. I sometimes wonder
if I might have been an artist in my own right in a different life.
But like mothers everywhere, I gave everything up for the children. They're all over the world now, doing wonderful things,
and I miss each and every one of them.' She smiled proudly, and
a tranquil expression settled on her face. 'I always encouraged
them to look at work by established artists before developing
their own style, which is why you see glimpses of the masters.
That seascape was painted by one of my most brilliant students,
a man named Callum Oak.'

Shanti returned with three steaming mugs. 'We've met Mr
Oak,' she said.

'And how was he?' asked Marlene. 'Poor dear Callum.'

'I'm afraid it's hit him hard,' said Caine.

'It was never a conventional marriage. But Callum was
devoted from the start, however unorthodox the beginning of
their relationship was.'

'You're referring to the performance at the art school
– *Preconception?*'

With a quivering hand, Marlene took a last pull on her cigarette, then stubbed it out and reached for her mug. 'I am a lover of culture, as you know, and I have an open mind about what is and what isn't art. But I confess that I have never seen anything quite like that exhibition.'

'You were there?' asked Caine.

'Oh yes. I was at the back, but that was close enough, thank you very much.' She set the quaking mug on a table. 'Performance art was never really my thing, and it was a distinctly uncomfortable afternoon. Animalistic, that's the way I describe it. I don't know if this is of any interest ...'

'It's of great interest, if you don't mind ...'

'Well, Kristal always had this notion about finding what she called the Immortal Idea – a bit pretentious, I always thought. I suppose she meant something so unique and shocking that it would never be forgotten.'

'Perhaps she achieved it in the end,' said Caine.

'Quite so. But when she took up with Callum, he began to lose his way as an artist – mixing sand in the paint and so on. He seemed to forget all the techniques I had taught him and began to talk a lot of baloney about "happenings" and releasing his "inner Shaman". It was a terrible waste of his talent, but he was completely under her spell. He certainly never painted like *that* again. Before the day in question, Kristal sent her minions around the campus putting up posters, and *Preconception* generated a huge amount of excitement. There was a mattress on a little stage at one end of the life room ... I realise this seems bizarre, but it was a time of experimentation and Kristal always got her way. And then when it happened, it was sad, actually. Callum was appallingly self-conscious at being naked in front of that crowd. They were such beautiful people in their prime, but it's not right, is it, Ms Joyce? Some things should happen behind closed doors.'

'I completely agree. But I suppose no one *had* to watch.'

'You would think so. I've thought about this many times, but it was magnetic. Everyone was caught up in it. There was almost a cult around Kristal Havfruen. And then of course the media got hold of the story and she gave interviews to art magazines and even the BBC . . . *Arena*, I think it was.'

'And then nine months later . . .'

'Nine months later came the performance known as *A Boy Named Art*. Of course Kristal was awarded a first-class honours degree, but as for poor Callum . . . he got a baby to care for and a 2:2. He seemed absolutely crushed. His father was a senior clergyman, so you can imagine what he made of it all.'

'Kristal clearly offended a lot of people . . . and you must have been upset too?'

'It takes a lot to upset me, Ms Joyce. You see it all at an art school. But it's a dilemma. Art is meant to provoke and challenge – one thinks of Picasso's *Guernica*, Munch's *Scream* and any number of works by Francis Bacon. Even Degas' *Little Dancer* caused a scandal in its time, did you know that?'

'I didn't. But I do know *The Scream*. My son did a project . . .'

'It was a turbulent time at the college. Perhaps you've heard that one of our tutors, Charles Ratakin, took his own life a few days later?'

'I didn't know that.'

'Well, it may have been coincidental. Poor Ratty suffered from terrible depression. They found his easel on a clifftop. But I'm trying to explain how much consternation Kristal created.

All the tabloids talked about was sex, sex, sex, but I believe she was trying to make a more intelligent point about voyeurism and the objectification of the female body. And we shouldn't forget the intense interest the event brought to the college and the funds that followed. The Havfruen Building was donated by Kristal's stepfather, a wealthy Danish industrialist. It was a major turning point for Falmouth. We went from two hundred students working in a rather traditional way, to several thousand students on various campuses studying everything from hairstyling to hovercraft design.'

'And is that a good thing?' asked Caine.

She turned her bright eyes on him. 'I'm a socialist, young man. I believe in equal opportunities for everybody. Who am I, a decrepit old lady, to say what is good art and what is not?'

'And how did you get on with her?' asked Caine. 'Kristal, I mean.'

'To be honest, our paths rarely crossed. I taught painting and life drawing. Neither was her cup of tea. But I remember her charisma and her striking looks. It takes balls to succeed as a woman in the art world, Mr Caine. Frida Kahlo, Georgia O'Keeffe, Barbara Hepworth, Louise Bourgeois led the way. But I can think of many talented female artists who have not enjoyed the acclaim they deserved because they lacked the necessary grit to rise in a world dominated by men with very large egos.'

'Amen to that,' said Shanti. 'Now I hope you won't mind us asking about the night of Kristal's death ...'

'Awful! Awful! Awful!' Marlene fumbled for her cigarettes.

'We have the statement you gave to Sergeant Bennett. But I'm wondering if there's anything else you'd like to add.

Something you've since remembered about the evening, no matter how insignificant.'

'Well, I had been looking forward to it for a long time, because many of my old students were going to be there. I felt rather proud of myself because I drove all the way to Somerset, which is quite something for me. I doubt if I'll ever manage that again. The guests were the usual creative types, but no, I don't remember anything untoward, aside from the tragic climax to the evening. I can't get that sight out of my mind – the foetal body in the tank with those red boots on top. I've had nightmares ever since of poor Callum dragging Kristal out of the tank and attempting to resuscitate her. Then dear Ollie pushed me outside because the fumes set off my coughing.'

She was beginning to look drained and Caine caught Shanti's eye. She nodded in his direction.

'Miss Moss, thank you so much for your time. We'll leave you in peace now.'

'Oh, but won't you stay for something to eat? I could make an omelette . . .'

'You're very kind. But we've already eaten. By the way, we were down at the harbour looking at Rock Cottage, which Kristal rented. We learnt that Kristal was frequently visited by two male students, one of whom was Callum Oak. The other was described – how can I put it? – in less flattering terms: like an oversized fish in appearance.'

Marlene tensed in her seat. 'Ugh! What a ghastly thing to say. I think you're referring to Oliver Sweetman, whom I've just mentioned. Ollie may not be blessed with conventional looks, but a kinder man I've yet to encounter. He was also one of my students, though not quite as able as Callum. The extraordinary thing is that when he suffered his head injury a few years ago, he was suddenly able to design and create beautiful objects with his hands: sculptures and furniture and astonishingly elaborate bird houses.

'I'm afraid that Ollie was another young man who became infatuated with Kristal, but you have to understand, Ms Joyce, that she hooked everyone in. As soon as he understood that she had chosen Callum as her ... as her partner, Ollie backed away and remained loyal to Kristal for the rest of her life. He would have done anything for her. Look over there in the bookshelf ... the big hardcover. That's her biography, *The Mother of Art*, which poor Ollie spent years compiling. And little thanks he received, I should imagine.'

'I've heard about this book.'

'It was conceived by Kristal but it's full of Ollie's photos, plus a few film frames. I shan't be looking at it again, so I don't mind lending it to you. But it is signed by both Kristal and Ollie, so I suppose it has some value.'

'I would appreciate that very much,' said Shanti. 'And you can be sure that I'll return it. I'll put it in the post if we don't ... if we don't meet again.'

Caine was crouching in front of the bookcase.

'You obviously enjoy reading, Marlene,' he said. 'Lots of Agatha Christie.'

'Yes, it's something Callum and I have in common. We both love West Country authors. He steers towards Thomas Hardy and I steer more towards crime and thrillers, but I enjoy a nice Hardy story on the television.'

They shook the old lady's birdlike claw.

'The paintings must be a great comfort,' said Caine.

'They are indeed, young man,' said Marlene. 'That and my naughty little habits. I'm a bad girl, I know. But don't be too cross with me, Mr Caine.' The impish smile of a teenager alighted on her face, which appeared to Caine as nothing more than thin skin stretched over a skull.

Chapter 11

The Doves of Paradise

'What did you make of her?' asked Shanti as they walked back towards the car.

'It's hard to believe she did it.'

'And there's me thinking she wrestled Kristal to the ground and stuffed her in a tank of formaldehyde.'

'I liked her. And her art collection is stunning.'

'She's dying, isn't she?'

'We're all dying, Shanti. But yes, I'd give her a year at the outside, poor old girl.'

The Saab climbed out of Falmouth, past Truro and onto the A30 in the direction of Exeter.

'Is there any chance you could share the driving?' said Shanti.

'I'm sorry. I don't really drive.'

'Don't or won't?'

'Driving isn't my thing.'

'Not your thing? What the hell does that mean? Every cop drives. It's what we do.'

'As I said, Shanti, I don't know if I am a cop.'

'I'll tell you what – you're a big boy now, Vincent Caine. Maybe it's time you made your mind up. In the meantime, if I fall asleep at the wheel and many people die, it's your fault, OK?'

As they crossed Bodmin Moor, Caine leafed through *The Mother of Art*.

'It's just as I remember – hundreds of photos of Kristal in her red boots and little white dress, or naked and beautiful.'

'You like that, eh, Caine?'

'Too much posing for me. I prefer natural women. There's a series here of Kristal topless on the beach with seaweed and bin bags wrapped around her legs. I suppose she's meant to be some kind of sea creature. What's hilarious is the figures in the background ... Don't look! Keep your eyes on the road! There are several locals who've obviously never seen a "happening". Some look outraged while others are riveted.'

'Perhaps our friend the crabber was there.'

'One thing's for sure, Kristal loved to be the centre of attention.'

'She was insufferable.'

'OK, here's an early photo of the three of them together in the college gardens, exactly where we walked this morning. Here's Callum, Kristal and Ollie Sweetman on the right ... he's a big lad, isn't he? And those boys can't take their eyes off her. But she's not much of a smiler. It makes me wonder, Shanti – Marlene talked about the crush that Oliver had on Kristal. But when Kristal rejected him, he just seemed to accept it. He simply withdrew and remained loyal to her and Callum for the rest of her life, becoming Kristal's studio assistant and photographer. That doesn't sound quite normal, does it? Surely he would have retained some resentment towards her – or to Callum, at least. I suggest we pay Mr Sweetman a visit.'

'Yes, he was next on my list, but Callum talked about some kind of head injury, so he may be an unreliable witness.'

'Marlene mentioned that too.'

'But I agree, there's no harm in paying him a visit. Shanti tossed him her phone. 'You're good at this, Caine. Have a word with your pal Callum. See how he's getting along, and get some details about Oliver.'

The phone rang for a long time before Oak answered in a sad, formal voice.

'Mangrove House. Oak speaking.'

'Mr Oak, it's DI Vincent Caine. How are you today, sir?'

'Well, I have an encampment of journalists at my gate. Every time I step outside, they shout, "Who killed Kristal? Who killed Kristal?" Like a hysterical pack of idiots.'

'I'm so sorry. It's a big story, I suppose. But they have no right to enter the grounds.'

'Anyway, I'm better for seeing Art. We had dinner together last night.'

'Ah, that's good. Is he staying with you?'

'No, he'll be staying at his weekend apartment in Charmouth until after the funeral, assuming the police eventually grant us that comfort . . . When will that be, Mr Caine?'

'I assure you that your wife's body will be released very soon.'

'Art is extremely unhappy with the way he has been treated. I had to talk him out of making a formal complaint against your colleague, DI Joyce.'

'I don't think a complaint would help anything. It would just slow everything down. We need to find out what happened and then you can all begin to move on. We're planning to visit Oliver Sweetman today. I understand he worked for Kristal, so I suppose that arrangement has come to an end?'

'I've promised to find him a little work here and there, and I'll continue to pay him something, although it won't be a great deal. Fortunately Ollie lives very modestly. But I must warn you, you won't get a great deal of sense out of him. The accident . . .'

'Yes, we heard about that. Can you tell me more?'

'It must have been seven or eight years ago. Ollie was helping to unload a polished steel sculpture here at Mangrove House. It was being lowered on a small crane from the back of a truck when suddenly a rope broke and the pallet swung free. Struck him right on the temple. We thought we'd lost him, but Ollie is made of tougher stuff than most and he pulled through, although he changed considerably.'

'In what way?'

'You'd need to talk to a doctor for a full explanation. I believe that brain injury can occasionally liberate certain skills. But in my perception it was a miracle.'

'A miracle?'

'That's how I see it, yes. For a start, it was remarkable that he wasn't killed outright. When he returned from hospital, I began to notice some comprehension difficulties.'

'I see . . . but why do you describe this as a miracle?'

'Ah, well, when Ollie and I shared student accommodation back in Falmouth, he was an average student, to put it kindly. I believe the art school had an onus to admit a certain number of local students, and Ollie is a Cornish boy. But the remarkable thing is that after the accident, he began to create things that were truly astonishing – furniture, children's toys, dovecotes and miniature buildings. He was never able to do this before, so I thought of it as divine compensation for that appalling incident with the sculpture.'

'Was the injury caused by one of the sculptures in your garden?'

'That's correct. An image of me and Kris ... an image of a couple making love.'

'Is that the piece called *Preconception2*?'

'Yes. It was an interpretation of that dreadful student performance. I loathed the thing, but Kristal always got her way. I honestly think that sculpture was a deliberate and constant reminder to all of us – me, Art and poor Ollie – of her influence in our lives. It became an ongoing battle, actually. After the accident, I had a fence erected and tried to grow bushes to conceal it, but Kristal would order Ollie to cut them back. I think it was terribly cruel, considering how much suffering it caused.'

'How has Oliver reacted to her death?'

'Like all of us, he hasn't really accepted that she's gone. He's unbelievably calm about it at the moment, but I suppose the reality will sink in sooner or later. He was absolutely devoted to Kristal.'

By the time the call had finished, Caine had obtained a description of Paradise Park, where Oliver Sweetman had resided for the last fifteen years.

He seemed to know the area like the back of his hand, and he guided Shanti through the Blackdown Hills from Honiton. In a little over two hours, they were skirting Chard, and a mile along a single-track lane they found the holiday park, where two magnificent driftwood angels stood sentinel at the gates.

They parked in front of a log cabin reception, where a tidy

man in shorts, sandals and a khaki shirt was sitting behind a desk. 'Welcome to Paradise,' he said.

He examined Shanti's warrant card with great interest, stroking his carefully trimmed beard.

'Police, eh! We've never had police before.'

It was true that Paradise Park did not look like a hub of gang warfare. Set on the edge of a wood, with a Japanese bridge spanning a trickling stream, the place was immaculate, with regimented rows of pastel-coloured static homes, accessed by narrow tarmac drives. Each home was bordered by a cheery flower garden behind a picket fence. And throughout the site, ethereal doves flirted and kissed and cooed.

'We're not looking into a crime on the site, Mr ...?' said Shanti.

The man's features seemed as neatly arranged as his campsite. 'Colin Leggit, proprietor of Paradise.'

'Mr Leggit. We're here to speak to Oliver Sweetman.'

Leggit's face fell. 'Ah! My wife guessed that you'd want to speak with Ollie. He's not in trouble, is he? Not our Ollie.'

'Why did your wife think we'd want to speak to him?' asked Caine.

'Ollie knew that woman, didn't he? That sick artist who's been in the paper.' Leggit tapped a copy of the *Daily Mail*.

WHO KILLED KRISTAL? Our readers DEMAND to know!
Four-page pullout special. All her SAUCIEST works!

He glanced at a clock on the log wall. 'Well, it's not an ideal time. What you need to understand about Ollie is that his day runs like clockwork. At eight fifteen every morning he feeds his doves. Then he mows the lawns, and works on his models until two. All the figures and buildings in Paradise are made by Ollie's own hands. The children love him and many families come back year after year just to see what he's made. We give him free accommodation in return and he's never caused us the slightest bother.'

'But it's after two now.'

'Mini golf time.'

'OK, well could we talk to him while he's playing?' asked Caine.

'You could try. Best thing is to have a game yourself. He'd like that, would Ollie.'

Leggit reached behind the desk and handed each of the DIs a half-sized golf club and a ball. 'It's normally three pounds to play, but seeing as you're police, I'll let you have them for a quid each. Is that fair? Now, you follow the path through the children's activity area. I'm sorry to tell you that the model railway isn't operating this season due to moles beneath the track. You'll find the mini golf towards the end of Paradise. Can't miss it. But I should warn you that Ollie's a terrible softie, so don't upset him, will you? Had him sobbing in here for an hour yesterday on account of a frog under the mower. Give me a shout if he gets tearful. I know how to manage him.'

Swinging their golf clubs, they made their way along the drive, past a sign saying, *CAUTION, FREE RANGE CHILDREN!* and another declaring, *NO SMOKING ANYWHERE ON SITE!*

Throughout the site stood beautifully constructed wooden trellises, hand-built benches and driftwood animals. They passed a heavily pregnant mother hanging out washing by her caravan, who gave Caine a broad smile; an old couple were tanning themselves on plastic chairs; children sped past on tricycles, sending doves fluttering like an explosion in a bookshop.

'If the crew from Camden could see me now,' sighed Shanti.

'Do you miss London?' asked Caine.

'I loved London, Caine. London is a beautiful, tolerant melting pot, and except for a few nutters, everyone gets on very well.'

'It's a very expensive melting pot.'

'That's true. It's impossible for young people nowadays. Anyway, Paul and I had some great times . . . but as you know, it didn't end well.'

'If you ever feel like talking about it . . .'

'Thanks. I handled it. And I'm handling it now.'

They could hear the shouts of children, and a woodchip path led to the activity area, which was filled with ingeniously constructed play equipment – climbing frames, tree houses, a pirate ship, a castle, swings and rope walkways, where children of all ages cavorted and ran.

The path led eventually to an elaborate mini golf range, spilling in every direction like a fantastical city. Shanti and Caine saw rows of Lilliputian houses, a cathedral, a lighthouse on a rock, and a toy airport. In puddle-sized ponds, pint-sized hippos and crocodiles lurked motionless. And on top of an artificial hill, beside a waist-high fairy castle, stood the red-headed architect of this elaborate fantasy land.

Even without the peculiar scale of his environment, Oliver Sweetman was a beaming giant of a man. In cream slacks and a short-sleeved shirt, with a paunch breaking over his belt like a wave, he bent over his dinky golf club, concentrating gleefully on the tricky shot he was about to take – down a meandering ramp towards a windmill. When it finally came, the shot was perfect and the ball flipped precisely through the windmill's door.

Sweetman punched the air, and his ever-present grin spread even wider. 'Nice one!' he said in a soft West Country lilt.

'Great shot!' said Caine. 'Can we join you?'

The cruel description the Falmouth crabber had given had some validity. Sweetman's lips were full and fleshy, his nose was softly sprinkled with freckles, and his spherical head was crowned with a mop of flaming orange.

'Well you'll have to be quick to catch up. I have to get to the Eiffel Tower before the end of my break or my doves will miss their supper.'

'We've never played before,' said Shanti. 'Perhaps you could give us a few tips?'

'Never played?' said Oliver in disbelief. 'Well, for starters you need to hold the club properly. Here, let me show you . . .'

He stood behind her and placed her hands gently on the club. Shanti felt the soft embrace of his body on her back and his steady breath on the nape of her neck, but she also sensed the gentle innocence of the man.

'I'll tell you a secret,' he whispered into her hair. 'I say it to everyone: not too hard and not too soft. Now you're learning, see.'

'My name's Shanti Joyce. And this is my friend, Vincent Caine.'

'Pleased to meet you, Shanti Joyce and Vincent Caine. Which caravan are you in? Mine's the blue one – Shangri-La, near the dovecote.'

'No, we're not staying,' said Shanti. 'We came to ask a few questions, if that's all right. We're actually detectives, Oliver, from Yeovil police station. We wanted to ask about Kristal. She was your friend, wasn't she?'

'Oh, Kristal's very well indeed, thank you,' said Oliver. 'Not too hard and not too soft, that's the secret.'

Caine and Shanti exchanged puzzled glances.

'What do you mean, Kristal's very well?'

'Fit as a fiddle, she is. Although, being a musical instrument, it's hard to see how a fiddle could be either fit or unfit.'

'I'm sorry. I'm confused . . .'

Shanti took a swing, and to her amazement, the ball popped through the windmill's door. Oliver was delighted. 'That's it! Now you've got it, Shanti Joyce! Not too hard and not too soft. As a matter of fact, you're lucky there's no wind today. When it's windy, the sails turn and it makes it twice as hard to get the ball inside.'

Caine was struggling in the foothills. After several missed shots, his ball became entangled in the legs of a giraffe. Eventually he lifted it out and placed it further up the hill by the castle.

'He cheated! You cheated! I saw him!'

'Vincent Caine!' scolded Shanti. 'I'm surprised at you. Now you have to go right back to the beginning.'

Shanti found she had a knack for the game. Sweetman was right – not too hard and not too soft. 'We've been looking at your book, Ollie. *The Mother of Art* . . .'

He paused and stared into space, as if he were searching for something from another lifetime. 'I made that book,' he said after a while.

'You did. You took all the photos. And you helped to organise Kristal's show at the Meat Hook, didn't you? Did you place the boots on top of the tank?'

'Yes, I put them there. Kristal thought they would look nice. I'll ask her why when I see her. Also I made sure the glass was polished, otherwise she gets upset.'

'Would she shout at you, Ollie?'

'Just a little smack on the hand when things aren't right.'

'I'll bet she was excited about that show, wasn't she?'

'Kristal gets in an awful fluster,' he said, laughing. 'But she's much happier now. She tells me all the time how happy she is. She's clever and beautiful and kind and happy.'

Shanti took another shot. The ball flew towards the bridge but landed in the water, where a family of koi carp sailed half-heartedly away. 'Damn!' she exclaimed.

'Too hard,' said Oliver. 'You done it too hard.'

Caine knew it wasn't a dropped shot that had frustrated Shanti. They were getting nowhere. Callum Oak had been right: this cheerful, confusing man-child wasn't even close to accepting that his beloved idol had gone. That was sad, but it wasn't their job to puzzle it out.

Oliver put his golf club over his shoulder and shook their hands.

'Well, nice to meet you, Shanti Joyce and Vincent Caine. See the clock on the cathedral? That's a real clock, that is. I built it. I've got to go now, but you make sure you put the clubs back in reception when you're finished. Some folks just leave them lying anywhere, and it's always Ollie that has to clear up after.'

They stood watching his mountainous frame lumbering up the driveway, waving at holidaymakers and patting small children as the doves settled on his flaming head and huge sloping shoulders.

'You were rubbish,' said Shanti. 'A five-year-old could beat you.'

In the Saab, Caine ticked off the suspects in his notebook.

'OK, we've talked to Art Havfruen, the Boy Named Art. He definitely had some issues with his mother and a fondness for a drug, a derivative of which was found in her bloodstream.'

'Still the bookies' favourite,' said Shanti.

'You've got a grudge against him, Shanti, and that doesn't help. OK, then there's Callum Oak, the husband. He's aware of his wife's shortcomings, but clearly loyal and devoted. Then we have Marlene Moss, the terminally ill former tutor. She'd have every right to resent Kristal, but she didn't. And finally, poor old Ollie Sweetman, who seems to believe that Kristal is still alive.'

'He's got the strength to do it, though . . .'

'Yes, but I've never seen a man with less malice. And surely that accident deprived him of the capacity to plan a sophisticated crime.'

'You may be wrong there, Caine. I mean, Sweetman built all that crazy stuff – the windmill, the clock tower and the pirate ship. I think he's incredibly smart.'

'His intelligence is all in his hands,' said Caine. 'Anyway, he adored Kristal. Why would he want to hurt her? Besides, he's too emotional. He wouldn't be able to hide it if he'd done something like that.'

'Well thanks for nothing, Caine. I've spent three days being your chauffeur and we're right back where we started. But don't worry, there are still a hundred and ninety-five more witnesses to question. And now I suppose you want a lift back to Lyme. That's fine, it's only an hour out of my way.'

Shanti ached to see Paul again. She glanced at the clock on the dashboard. If she put her foot down, she might just make it to school for pick-up.

She dropped Caine near the cinema at the top of the high street, promising to be in touch when she next needed his help.

The situation was absurd. How could she work with a partner who didn't drive? She thought of all the hours she had wasted at the wheel, and as she meandered past Lambert's Castle on the thickly wooded road to Yeovil, she considered the possibility of quietly dropping Caine from the case and proceeding on her own. After all, where had their combined talents got them? She was yet to witness those legendary detective skills or that intuitive feel for a case that had so impressed Benno.

And yet there was something intriguing about the man. She pictured Caine cross-legged in meditation, the subtle way he had of questioning. His knowledge of unlikely subjects, such as art and nature.

For the first time since Paul had started at the school, she managed to grab a parking space. She spotted her mum chatting to a group of parents in the playground and was about to join them when her phone rang.

'Hello, Benno. I've had a shocking couple of days, so please make this good news.'

'You be the judge.'

Shanti heard a note of enthusiasm in his voice, and a feeling of hope soared in her chest. 'You've got something for me?'

'Well, the body has been released for burial, so the family will be relieved. No more big developments from the final autopsy. As Dawn suspected, the pathologist couldn't pin down the time of death because the formaldehyde slowed the process of decomposition. Every organ is infused with the stuff. All we can say for certain is that we're still talking about a victim who was administered a massive dose of ketamine and drowned in a tank of formaldehyde.'

'Right . . .'

'But here's some information you might find interesting. We've seen details of the will. And guess who's just inherited a couple of million shares in Rasmussen Holdings?'

'Art Havfruen?'

'Wrong. It's the husband, Callum.'

'Jesus!'

This changed everything.

'I want a search warrant for Mangrove House.'

'I'm on it, boss.'

'I've got some fresh questions for our grieving widower.'

That boyish English reserve. The curly hair. The whole mournful Christian thing. Shanti didn't know much about art, but even she could tell that there was something disturbed about the scrawled words in Callum Oak's paintings. Kristal had humiliated and tormented him all his life, and that bizarre murder might be his revenge. The case was weird, but there was nothing unusual about the motive – old-fashioned male ego, frustrated by a powerful woman.

The children were coming out of school, shirts hanging, satchels swinging, buttons done up wrong, and when Shanti spotted Paul's apple face, she felt her heart leap. She'd made it back in time to be a mother.

And before the week was out, she was going to nail a murderer.

Chapter 12

The Cold Chamber of Death

The dawn was still a dewy promise when the constables – two women and two men – pulled up in a lay-by on the deserted A375 near Sidmouth. They climbed unenthusiastically from their vehicles and huddled against a gate, where a herd of loose-bowelled bullocks snorted and grazed in the half-light.

Ten minutes later, Shanti's Saab drew up alongside the patrol cars, and as she and Benno walked over to join the uniforms, the dawn chorus spewed from every hedgerow.

'Right, morning, everyone,' said Shanti. 'Sorry it's early, but I think this could be a critical day. As you know, this is now officially a murder inquiry. Sergeant Bennett and I have reason to believe there could be interesting evidence at Mangrove House, which is where the victim, Kristal Havfruen, lived with her husband, Callum Oak, until her murder last Saturday.'

The two younger constables were still keen enough to make notes.

'You're all familiar with the details of this case. You also know that it's attracting a stupid amount of media interest, and that's why I will seize every opportunity, including a lay-by at five forty-five in the morning, to remind you that if any one of you so much as texts your mum about this case, you will be queuing at the Job Centre before you know what's hit you. Is that clear?'

A mumble of assent.

'So, we've got a warrant, and as far as I know, Mr Oak will be there on his own. Far be it from me to jump to conclusions, but I would remind you that statistically, more than half of female homicide victims are murdered by their partners.

'I should mention that there are two dogs, but they are more likely to fart in your face than bite you. A reminder that Oak and Kristal Havfruen were both artists, so the place is full of what is commonly called modern art. It may look like garbage, but trust me, some of these pieces are worth more than your annual salary. What you break, you buy. Is that understood, Dunster?

'I'll tell you what we're looking for: anything to do with a legacy from a Danish company called Rasmussen Holdings … Benno will give you the spelling. Also any clues about hostility between Oak and Kristal. Keep your eyes open for narcotics, which might belong to our friend Art Havfruen. We're also particularly interested in hypodermic syringes, which might have been used to sedate the deceased. Keep a careful look-out for miscellaneous letters or documents that might give some clues. Finally – and forgive me if this sounds completely barking – I'm hoping to locate a super-realistic effigy of Kristal that was substituted for her body. Normally a thing like that would be easy enough to spot, but the whole place is like a bloody temple to Kristal Havfruen – there are replicas of her everywhere. The one we're looking for, however, is precisely life-size and it's likely to have that smell ... you know, the stuff we all had a blast of the other night. Formaldehyde. Any questions?'

'Where's VC, boss?'

'Right, it's very early. Who's VC, Spalding?'

'Veggie Cop.'

'If you mean DI Vincent Caine, I'm the lead officer on this case, and although Caine is a first-rate detective, I do some things better on my own. Are we all clear?'

Within an hour, the already world-weary interior of Mangrove House looked as if a small typhoon had passed through, disgorging drawers and bookshelves, scattering paperwork, magazines and *objets d'art*. Even the senders of a row of sympathy cards had been carefully noted.

Callum Oak, in an indigo and gold dressing gown, sat slumped in a leather armchair, clutching his curly head in his hands. The dogs waddled and thumped their tails nervously by his long bare feet.

'Privacy is the last bastion of a decent society,' he wailed. 'If you had simply telephoned and told me you were coming, I would have been glad to invite you in. As I keep telling you, Inspector Joyce, I have nothing to hide. But these people are violating ... *violating* my property! I will remind you that it is less than four days since my wife was brutally murdered. I am a man in mourning!'

'Mr Oak, I am acutely aware of the circumstances, but my job is to ascertain who did this to your wife, and therefore, even in a decent society, it is necessary to gather evidence. I realise that may appear intrusive, but I assure you my team have been trained to cause minimum disruption—'

'*Disruption!* That boy is manhandling an original Bernard Leach fish platter!'

'I understand your finances have recently had a bit of a turn-around, Mr Oak. Can you tell me about your inheritance – the shares in Rasmussen Holdings?'

'Look, I swear to you, the first I knew of these shares was two days ago, when my solicitor called. I very much doubt that even Kristal knew about them. She hadn't spoken to her stepfather in years. She had a lifelong grudge against Rasmussen, to the extent that she refused to attend his funeral. Believe me, she never mentioned his name, let alone these shares.'

Shanti tried to imagine what it would be like to forget an inheritance of that magnitude. 'All right, Mr Oak, that's all for the time being. You are free to wait here or have some breakfast, but I would ask you not to leave the house and to remain in plain sight at all times. I'm going to look upstairs, if you don't mind.'

'I do mind. In any case, I have to walk my dogs, damn you.'

'Just let them outside into the garden and later one of my team will accompany you if you need to go out. Please try to cooperate, sir. It will make everything so much easier.'

Having indicated to Benno where she was going, Shanti ascended the sweeping staircase. A carpeted, art-filled landing was lined with white doors, the last of which opened into an airy white bedroom dominated by several elaborately framed full-length mirrors, like those at a ballet school. This was Kristal's room. At the far end, a pair of French doors opened onto a balcony, and Shanti peered out across a tennis court and unkempt lawns, and over the sandy cliff edge to the gunmetal expanse of Lyme Bay.

The room had the same neglected atmosphere as the rest of

the house, and the duvet on the vast double bed lay cold and crumpled. On a cluttered dressing table, a vase of withered red and white roses stood amidst a pile of jewellery and expensive make-up. There was that rosy lipstick that Kristal so artfully smeared around her lips each day. In an oversized wardrobe, Shanti discovered a row of lacy white dresses, as if a multitude of bridesmaids lived here. Besides a few shawls, coats and cardigans, the only other items were a parade of Kristal's distinctive red Dr Marten boots. There was nothing in the room that belonged to Oak.

Adjoining the bedroom was a spa-like bathroom, littered with discarded lingerie, where countless weeping candlesticks were reflected in the many mirrors. On the porcelain surface beside the double sink, Shanti noted half a line of white powder and a rolled banknote. Had Kristal been a user? Or was her son in the habit of utilising any smooth surface in the house? She imagined the lonely, angry young man wandering through the empty rooms, numbing himself with narcotics and longing for the mother he never had.

Retracing her steps along the landing, Shanti peered into several rooms before entering a dingy north-facing bedroom that overlooked the gloomy courtyard where Oak's Volvo, the Saab and the two pandas were parked. She placed a latex-gloved hand within the single bed and found it warm to the touch. Here was a man who was used to sleeping alone.

On the bedside table was a stack of books by writers she had heard of but would never read. Novels and collections of poetry by local authors: Thomas Hardy, John Fowles, Samuel Taylor Coleridge, Daphne du Maurier. She lifted each book in turn and flipped through the pages – amazing how often a telltale note or receipt was used as a bookmark. But there was nothing. In the drawer she found the usual bedside detritus – a phone charger, a dead torch, a few old supermarket receipts, aspirins, cufflinks, loose change, nail clippers. There was also a silver cross and a stubby black bible.

On hands and knees she explored beneath the bed and in the dark recess discovered two large cardboard boxes. When she pulled them out and brushed away the dust and cobwebs, she saw that each had been labelled with the word *FALMOUTH*.

Inside was material from Oak's student days, and for fifteen minutes Shanti wandered through fragments of a strange tale of a steadfast student who had stumbled into the path of an irresistible but controlling woman. She found increasingly anxious letters from Oak's alarmed parents and apprehensive warnings from his head of department, Marlene Moss, who worried that he was wasting his ability. At the very bottom of the pile was an extraordinary flattened A4 document signed by Callum Oak and Kristal Havfruen, and witnessed by a twenty-year-old Oliver Sweetman. As she read it, Shanti didn't know whether to laugh or cry.

> I, the undersigned, CALLUM OAK, being of sound
> mind and body, having repeatedly expressed an interest
> in a physical relationship with KRISTAL HAVFRUEN,
> hereafter known as The Artist, do agree that a single
> act of sexual union shall take place strictly under the
> following Terms and Conditions:
>
> 1. That the Union shall be carried out in a public space
> – specifically the life room at Falmouth School of Art
> – at a time and date determined by The Artist.

2. That the Union is understood to be a Happening, or Work of Art, created by The Artist, to be entitled: *Preconception.*

3. That this Happening shall be witnessed by an invited audience of The Artist's choosing, to include, but not restricted to, members of the press and public.

4. That all recordings of the event, to include video, photography and sound, shall forever remain the property of The Artist, and may be disseminated in whatever manner she deems appropriate.

5. That any consequences of *Preconception*, in any form, shall be seen an integral element of The Artist's work and shall therefore remain her property in perpetuity according to the terms of this agreement.

6. That The Artist and her appointed agent alone will manage any contact with the media that may arise from the work.

7. That any financial remuneration from the work belongs exclusively to The Artist.

8. That I will be irrevocably bound by the terms of this agreement, which shall be binding on my executors, administrators, successors, heirs and assignees.

9. That I, Callum Oak, am free to enter into this agreement. I accept full responsibility for my actions and agree not to pursue any legal proceedings against The Artist, in perpetuity.

10. That I have read and fully understood the terms of this contract.

Signed: Callum Oak
And also by: The Artist, Kristal Havfruen
Witnessed by: Oliver Sweetman, Assistant

Shanti prided herself on a professional approach to her work, but this strange document threw up a multitude of sensations: pity for the pathetic student, Callum Oak; bemusement at the pseudo-legal wording by which he had been ensnared; and something approaching revulsion at the ruthlessness of that arch-manipulator, Kristal Havfruen. But here, surely, within this puerile document, lay the root of Callum Oak's emasculation and subsequent simmering resentment of his wife.

Shanti photographed the manuscript and was in the process of returning it to its place beneath a pile of faded magazines when the bedroom door opened and the Labrador nosed and wagged its way into the room, followed by its master, who was seething with indignation.

'Do you not have one shred of decency, Ms Joyce? I have just been robbed of my wife and now you are sacking my home. What is it that you hope to find?'

'Is this your copy of *Asian Nuns*?' asked Shanti, rising to her feet.

'DI Joyce,' he hissed, snatching the magazine from her hand, 'you may be interested to know that you have something in common with my wife – you are a bully. Now please leave me so that I can get dressed. And let me make myself quite clear – any further communication between you and me will be through my solicitor.'

Downstairs, in the faint formaldehyde fug of the big studio, Benno and two uniforms were working their way painstakingly through portfolios and plan chests.

'Find anything, boss?' said Benno.

'Kristal and Oak slept separately. I checked both bedrooms but I couldn't find anything incriminating, although there's been a lot of powder consumed on the premises. I feel so frustrated, Benno. I was sure we'd get a breakthrough today, but I'm afraid any dialogue with Oak has broken down since I rumbled his porn stash.'

'Listen, boss . . . as a colleague and a friend – you've been on this case 24/7 and you look terrible.'

'Thanks, Benno, that's cheered me up no end.'

'I thought Vince was helping you. He's good at this kind of thing. He'd get Oak to open up.'

'Maybe. But I'm buggered if I'm going to drive to Lyme or embark on a full-scale jungle trek just to beg him to come back on board.'

'You won't need to do that, Shanti.'

He was standing by the open French doors, like a vertical shadow.

'Caine! How the hell did you . . .? Oh, never mind. As you're here, you might as well see if you can squeeze anything out of Oak. He should be down in a mo. He was looking for someone to walk the dogs with him.'

The tall men strode beside the wild, salt-spitting sea, where the wind was so strong you could lean on it. High in the ether, sea-birds circled like boomerangs. At their feet, the old dogs lumbered like joyous sea lions.

'I will not . . . I cannot talk to that woman again,' Oak bellowed above the surf. 'Your friend, DI Joyce. Don't they teach basic communication skills at the police academy?'

'She doesn't mean to offend. Look, it's a tough job and sometimes the only way to survive is to be tough yourself.'

'But you, at least, have retained a little civility.'

'I'm more of a locum cop, Mr Oak. I spend most of my time on the Undercliff.'

'One of our favourite walks too.'

'You mean you and Kristal?'

'I mean me and the dogs. Kristal was never a walker.'

'Can I ask you something, sir?'

'Call me Callum, for goodness' sake.'

'Callum. Did you and Kristal love each other?'

Oak stopped and inhaled a chestful of ozone. 'Physically, you mean? Look, I'm going to tell you something I've never told anyone before. God knows why, but there's something about you I trust.'

'Thank you.'

'This may sound bizarre, but I'm forty-six years old and apart from that one ghastly time in the life room, I have never known a woman. Aside from *Preconception*, I remain a virgin.'

'Celibacy can be a strength.'

'Not when there is no choice. Kristal was as cold as the models in her studio. Do you know the Bible? "A man will leave his father and mother and be united to his wife, and the two will become one flesh. Therefore what God has joined, let no one separate." Mark 10, verses 7 to 9. The point is, we were not one flesh and I have been lonely all my life.'

'But she was clearly attracted to you when you met?'

'I was completely absorbed in my work when we met. I was the last person at the college to notice Kristal. I sometimes wonder if that was what drew her to me – she always wanted what she could not have. It bothered her when people didn't pay her enough attention.'

'You discredit yourself, Callum. I've seen photos – you were a handsome man.'

'I notice you use the past tense. But thank you.'

'I'd like to know a little more about the happening called *Preconception*. Why did you agree to that?'

'Because Kristal taunted me mercilessly with her sexuality. She drove me insane with desire. But she pushed me away again and again. In the end, I would have done anything to have her.'

'And afterwards? How did you feel?'

'Humiliated. Shamed. Degraded. I despised myself for my weakness. I mortified myself by sleeping on a stone floor and praying to God for forgiveness.'

'And you were still a student when Art was born.'

'I was. I was far from ready to be a father. If it hadn't been for the selfless support of my head of department, Marlene Moss, I don't know what I would have done. She was kindness itself.'

'Forgive me, but I'd like to ask you a very direct question, if I may.'

'Fire away.'

'Who killed Kristal, Callum? Who do you think it was?'

'Do you think I haven't turned it over endlessly in my mind? I genuinely have no idea.'

'Oliver Sweetman?'

'Ollie? Ollie wouldn't hurt a fly. He worshipped Kristal.'

'Someone from her family, then? They are wealthy and influential. I believe she hated her stepfather, isn't that the case?'

'It's true she loathed Rasmussen. Never accepted him as her stepfather. Between you and me, she accused him of some kind of abuse in her childhood. He sent endless letters trying to win her round – he even funded that magnificent building at Falmouth in her name. When he died five years ago, he left her a generous inheritance, which, as I've been trying to explain to your ill-mannered colleague, I heard about for the first time when it passed to me on Kristal's death. I honestly don't care about the money. I'd give it all back to have things as they were. Love or no love, at least there was peace.'

'It's hard to see now, but peace will return, Callum. At least the legacy will enable you to paint. It's not for me to say, but I saw some of your early work in Falmouth and it was astonishing. Perhaps this may be a new beginning.'

They had reached the sandy cliff that led to the elevated gardens of Mangrove House. Caine followed the wretched artist and the lumbering dogs up the bone-white wooden steps and his heart went out to him.

Near the abandoned tennis court, Oak said, 'Caine, in another life, I'd have liked to get to know you. Perhaps we could have been friends.'

Caine turned and embraced him, allowing the widower to sob in his arms. 'Underneath, we are all the same, Callum. We yearn for love and we grieve when someone dies.'

'Come to the funeral, Caine.'

'I'd like that. Thank you.'

Oak pulled out a handkerchief and blew his nose.

'But you'd better keep a lowish profile. One never quite

LAURENCE ANHOLT

knows how Art might behave. I'm afraid he may be planning something.'

'Such as ...?'

'As I told you, I wanted a simple, dignified Christian ceremony – a few prayers and eulogies. But it seems my son wants his mother to go out in style. I fear there may be another happening.'

132

Chapter 13

The Crystal Coffin

The hamlet of Branscombe nestled like a hidden emerald on the Devon coast. But two factors prevented Shanti from appreciating the timeless charm of the place. The first was that the entire valley was swathed in sea fog, as if Kristal herself had planned a send-off as melodramatic as her life. The second was that Shanti herself was swathed in a fog of gloom and confusion.

She sat with a Diet Coke, waiting for Caine beneath a thatched parasol outside the Mason's Arms. She was wearing what she had thought would be appropriate clothes for a funeral – a dark coat and a sleek black dress that she had loved when she bought it, but that now required a safety pin where the zip did not meet at the back.

As she fought her way to the bar, however, she discovered that the dense crowd of mourners had chosen a different style. The place was a riot of showy couture, with a noticeable red and white theme. The din was unbearable, so Shanti had grabbed her drink and two packets of cheese and onion crisps and battled her way into the welcome air.

In front of her, the fog drifted along the village street, as if the Mason's Arms were a ghost ship rolling through the waves.

Prodding a lemon slice with a straw, Shanti reflected on how naïve she had been in the early days of the case, when she thought everything would simply fall into place. Now the riddle of the floating foetal artist kept her awake at night and haunted her every waking hour. Her darkest fear was that the killer would elude her and she would be responsible for another botched case. Even now, she could feel the shame of that episode, which had almost negated fifteen years of outstanding service. In reality, it had been nothing more than a series of small errors brought about by the fact that she was frazzled by the divorce and desperately trying to cope as a single mum. Nonetheless, a lack of attention to detail had given the defence barrister the opportunity to pick holes in her record-keeping, and as a result, a major north London dealer had walked free. Shanti would never forget the blatant smirk that bastard had given her as he walked out of the court. She simply could not let that happen again. It would be too depressing for words.

There was still no sign of Caine, but all around, more and more red and white mourners poured from cars, some on teetering heels, a few in the inevitable red DM boots. Alongside the ubiquitous journalists and photographers inside the pub, Shanti had noticed many familiar figures – Saul Spencer, angular as a jar of pencils; and the huge form of Oliver Sweetman bent beneath the black beams, merrily supping his beer. Now a taxi pulled up and a striking group of outrageously healthy Aryans emerged – Kristal's family from Copenhagen, she assumed.

But there was more to her dejected mood than lack of sleep or a tricky case to be solved. She was increasingly worried about

Paul. As far as Shanti was concerned, her son was still a child who loved the same picture books he had enjoyed when he was little. But at school, Ms Khan, the head teacher, had taken her aside and asked if there were problems at home. Paul, it seemed, had been rude to his teacher on more than one occasion. And some of the language he had brought from London was an unwelcome novelty to his new classmates.

Last night, Shanti had broached the subject, which had led to tantrums and sobbing from Paul. And reassurances from her about spending more time together, until he had fallen into a half-weeping half-sleep against her chest, reciting a heart-rending list of her failings: 'You're always at work . . . you're never home after school . . . you're always stressed . . . you promised to take me out . . .'

Shanti's mum did her best, but they both knew what was at the heart of it – the boy missed his dad and blamed his mother for the move, which had meant leaving all his old friends behind.

Being a DI and a single mum was an impossible circle to square. But she simply could not miss this funeral.

'You look a bit low,' said Caine, pulling up a chair beside her. 'Can I get you another drink?'

'Just tired, Caine.'

'I hope you won't mind me saying – I've never seen you in a dress before. You look absolutely stunning.'

She searched for a hint of sarcasm or lechery. But there was none.

'Yeah, well the only chance I get to dress up is a funeral.'

At least Caine had taken the trouble to tidy himself up. Nothing fussy – skinny black jeans, a tight belt and a spotless white shirt, in striking contrast to his dark curls. As he placed his drink on the table, Shanti noticed a dozen pairs of female eyes swivelling in his direction.

'What's that you're drinking, Caine? I didn't think Buddhists were allowed intoxicants.'

'Local cider. Try some. It's delicious. And I reckon Buddhists are free to do whatever makes them happy. There's this thing called the Middle Way. You see, the Buddha—'

'Right. Listen, have you seen Art and Callum?'

'The immediate family usually arrive separately, don't they?'

'Probably. What about Marlene Moss?'

'Too far for the old girl, I should think. Besides, she didn't know Kristal very well. It was Callum and Oliver who were her students, remember.'

'OK, the service is scheduled for two p.m. at St Winifred's, just up the road, followed by a wake at Mangrove House. I'll hang around outside to avoid any possible confrontation, so you'll have to be my eyes and ears. Is that OK?'

'I'll be any part of you you like.'

'I've noticed that people often let their guard down at events like weddings and funerals, so there's every chance that someone will mention something significant.'

'I'm on it, Shanti.'

Their conversation was interrupted by a timeless sound – the hollow clip-clop of hooves on hard ground and the whinny of horses. Shanti strained her eyes, and to her utter amazement, four white mares loomed out of the fog, breathing steam from their nostrils like spectral creatures, their bowed heads crowned with red and white feathers. The procession halted directly in front of her, and she could see that the horses were hauling a white lacquered carriage.

She had seen the occasional horse-drawn funeral in the East End – old-school gangsters were particularly fond of them – but this was something else.

It was one of those flatbed gun carriages that you saw at royal funerals, garlanded with white and red roses. Two poker-faced undertakers sat stiffly at the front, with long whips in their gloved hands and ribbons on their top hats.

The customers at the other tables had risen to their feet, and immediately the pub doors opened and a scrum of media hounds surged out, firing off film and talking rapidly into mobile phones.

It was at this point that Shanti noticed the coffin lying on the platform, and before she could completely process what she was seeing, her stomach lurched in a sickly series of acrobatic manoeuvres.

At her side, a wide-eyed teenage girl gasped, 'It's the most beautiful thing I've ever seen!'

'It's an abomination!' roared an elderly gentleman behind her.

'Oh Kristal!' breathed Caine. 'You were never going to go quietly.'

Shanti gawped in disbelief. The coffin was constructed entirely of glass, and inside, for all the world to see, lay the perfectly preserved body of Kristal Havfruen, dressed in lacy white. Her impeccably manicured hands clutched a single red rose against her slim body. Her face was thickly made up with creamy foundation and her mouth was smeared with an angry slash of blood-red lipstick. Perched cheekily on the coffin lid sat a pair of red Dr Marten boots.

'Like Sleeping bloody Beauty!' sighed the teenage girl.

As TV cameras whirred and the crowds pressed forward,

Shanti felt a wave of nausea – not enough sleep, a stupid diet, too much stress and an excess of weirdness. She was relieved when Caine took her arm and steered her gently towards the back of the throng as the river of mourners, led by Callum Oak and Art Havfruen, began to trudge up the lane behind the slow-moving carriage with its creepy cargo.

The wheels groaned and creaked; the hooves tapped out their tattoo as the procession inched up the narrow street past wide-eyed villagers and slack-jawed holidaymakers.

They filed past the village hall, past stone cottages festooned with hanging baskets, past a teashop; even a working forge where, like a scene from another century, an aproned blacksmith ceased his hammering and removed his cap to watch the morbid cavalcade.

Towards the front of the procession some kind of altercation was taking place between Callum Oak and the vicar of Branscombe, who had just arrived.

'This is most irregular,' she protested. 'I'm sorry, Callum, but you didn't tell me about this. I'll have to consult with the church authorities. There are strict guidelines about appropriate caskets. This is completely unprecedented.'

'I suppose you think I knew about it?' wailed Oak. 'You'd better speak to my son ... Where is he? Art!'

'Yeah? You got a problem?' said Art, dancing backwards on his pointed boots like a boxer. 'Just give us a break, man! She'll be six foot under soon. Then no one will give a fuck what the coffin is made of!'

Catching a glimpse of Art's wild gestures and dilated pupils, Shanti guessed that his mood was induced more by chemicals than cider.

The vicar was so taken aback by this aggressive outburst that she stopped in her tracks, creating an instant gridlock of grievers. It took one of the solemn Danes to step forward and soothe the situation in meticulous diplomatic English.

'Please forgive Art – he is of course in a state of shock, as we all are. On behalf of Kristal's family, I would like to apologise for the oversight with the coffin, but presumably we can proceed with the ceremony and discuss the details of the burial at a later stage?'

On the outskirts of the village, the procession eventually came to a halt, and Shanti saw the ancient tower of Oak's place of worship, St Winifred's, looming through the clouds.

'Does all of this pass as normal in your part of the world?' she asked Caine. She nodded towards the hearse, where an undertaker was steadying the horses.

The glass coffin was nudged carefully onto the shoulders of the pallbearers – the stony-faced widower, Callum Oak; Oliver Sweetman, the gentle freckled giant; and the burly Scandinavians. When they were ready, Art Havfruen led the way, pale-faced, with the red boots in hand.

Flash bulbs exploded as the casket was borne along the steep path towards the church, with Oak gripping tightly to Sweetman's shoulder in an effort to steady his lurching emotions. Lingering at the back of the crowd, Shanti and Caine followed beneath primeval elm trees, where antique headstones burst through the soil like the broken teeth of the world.

As the mourners filed into the cool interior of the church, Shanti and Caine paused in the porch. The main door had been hooked open, and for the second time that afternoon, Shanti's stomach reeled. In the nave, a flickering hologram the size of a child greeted the mourners with outspread arms. It was a perfect three-dimensional image of Kristal, her eyes flashing, and from her smeary blood-red lips a tiny childlike voice repeated again and again: 'I will never leave you! I am with you forever!'

For once, Shanti welcomed the touch of Caine's warm hand on hers as he whispered that he would meet her after the service. He stepped inside the overcrowded church and the door closed behind him.

Suddenly alone, Shanti wandered the cloudy cemetery, surveying the sinister gargoyles and the worn faces of medieval skulls on headstones. A family of crows flapped over the tombs like scraps of night. From behind the kaleidoscopic windows, she heard the occasional organ drone or muttered prayer. And then silence consumed her, like the drizzle in the air.

At the far end of the cemetery, two figures stood near an open grave – a sextant and a gravedigger by the look of them. Moving unnoticed in their direction, Shanti was able to overhear their peculiar joking conversation, the gallows banter of those who interacted daily with the dead.

'Vicar says there'll be a delay until she finds out if that glass casket is allowed.'

'Did you see that thing inside the church? That hologram? *I will never leave you! I am with you forever!* Gave me the willies.'

'Mind you . . . ha, ha . . . !'

'What's so funny?'

'She were right, weren't she!'

'Who were right?'

'Kristal.'

'What d'you mean?'

'She *will* be with us forever. Soaked in formaldehyde she is. Fair pickled through an' through. Dig up that glass casket in ten years and I'll wager ten to one she won't have aged a day.'

'Forever young, you might say, Daniel. Forever young.'

They wandered away chuckling.

All these bodies, sleeping forever. The crossbones, cherubs and hourglasses etched into ivy-clad tombstones. The soothing platitudes – *dearly beloved . . . taken from us . . . at peace with his Maker.* The mothers, the fathers, the stillborn.

Shanti was woken from her reverie by a faint movement in the lower level of the plot. Someone was sitting on a wall with legs swinging. Shanti wandered slowly along a cinder path amongst dead flowers and rusting mowers. As she approached the seated figure, she felt her mouth go dry. Surely she was mistaken! She blinked her eyes. But when she reopened them, the person was still there, sitting on the stone wall, swinging her red boots.

It was a petite blonde-haired woman in a short lacy dress, with a smear of red lipstick on her white face. It was another hologram, of course . . . it must be! Or one of those damned mannequins that were so true to life . . . or true to death, Shanti mused.

She shook her head. What a day she was having! Since the appalling week of her divorce and the collapse of her case, she couldn't remember feeling more psychologically frayed.

The woman on the wall lifted a pale hand and ran her fingers through her blonde hair.

I'm going mad, Shanti realised with sudden certainty. I am actually losing it completely. I have reached the point where I cannot tell the difference between illusion and reality. And once that point is passed, then nothing is possible.

But she was no coward. She willed her leaden limbs to carry her closer, down the path amongst the weeds and smashed flowerpots, past a broken shed on the hillside. Behind her, the muffled words of Blake's 'Jerusalem' droned:

And did those feet in ancient time
Walk upon England's mountains green?

Shanti's grandmother had believed in spirits that rowed deathly canoes in the Keralan backwaters. Ever logical, ever cynical, Shanti had scoffed, even as a child. But now, as she approached this apparition, her heart pounded like the blacksmith's hammer.

Searching for sufficient saliva to form a word, she managed, 'Hello.'

In return, the woman giggled faintly and slithered off the wall onto the ground.

'Don't be frightened,' said Shanti, more to herself than anyone else. It was not just her heart that pulsated – her entire bloodstream pummelled like floodwaters.

The figure turned, pivoting, dancing, darting through the mist. Shanti was wearing the wrong shoes for this, but she gave chase, along a track and over a stile. Here, at the lowest point of the valley, the fog was so dense, that she could see nothing of the woman except those boots – those blood-red boots rising and falling like pistons in the dew-soaked grass, down the hillside towards the stream, blanketed in cloud like the ghost of a river.

Every part of her wanted to run in the opposite direction, back towards the church. She wanted to scream her lungs out and burst through the iron-riveted door where Caine sat – the warm-blooded, warm-hearted Buddhist, comfortably respectful of a Christian ceremony.

But the phantom trampled lightly over a wooden bridge and on to the other side, where the ground rose steeply. Shanti saw the red flashes ascending a set of steps cut into the hillside.

As she ran onto the bridge, her dress snagged on a nail, and to her dismay, she heard the fabric rip. She pulled off her shoes, feeling the wet ground squelch through her stockings, and leapt the grassy stairs two at a time, but lost her footing and tumbled onto the muddy ground, crying out as a flint gashed her hand.

'I just want to talk to you!' she wailed. 'Please . . . wait for me!'

But the crimson boots kept moving, up the other side of the valley, where they disappeared into the labyrinthine forest interior.

Bloodied and defeated, Shanti pulled on her shoes and hobbled back across the bridge. She hauled herself breathlessly over the stile, returning to the graveyard just as the final booming notes of the organ released the mourners into the dripping evening.

And behind a sad black yew tree, Shanti Joyce hid herself away. Because she looked a mess. Because the tears were streaming down her face. Because her dress was torn. Because she had mud and blood on her hands. Because she had a reputation for being the solid, sane cop who would exhaust every line of inquiry and crack any case.

Instead it was she who was exhausted.

And she who had cracked.

Chapter 14

A Loosened Tongue

Vincent Caine sat crammed between Danes in the back seat of Saul Spencer's overcrowded vintage Mercedes.

To his left were the muscular flanks of two brothers called Carl and Aksel, and to his right the athletic form of another relative, Anja.

An equally striking young woman, Freja, had taken the front passenger seat, while behind the leather-trimmed steering wheel and walnut dashboard sat the spindly form of the driver, Saul Spencer, his neck so thin it barely touched his shirt collar.

After the funeral, Caine had searched everywhere for Shanti, but she was nowhere to be seen. He had no doubt that she could look after herself – she'd probably returned to Yeovil to be with her son – and yet something about her absence made him anxious.

Outside the church, Callum and Art had tried to organise lift shares in their own inimitable ways.

'My dear friends, Kristal would be touched that so many of

you have joined us to say goodbye. And now Art and I would like to invite you to Mangrove House for refreshments.'

'Yo, refreshments! Bring it on!'

'Thank you, Art. Unfortunately, we can only accommodate Kristal's family and friends.'

'What my dad means is that you fuckers from the tabloids can fuck right off back to London, and when you get there, you can fuck off again, and while you're at it, you may as well keep fucking off until you get back here, then you can fuck off all over again!'

People laughed awkwardly. The living artwork was like an overindulged football star.

Caine continuously scanned the shadows at the edge of the cemetery, but there was no sign of Shanti. And now, cramped on the cracked leather seats of Spencer's car, he resolved to do his job and obtain whatever information he could find.

'Strange service,' said Freja in the front, turning her glowing face towards them.

'What? Did you expect normal?' laughed Anja. 'Kristal would have loved it. The hologram ... the glass coffin. It was awesome!'

'Did you know her well? I'm Vincent, by the way, Vincent Caine. I'm a friend of Callum's.'

'Sure. We all knew Kristal,' said Carl. 'Aksel and I are actually nephews of her stepdad, Rasmussen. Anja and Freja are her mother's nieces ... Sorry, it's a complicated family.'

'Kristal had no siblings, then?'

'No, she was always the special one!'

'Tell me if it's none of my business, but Callum mentioned a rift between Kristal and her stepdad.'

'That was bullshit!' said Freja. 'Listen, all of us knew Rasmussen well and he was a lovely guy.'

'A true gent,' agreed Aksel. 'I don't know how well you knew Kristal, but she had a . . . a creative way of looking at the world.'

'My brother means she was a liar,' said Carl. 'Look, let's be honest – when her parents split up, Kristal felt abandoned. Her mother was a director at the Rasmussen plant in Aalborg and she fell in love with the boss. It was the best thing that happened to both of them. Everyone loved our uncle . . .'

'Except Kristal,' said Anja. 'She thought no one could replace her daddy, and no matter how kind Rasmussen was to her – and trust me, he spoiled her rotten – she resented him more and more.'

'The truth is, Kristal never forgave her mother,' said Carl. 'She wanted to destroy the happiness she'd found with Rasmussen. Kristal was an incredibly difficult kid, and an even more trouble-some teenager. In the end, our uncle sent her to boarding school near Copenhagen.'

'That's when the allegations began – that Rasmussen had behaved inappropriately and so on. It was a nightmare for him. Our father is a psychologist – he talked to Rasmussen very directly, and he was always convinced that the accusations were unfounded.'

'That must have been very distressing,' said Caine.

'Yeah, and when Kristal turned eighteen, she reported Rasmussen to the authorities and the poor guy was arrested. Of course the papers picked up the story and he had to stand up in court and defend himself. It turned out he had a reliable alibi on every occasion and the case was thrown out.'

'But that story about abuse would have suited her,' said Freja. 'The innocent child assaulted by the evil billionaire.'

'Even then, our uncle forgave her,' said Aksel. 'He was determined to make his peace, but once Kristal had a hold of something, she could never let it go. The poor man had this hanging over him for the rest of his days.'

'It sounds like none of you had much sympathy for Kristal,' said Caine.

There was a long silence. And then all the passengers began talking at once, about what a talented artist she had been . . .

'Always inventive.'

'So brave.'

'Determined. That's the word I'd use.'

'I must admit, we're not only here for the funeral,' said Carl. 'Aksel and I are setting up a modern art museum in Copenhagen, and we're hoping to get hold of one or two really fine pieces of Kristal's work, if Saul here can help us.'

'As I said, I'll help if I can,' said Spencer as he steered between the rising-sun gates of Mangrove House. 'But right now, everyone wants an original Havfruen. One thing's for sure, Kristal will get her place in the art history books after all.'

In the drawing room, caterers bearing canapés drifted amongst the subdued red and white guests. In recent days, Caine had studied the CCTV footage from the Meat Hook Gallery many times, and he was pretty sure he recognised several of the art lovers from the night of the private view. Even the team from the removal company, MasterMoves, were here. Caine mingled, listening to the gossip, chatting to friends and family of the deceased. He appeared casual, but his senses were on high alert.

By the huge woodburner, Callum Oak was making a brave attempt to be polite and cordial, but Caine noticed the anguish on his boyish face. He wandered over and they shook hands warmly.

'A beautiful service,' said Caine.

'Inevitably hijacked by Art,' sighed Oak. 'Listen, Caine, all I want is for you to resolve this case. Then we can all find some peace.'

'We're working on it, Callum, believe me.' But as he said the words, Caine wondered how far they had truly come. This room had been turned upside down to no avail. Was Kristal's murderer wandering amongst them now, sipping wine and pretending to grieve?

Through the French doors, Caine noticed that the weather had cleared and a silvery sheen had settled over the sea. Then he spotted two figures on the terrace in heated conversation: Art Havfruen and Saul Spencer. Caine strolled over, but by the time he reached the door, Art had burst back into the room, shoving aggressively past him.

After many bottles had been consumed, the noise level in the room began to increase. Callum called for attention, and one by one, various friends and acquaintances stepped forward to offer eulogies to Kristal. The vicar spoke enthusiastically of the unique spirit and energy that lived on in her work, but Caine felt that many of the benevolent words were offered more for Callum's comfort.

'And who else would like to say something?' said Oak.

'I would!' called Oliver Sweetman, a megawatt smile beaming on his round freckled face.

'Oh, Ollie ... perhaps later,' said Callum anxiously. But Sweetman was bumbling drunkenly towards the front of the crowd, a large glass of wine in his hand.

'Look at you!' he said. 'All them long faces. Like those horses, you are. I don't know why you're so sad, truly I don't. I'm having a whale of a time!' To prove it he performed a small tap dance in front of the stove.

'Righto, Ollie,' said Oak, taking his elbow firmly. 'That'll do for now.'

But the big man was enjoying the attention. 'I got a message for you from Kristal – she says cheer up, the lot of you. Especially you, Callum Oak. You're all talking like she's gone forever. But she'll be along soon enough, you wait and see.'

'I said that will do!' said Oak sharply.

'No need to get your knickers in a twist!' grinned the giant. 'Always so serious, you were – a bit self-important if you ask me. Well, thanks for your attention, ladies. This is big Ollie Sweetman wishing you cheerio and goodnight!'

Saul Spencer had returned from the terrace looking flushed and anxious.

'Ah, here's Saul,' said Oak, 'I'm sure he'll have something sensible to contribute. As you all know, Saul Spencer is the curator of Kristal's wonderful and ... and ... tragic retrospective show. Saul, you understood her work better than anyone. Do you have a few words you could share?'

Spencer stepped forward, unfolding a sheet of paper as he collected himself. He wore a tight red tartan suit with a white shirt and red bow tie, his hair slicked back off his slim face. A moustache so thin it could have been drawn with a biro.

'Of course, Callum ... It has been the privilege of my life to work with Kristal. And so I think the most appropriate words would be her own. I'd like to read an extract from the famous Declaration, which was part of the fabled student work known as *A Boy Named Art*.'

149

'Oh for fuck's sake, Spencer!' yelled Art from the back of the room.

'I'm sorry, Art. I know you've heard this countless times, but the words are so resonant. I think your mother would want this.'

'Yeah, Mum always got what she wanted. Right, well if anyone needs me, I'll be in the lav!' And he stormed out of the room, swearing violently as he tripped headlong over the sleeping Labrador, who squealed beneath his pointy toes.

Coughing nervously, the thin man began.

'A Declaration.

I, Kristal Havfruen, Artist,

Make this Declaration on

The Birth Day of my son.

That this boy shall be named Art.

That from this moment everything he does . . .

Yes, even these cries . . .

Shall be a work of art.

That every word he speaks,

And every action, in every waking moment,

Shall be a work of Art.

That even the dreams he dreams

And the deepest thoughts of his subconscious mind

Shall be works of Art.

Because he is Art, he cannot do any thing that is not Art.

Yes, even the breath he breathes

And the fluids he emits from his body

Shall be Artworks.

And if in turn he produces children of his own,

Those children shall be living artworks too,

And their children forever.

And when this boy grows old and senile,

That also shall be Art.

And when he dies,

Even his passing shall be a Work of Art.'

As the poignant words reverberated, a few guests lifted handkerchiefs to tear-stained eyes, and enthusiastic applause rippled around the room.

What they could not see was the sickly living artwork hunched over a line of numbing powder at the sink unit in his mother's bathroom. Wound tightly around one hand was one of Kristal's lacy white dresses.

'Thank you, Saul,' said Callum. 'That was very moving. Now if everyone who wants to speak has done so, would you please raise your glasses to my wife, the unique and beautiful artist Kristal Havfruen.'

'To Kristal!'

'May she rest in peace, and may the person who ended her life in such a callous way be swiftly brought to justice.'

'Bottoms up and tits out!' shouted Oliver.

Caine, with glass raised, noticed the living-room door burst open and Art storm wild-eyed into the room.

'Think you forgot someone, Dad!' he shouted. 'Maybe I've got a few things to say.'

In an instant, the atmosphere turned dangerous.

'Cheers everyone, you fuckers. Yeah, Mum. What can I say? Love you, bitch. Thing about you, Mum, is you're dead, right, but nothing has changed. I mean, when I was a kid, you were my whole fucking world, but you were never there. Know what I mean? Now it's the same – you're the centre of attention, everyone talking about you, but you ain't there again. Fuck it ... let's get smashed.'

Nervous laughter from the crowd, with a few isolated whoops and catcalls of support. But Art had not quite finished.

'By the way, just so's you know ... see the fella over there? The tall one with the long hair?'

He pointed straight at Caine.

'He's a cop. Yeah, that's right. He don't look like it, but he is. So you'd better watch what you say, otherwise Mr Piggy will nick you and take you back to the piggery, just like he nicked me. He thought I done it – thought I killed me own mum. Well I didn't. But we all know who did, don't we, Saul? Had to get the punters through the door, didn't you. Boost up them prices. Well go on, Officer Dibble, why don't you arrest Saul Spencer?'

Chapter 15

How to Make a Killing

'It seems Art was correct,' said Saul Spencer.

It was the Monday after the funeral, and Shanti and Caine were in the curator's office at the Meat Hook, seated in front of what passed for a desk but was in reality a large sheet of toughened glass resting on two trestles, with a MacBook and a few tidy stacks of paper on its surface.

'Correct about what?' asked Caine.

'He accused you of being a policeman – something you omitted to mention when I gave you a lift from the funeral. I think you told us you were a friend of Callum Oak.'

'Both things could be true. But as I remember, that wasn't the only accusation he made . . .'

'I have known Art a long time, Detective Inspector Caine . . . is that what you are – a detective inspector? We were at school together, as a matter of fact. He is a lovely, confused and silly man. But he's also a very smart advertising creative whose job is to get people's attention with random statements in order for them to buy things they don't actually need. He loves to shock, it's as simple as that.'

Shanti stared at the arachnid man in the red suit. Unless she was mistaken, the curator seemed restless, and minute beads were forming around his meagre moustache.

'Nonetheless,' she said, 'it seems very strange to accuse a friend of being involved with his mother's death. Why would he do that?'

'I'd say that was a mystery shared between Art and a couple of toots of powder. Look, I'm not trying to avoid your questions, but I'm gasping for a coffee. Why don't we walk over to the restaurant? So long as I have a latte and a croissant in front of me, you can ask me anything you want.'

They trailed behind him across the yard and Shanti noted his peculiar walk – like a marionette operated by a drunken puppeteer.

What she had observed when they arrived at the gallery was that the car parks were filled to overflowing. What she noticed now, as they approached the main building, was a large queue in front of the ticket desk that snaked into the courtyard, where children chased each other around the giant *Pissing Kristal*.

Inside the main building, the gift shop was humming with customers. A poster with a smouldering black and white image of Kristal and the words *KRISTAL HAVFRUEN – A Life* was selling rapidly. There was also a large stack of *The Mother of Art* by the till, republished in a striking new format. There were cute little resin foetus key rings, and on low stools around a large shoe rack, teenagers were trying on raspberry-red Doc Martens in many sizes.

As they sidestepped the crowds and followed Saul Spencer

along the corridor towards the restaurant, Shanti could have sworn she detected a faint after-note beneath the aroma of roasted coffee beans – the lingering whiff of formaldehyde.

'Oh, before we have coffee, Mr Spencer . . . isn't the master gallery down this way? Do you think my colleague could take a quick look? Just to get his bearings.'

For reasons unknown, Spencer flushed with embarrassment. 'To be honest, I'd rather have coffee first if you don't mind. As I said, I'm gasping.'

'I'm sure the coffee can wait for ten minutes,' insisted Shanti.

'You'll be wasting your time really. It's more or less an empty room.'

'I like a little emptiness,' said Caine.

Spencer stood squirming like a schoolboy outside a toilet.

'Look, I'll tell you what – why don't I pick up some visitor passes and you can wander wherever you like? I'm pretty busy anyway.'

'Oh, but we'd like your company, Mr Spencer. I don't know much about art, so it's nice to have an expert on hand.'

Spencer was noticeably irritated, but he pulled himself together and jitterbugged past the restaurant and along the corridor, through the galleries, past the garish Day-glo tree called *Forbidden Fruit*, festooned with multicoloured foetuses, and between the dozens of Kristal Havfruens – naked and tiny, or huge and lacy white, with red boots in corresponding sizes.

They followed the back of his neatly cropped head through crowds of art students and holidaying families, Spencer indifferent to the exhibits, Caine gazing in fascination, Shanti shaking her head in disbelief.

At last they arrived at the huge theatrical doors of the master gallery, which Shanti had assumed would be closed but which were instead flung wide, watched over by two attendants. A dense crowd waited outside.

'Only six at a time, please,' instructed one of the attendants, a young Sikh, and he counted them as they filed in.

Shanti, Caine and Spencer waited their turn, as flashing iPhones sent surges of light from the vaulted room.

Shanti caught brief snatches of conversation around her.

'And this is the room where they found her. Floating in the tank. Stone dead.'

'Mum, it's like a shrine in there!'

'Well actually our Hannah is doing a project at college. She's collected every news cutting and she saved up for the red Docs and the white mini dress. She even does the thing with the smudged lipstick.'

'Who d'you think done it?'

'The son, of course.'

'No, not Art. That would be too obvious.'

'Go on then, clever. Who killed Kristal?'

At last it was their turn. When the six visitors had shuffled out of the gallery, looking visibly moved, the attendant admitted a family of four, plus Spencer and Caine.

'Would you mind waiting?' he asked Shanti.

'It's all right, Akash. She's with me,' said the increasingly flustered Spencer.

'OK, Saul. In you go, miss.'

Shanti entered the dark interior. A few feet in front of her, a ribbon of police tape prevented visitors from stepping into the main space. On the floor below the tape, a mountain of red and white roses in cellophane wrappers exuded a sickly-sweet smell of dying vegetation – a perfume so dense it almost overwhelmed the dull stench of formaldehyde.

'I'm a bit confused, Mr Spencer,' said Shanti as her eyes adjusted to the gloom. 'I authorised that tape to be removed. This is no longer a crime scene, so presumably visitors can go right inside.'

'It's a sort of tribute,' snapped Spencer. 'It's what people want. They've read about nothing else for the last two weeks. It's like a soap opera.'

The young attendant stepped forward. 'Ready for the lights, Saul?'

'Oh . . . we won't bother with the lights, Akash,' said Spencer, backing out of the room.

'Oh yes, let's have the lights, Mr Spencer. We like lights, don't we, Caine?'

The attendant, Akash, raised his arm to activate a motion sensor, and suddenly the silent black space before them exploded into life, Beethoven's Choral Symphony blaring out and the jagged beams of laser lights leaping onto the podium at the centre of the vast room.

There was an intake of breath from the audience.

'Ooh, look! There are her boots!'

'And the glass case tipped on its side!'

'With . . . Oh my God!'

'What's that spilling from the tank, Dad?'

'Here's the curator,' said Shanti, 'let's ask him. What is that spilling from the tank, sir?'

'It's nothing. Just a neutral liquid. It's perfectly harmless. It's supposed to look like . . . you know . . .'

'Formaldehyde. That's pretty sick, isn't it?'

'Like I say, it's what the public want.'

'Boosted ticket sales, has it?'

'A little. We're always busy in the holiday season. Look, can we step out of the way, please? There are people waiting to get inside. I'm trying to run an art gallery.'

Out in the corridor, Shanti pressed the flustered curator a little more.

'I seem to recall that you were initially nervous about hosting a Kristal Havfruen show, Mr Spencer. Isn't that the case? I believe you only agreed to do it if Kristal produced a brand-new exhibit for the master gallery. A happening, isn't that what it's called?'

'I did it to help Art, and his mother, dammit. It was more or less an act of charity. She was forgotten until I got involved.'

'But this . . . this event turned out to be more than you could have hoped for.'

'That's a disgraceful thing to say!' said Spencer, his face livid with crimson angles.

'Yes,' said Caine calmly. 'It's the kind of idea a really smart advertising executive might think up. An incredibly dramatic way to promote a show. Imagine how much you'd pay for that kind of publicity!'

'What the hell are you accusing me of? You're forgetting the trauma of that night. It was me who first realised that Kristal was dead. I called the police. I ran to fetch a toolbox and I helped Callum lever off the lid. I watched that slippery body slithering out of the tank like one of those horrifying images by Goya or Bosch . . .'

'It's not an accusation,' said Caine. 'Just a hypothesis. One way or another, the value of Kristal's work has gone through the roof, and I think I'm right in saying that the Havfruen-Oak family have appointed you as Kristal's sole dealer.'

'I . . . need . . . coffee . . .' gasped Spencer.

'Will there be buns?' asked Shanti.

The Meat Hook Bar and Grill was an artwork in itself – bits and pieces of metalwork and wiring that spilled from wooden crates stacked with bottles of liquor. Assemblages of plastic toys, old television sets and kitchen utensils, dripping with paint in the style of Rauschenberg. Behind a gleaming counter, a muscular youth with his hair in a topknot and more than his share of tattoos and piercings prepared cappuccinos with many theatrical flourishes. As he worked, he charmed and chatted to four Japanese girls on bar stools, identically dressed as Kristal Havfruen, with blonde wigs and smudged red lips.

Shanti, Caine and Spencer found an empty table beneath a high-resolution print of a grizzled hobo sunbathing in a rubbish tip.

Shanti noticed that Spencer's delicate hands were trembling as he counted sugar lumps into his long-awaited latte.

'You say you went to school with Art Havfruen – was that a boarding school?'

'Bryanston, Inspector Joyce. A proper school. A proper education.'

'And did you meet up in the holidays?'

'Yes. Occasionally. I stayed at Mangrove House a few times.'

'That's interesting. And who was there when you visited?'

'Kristal was always in her studio, but she didn't come out much. She scared me a little, to be honest – she could be quite sharp with Art. Callum spent most of his time in his studio above the garage. A nice guy, but very timid – he left us to our own devices.'

'And what did you public school chaps get up to? Girlfriends? Drugs?'

'I'm a homosexual, Detective Inspector. But I seem to remember a bit of pot. That was more Art's thing than mine.'

'Nothing stronger, though?'

'We were schoolboys.'

'But who cared for Art? Made his meals and so on? Did they have staff?'

'No. There was a lovely woman who often stayed – Art's godmother, I believe ... looked like Charlotte Rampling ...'

'Marlene Moss?'

'That's right.'

Shanti shot Caine a glance.

'She was much older than Callum,' continued Spencer, 'but I often wondered if there was something between them. She was certainly mad about his paintings, I remember that. I've seen his early works – very good, if a little retro. I think I'm right in saying that Marlene had known Art all his life. She was a sort of auntie figure, and it was clear they adored each other. You have to remember, Art was starved of a mother, so Marlene's presence was comforting. At least when he was young. As he got older, he became angry with everyone, so she was in the firing line as much as the next person.'

'That's very helpful, Mr Spencer. Only a couple more questions from me and then I'll hand over to DI Caine. It's no secret that Art likes his powder and that makes him a bit volatile. Do you have any idea where he obtains his supplies?'

'Ha, ha! This is wonderful!'

'I'm sorry, I missed the joke . . .'

'Look, Art works in advertising, right?'

'So . . .?'

'Goodness me, what a naïve question! Surely you realise that if you work in the creative sector in London and you fancy pills, potions, poppers, uppers, downers, acid, crack, Ecstasy – anything at all with your tea break – well you browse a menu, send a text and within minutes there's a man on a scooter.'

'Art has a weekend place in Charmouth, near Bridport, is that correct?'

'I believe so.'

'You believe so? You've never visited?'

'Once or twice.'

'And did you ever see him with a syringe in his hands?'

'Never! Look, I'm sorry, but you've caught me on a particularly busy day.'

'Of course. Ten minutes more at most. I want to ask you something very important, something that's baffled me from the start. I wonder if you can shed any light on the CCTV images of the evening of the private view? It's absolutely central to this case.'

'Very well, I'll try.'

'At 18.30, we see Art arguing aggressively with Kristal just inside the master gallery. The tank is clearly visible in the background with the effigy of Kristal inside. Apart from Oliver Sweetman, who gives the tank a polish at 19.00, nobody goes near that tank until you lead the group of visitors into the master gallery and discover the body at 20.38. Can you explain that? I must admit it's giving me a headache.'

'A few minutes ago you seemed to be accusing me of Kristal's murder, and now you're asking me to help solve the crime. We all know about cutbacks in the police force, but surely this isn't my job! Anyway, since you ask, I have also wondered about that. I agree it's deeply confusing, but I simply have no idea.'

'Can I get you guys anything else?' asked a waitress who might have stepped off a Paris catwalk.

'Another latte,' snapped Spencer.

'OK, Saul. Anything for anyone else?'

'I'll take another latte too,' said Shanti. 'And a slice of that banana cake.'

'Sorry to be difficult,' said Caine. 'But do you have any honey? Just a spoonful for my tea.'

She beamed at him. 'I'll see what I can do.'

Caine sat for a long time with a calm half-smile on his face, which seemed to unnerve Spencer more than ever. When the drinks and a miniature jar of honey arrived, Caine stirred his tea and carefully placed the teaspoon on the saucer. At last he said:

'So, Mr Spencer . . . or may I call you Saul?'

'You can call me anything you like.'

'As you mentioned, Saul, you were kind enough to give me a lift to Mangrove House after the funeral, along with four of Kristal's relatives from Denmark.'

'That's correct.'

'The brothers, Aksel and Carl, are art collectors, isn't that right? Nice guys.'

'Yes.'

'I noticed that you had a long chat with them at the wake.'

'Is that a crime?'

'Not at all. But I couldn't help overhearing a few words, and it sounded as if they were negotiating for some original Havfruens – some substantial sums were mentioned.'

Both Spencer and his coffee cup seemed rattled.

'You said it yourself – they are art buyers and I'm a curator. Of course we discussed business.'

'I think you're being a little modest.'

'I don't understand.'

'You describe yourself as a curator, but in fact you are a partner in the business, isn't that correct? You are co-owner of Meat Hook International.'

'Unless this is directly relevant to the case, Inspector Caine, I would suggest that my business dealings are my own concern.'

'The thing is, I had the feeling that you were conducting something more than a general chat with Aksel and Carl. I noticed a lot of smiles and handshakes, as if you'd reached an agreement.'

'Look, I'm not sure what you're driving at, Inspector. It's no secret that we made a deal. I was able to sell them some works from Kristal's studio.'

'I'll need you to be more specific, if you don't mind. I've visited Mangrove House several times – there are some incomplete figures in Kristal's studio and a few pieces in the garden, but almost all her important works are in the retrospective here at the Meat Hook.'

'You are very observant. Well, I suppose there's no harm in telling you: Art and I came up with an idea. We managed to get hold of all the moulds for the figures. Some are actual life casts – inverted plaster negatives of Kristal's body. They're marvellous objects in their own right, and Carl and Aksel are going to display them in a special room at the new museum.'

'And that was the full extent of their purchase?'

'More or less,' said Spencer, crossing and uncrossing his lanky legs.

'More or less?'

'There's a slim possibility of a sale on another work. Something unique and almost priceless. I'm not trying to avoid your question, Inspector, but discussions are at an early stage and it may not happen at all.' Saul glanced at his watch and then around the café, which was beginning to empty. 'Look, I'm very sorry, I can see people waiting for me. I'm afraid that really is all the time I can spare. I'm sorry not to be more helpful.'

'Oh, but you were most helpful, Mr Spencer,' said Shanti. 'I've learnt so much about art today. But the trouble with our business is that the more questions you answer, the more questions arise. We may need to talk again, if you can spare some of your valuable time. But perhaps there would be fewer distractions at the station – it's what we undereducated coppers refer to as an interview under caution.'

Spencer scuttled away as if his hair was on fire.

'That giant red spider is so-o guilty!' said Shanti in the car.

'That giant red spider is a giant red herring,' responded Caine.

'What are you talking about? You said it yourself, he's made a mint out of Kristal's death. That was brilliant, by the way, when you pointed out that he was a co-owner of the gallery. How did you even know that?'

'It wasn't hard to find out.'

'Then he admitted that he'd flogged a truckload of plaster casts of her body. You know what, Caine? So long as there are rich, gullible people out there, self-satisfied schoolboys like Spencer are going to make a killing . . . if you'll forgive the phrase.'

'He's certainly benefited from her death, but that doesn't implicate him in her murder.'

'Come on, Caine, he was sweating like a snowman in a sauna. What about this unique and priceless artwork? Why's he so cagey about that?'

'Don't worry, Shanti. I'm on it.' He fumbled in his shoulder bag and pulled out his notebook. 'Now, where did I put those . . .? Ah, here we are.'

Sandwiched between the pages were four business cards, which he laid out one by one along the dashboard of the car like playing cards. 'Now then, Carl, Aksel, Freja and Anja.'

'Smart work, Caine. You'll get a gold star today. Do you want me to contact them?'

'It's better if I do it – they know who I am. To be honest, I doubt it will help the case, but I'll send a few emails and see if I can find out any more about this unique piece of artwork. It does sounds intriguing.'

'Are Buddhists even allowed to use email?'

'So long as there are no attachments.'

Shanti groaned. 'Is that from one of your mugs?'

He smiled. 'Tell me, Shanti. How are you? I couldn't find you after the funeral.'

'I needed an early night. But since you ask, I had a lousy day. I was at my wits' end at the funeral. Don't worry, though, I've pulled myself together now.'

'Something freaked you, didn't it? Are you going to tell me what happened?'

'Ah! I must have imagined it . . . it seems insane now. You'll think I'm a fool.'

'Try me.'

'Well, when you were inside the church, I saw ... I saw ...'

'Saw what, Shanti?'

'I saw Kristal.'

'OK ...'

'I mean something exactly like Kristal. It was foggy, right? I saw a blonde-haired woman in a white dress sitting on a wall in the graveyard. She was even wearing those damned red boots.'

'Spooky.'

'It was spooky, Caine. Genuinely spooky. I must admit, it shook me up pretty bad. I gave chase, of course, but she got away and disappeared into the woods.'

'Maybe someone was trying to scare you.'

'Well, they succeeded. You know, I've never thought this in my life, but maybe there *are* ghosts. If anyone would want to create an impression after their death, it would be Kristal, right? You're a Buddhist, so you believe in reincarnation, don't you?'

'Well, not literally, necessarily. But here in the countryside, reincarnation is all around.'

'I suppose you're going to explain.'

'I mean in a few months, every one of these billions of leaves will die and fall to the ground. They'll rot into compost, and in the spring, a billion new leaves will grow. It's an endless cycle of life and death, which reaches way beyond our individual lives and this tiny planet. In reality, there's no end and no beginning. We humans like to think we are separate, but we are all part of that eternal life force – that never-ending stream of molecules.'

'That's very lovely, Caine, in an unhelpful sort of way. So do you believe I saw Kristal or not?'

'Listen, I believe you saw something in that graveyard that frightened you. Remember the thing about embracing uncertainty and not filling in the gaps? Well, I'm not going to guess exactly what you saw until I know for certain.'

'Could I make a suggestion, Caine? You need to get a life . . . obtainable from all good mothers everywhere.'

'I'm sorry, do I annoy you, Shanti?'

'All men annoy me. So come on, DI Dalai Lama. Where do we go from here?'

'Remember our day in Falmouth? It was nice, wasn't it? How about a return to our friend Marlene?'

'I'm sure she would be pleased to see us. She loves a bit of company. And you're right – it does seem that she was closer to the Oaks than we first realised. I'm not convinced it's the best use of our time, but perhaps she'll reveal a little more about the family dynamics.'

They drove in silence for a while, Caine making doodles in his notebook. Eventually Shanti said, 'I don't normally talk about my family life, but you may as well know that Paul has been having a few problems at school. Mum does her best, but I wish I could be around more. I suppose he misses his dad.'

'Boys need male mentors.'

'Are you applying for the job?'

'Listen, why don't we take him with us to Falmouth? A mini break.'

'It's a sweet idea, Caine. But you really don't get this. I can't mix family and work. Where's Paul while we're interviewing Marlene? Eating biscuits on my lap?'

'No. He'll be playing on the beach with his granny.'

'Jesus, Caine! You're planning a whole family outing!'

'I'd like to meet Paul. Your mum too. What's her name, by the way?'

Chapter 16

Milly, Molly and Murder

'Amma. Call me Amma,' said Shanti's mum.

She and Caine sat side by side in the back of the Saab, surrounded by piles of picnic paraphernalia, a windbreak, a bodyboard, a football and a kite. In the front, Paul was chatting happily to Shanti as they headed out of Devon towards Cornwall.

'Amma is Malayalam for mother,' she continued. 'And by the way, the words Amma and Malayalam are both palindromes – they are the same forwards and backwards.'

'You always say that, Amma!' groaned Paul.

'Well I haven't heard it before,' said Caine. 'It's very clever. I like that.'

'Have you visited Kerala, Inspector Caine?'

'Vincent, please. No, I've been to Bodh Gaya in the north, but never to the south. But in fact one of my favourite novels is set in Kerala. It's called *The God of Small Things*.'

'Ah, I could tell you were a reader. I'm so happy that Shanti has found a nice friend. She's a wonderful girl, as I'm sure you know . . . intelligent, beautiful—'

'Mum! Will you please be quiet!'

'I'm only saying what is true,' said Amma. 'I expect you saw Shanti on the news last night, Vincent? So impressive. Really, I think the whole country was impressed.'

'Caine hasn't got a TV, Amma,' said Paul. 'He lives in the woods. He's a wild man.'

'No TV. Imagine that.'

'Was it a press briefing, Shanti?' asked Caine.

'I apologise for my family, Caine. Yes, it was a press briefing. The Super made me do it. Seems half the country is obsessed with finding out who killed Kristal, which will be incredibly unhelpful if it comes to court.'

'Mum?'

'Yes, Paul.'

'Mum, who *did* kill Kristal?'

'Oh Jeez,' said Shanti. 'This is going to be a long day.'

It was a little after 10 a.m. when Shanti dropped Paul and Amma at Swanpool Beach in Falmouth. She and Caine helped them carry the beach equipment across the sand until Amma was finally satisfied with their position.

'Have a lovely morning,' said Shanti, giving Paul a kiss on the head. 'We shouldn't be long. A few hours at most.'

Caine finished banging in the poles of the windbreak with a rock.

'Are you and Mum going to catch bad guys?' asked Paul.

'You bet,' said Caine with a wink. 'A whole gang of big hairy bad guys.'

'You two take as long as you need,' said Amma. Then, making sure Caine was out of earshot, she whispered, 'He's perfect, Shanti. You make such a handsome couple.'

'Right, Mum, look at me . . . Read my lips: we are *not* a couple. I am not in a relationship. I do not want a relationship. Caine is my work colleague. *Nothing more!*'

'So you tell me, but a mother knows these things. The way he looks at you . . .'

Back at the car, Caine had moved into the passenger seat – 'I assume I'm allowed in the front if I behave!' – and they set off for their appointment at Vernon Place.

Caine pushed long and hard on the doorbell, but all he got in return was an asthmatic rasp. He leaned over and tapped on the window, and after a long, long time, Marlene Moss came to the door, swinging her Zimmer in front of her. She seemed frailer than ever.

'Ah ha, my favourite crime-fighting duo! Bringing excitement into my life.'

'Nice to see you, Marlene. Look, I remembered your book.'

'Oh, I'd completely forgotten . . .'

They followed her tiny shuffling form along the corridor and into the stuffy living room, where she parked her walking frame and fumbled for cigarettes.

'You make yourself comfortable, Ms Joyce. I think it's DI Caine's turn to make tea, isn't it? We women have waited a thousand years for that cuppa, so we may as well enjoy it.'

'Damn right,' said Shanti. 'So how are you, Marlene?'

'Well I'm dying, dear. But besides that, I'm extremely well.

Look, never mind me – have you discovered who killed Kristal? That's what we all want to know.'

'I think we're getting closer, that's all I can say. But I wanted to ask you – do you remember this photo in *The Mother of Art*? Isn't that you and Callum and baby Art?'

'Oh yes, Ollie took that photo. I always thought it was rather good of me.'

'You look stunning, Marlene. Like a movie star.'

'Without the Hollywood salary, unfortunately. Mind you, Callum looks a little apprehensive, doesn't he? Art was just few days old and the poor child had a media swarm around him from dawn to dusk. I don't know if it's true, but there was a rumour that his first nappy was auctioned at Christie's.'

'It may well be true. I'm beginning to learn that a lot of people will pay good money for sh—'

Caine put his head around the door. 'Sorry to interrupt. But would you mind if I had a quick word with DI Shanti?'

'Of course not, dear,' said Marlene. 'Do you need help with the kettle? Men often struggle with these things.'

Shanti followed him into the kitchen.

'What is it, Caine? That was just getting interesting.'

'Sorry, but close the door a minute . . .'

He led her across the kitchen and opened the door into a small conservatory at the back of the house.

'Jesus, Caine! It reeks in here!'

'It does. And here are the culprits . . .'

Sitting happily amongst geraniums, peppers, grape vines and tomatoes stood three dark green chest-high shrubs with distinctive spiky fingers.

'Jesus! Cannabis!'

'Who'd have thought it?'

'Well it's not exactly *Breaking Bad*, but I suppose we can't ignore it.'

'OK, grab the teapot and we'll have a little chat.'

They carried the tea things into the living room, where Marlene was balancing a precariously long line of ash on her Silk Cut.

'Marlene . . .'

'Yes, dear. Oh that's nice, you made toast too. I think toast and butter is one of life's little pleasures, don't you?'

'Yes. But talking of life's little pleasures, we couldn't help glancing in your conservatory.'

The ash teetered and tumbled.

'Oh dear, am I busted?'

'I think we were a bit surprised, that's all. Whatever were you thinking, Marlene?'

'I call them Milly, Molly and Mandy. But to be honest, I'm a little worried about Milly . . . I think she may actually be Billy, and a male cannabis plant is of no use to anyone, as you probably know. It has plenty of leaves, but no bud at all. What are your feelings, Inspector?'

'Marlene, did you know that it's actually a criminal offence to cultivate marijuana in the UK?' asked Caine gently.

'Have you brought handcuffs, dear?' She extended her skinny wrists. 'It's always been a secret dream of mine to be handcuffed by a strapping young policeman. And I wonder if you would use the lights and sirens in a case like this? You know, the blues and twos. Imagine how impressed the neighbours would be.'

'We won't be arresting you,' said Caine. 'But I suppose we are duty bound to report this, or at least destroy those plants.'

'That would be dreadful, Mr Caine! It's some of the best weed I've ever smoked. For a few hours it relieves the pain completely.'

'Ah! Now I understand – it's medicinal marijuana?'

'Well, yes, but you can still get pretty wasted. Come on, you two, let's skin one up. I won't tell a soul.'

'We are absolutely not allowed to do that. If you need cannabis oil for medical purposes, surely you could talk to your doctor?'

'But that's no fun at all.'

'Listen, Marlene,' said Shanti gently. 'Where did you get this from? I mean, how . . . ?'

'I grow it myself. I'm a one-woman operation.'

'But someone must have supplied the seeds.'

'Well, I don't want to get anyone in trouble, but Art introduced me to medicinal marijuana when I was first diagnosed. I loathe that super-strength skunk that all the kids smoke – it completely scrambles your brains. But Art was so considerate. He took the greatest trouble to source the right strain – high CBD, low THC, that's the thing. It's quite a skill, you know, but he was endlessly patient. He brought plant pots and carried in these huge sacks of compost, which practically ruined his suit. He'll be disappointed to hear about Billy, but at least he has two healthy sisters.'

'This puts us in a difficult position professionally. Surely you can see that, Marlene?'

'Oh, I wouldn't want that. I'm so sorry. I'm a bit of a terror, Ms Joyce. I've always done things my own way, and as Art always says, if the rest of the world doesn't like it, well fuck the lot of them!'

'OK, let's make a deal. If you give us a little background on the Havfruen-Oak family, then we'll pretend we haven't noticed. Now, you've known Art all his life, haven't you? In fact you're his godmother.'

'The godmother thing was Callum's idea – you know how churchy he is. But you're right. I was even present at the conception, which is more than most godmothers can say.'

'That's probably true. So tell us about Art. What kind of a man is he? I have to say he likes to kick out with those pointy boots.'

'That's all bluster. I agree he has become more volatile in recent years, but underneath it all, he is the kindest boy you ever met. I have no family of my own, but Art visits me as often as he can and never forgets a birthday. He was devastated when he heard about my diagnosis.'

'You say he took a lot of trouble to find the right medication for you,' said Shanti. 'Do you get the impression that he looks after other people's pharmaceutical needs as well?'

Marlene appeared flustered. 'I'm not sure what you mean.'

'Is Art a dealer?'

'Oh goodness! Goodness me! I couldn't possibly say. All I know is that he helped me. You're not planning to arrest him, are you? I beg you, take me instead. All I need is five minutes to pack a bag ...'

'No handcuffs, Marlene. No sirens. No police cars. Now, let's return to the early days with Art's family. You used to stay at Mangrove House when he was young?'

'Yes. Many times.'

'We went to see someone called Saul Spencer yesterday. Does that name ring a bell?'

'Of course, he's Kristal's curator. And Art's childhood friend. I knew him when he was a boy.'

'Saul suggested that you and Callum were very close.'

'Ms Joyce,' Marlene teased, 'whatever are you insinuating?'

'I'm sorry, but I have to ask these things. I just wondered if you and Callum had a relationship?'

'As you know, Callum Oak was the most talented student I ever had. I thought I recognised a direct line from Cézanne to Bomberg to Auerbach to Oak. And yes, I'd gladly have rogered him senseless.'

Shanti winced.

'Don't go all Miss Jean Brodie on me, DI Joyce. We're talking about art school in the nineties. What do you think we got up too? Macramé?'

Shanti re-tackled the question. 'So you had a sexual relationship?'

Marlene paused. 'Regretfully not. Callum is a man of old-fashioned values. No matter how poorly his partner treated him, he believed in the sanctity of marriage and suchlike oppressive nonsense. And of course once he discovered she was pregnant, he felt honour bound to marry her and be a steady father. He wanted her to take his name, but Kristal was having none of that.'

'How did that feel, that he'd chosen Kristal?' asked Shanti.

'Over me? Is that what you're trying to say? I do wish you'd spit it out, Ms Joyce.'

'Were you in love with Callum?'

'It's all a long time ago, but I dare say I was. He was so terribly good-looking, and more than anything, I loved him as an artist. On the other hand, I wasn't a fool. I was a good deal older than him, in addition to which, over the years I began to notice another side to him that was less appealing.'

'Meaning?'

'Meaning he was weak, Inspector Joyce. Like most men, he was cowardly inside, and that's why he let Kristal walk all over him. Maybe that's why I've been a singleton most of my life, because I've never found a strong enough man. A lucky escape, perhaps, but on the other hand, I managed to retain my friendship with Callum, which was – is – hugely important to me. I just wish I could put him in a time machine and take him back to *that*.' She stabbed a twig of a finger at the shimmering seascape.

Shanti glanced at the clock on the mantelpiece. They'd been there more than an hour, and Marlene appeared as grey and burnt out as cigarette ash. Shanti gave Caine a nudge and they rose to leave.

'Well, thank you once again, Marlene. We'll let ourselves out.'

'Before you go, I want you to promise that you won't give Art a hard time over those plants.'

'Plants?' said Caine. 'I didn't notice any plants. Did you, Shanti?'

'Must have escaped my attention, Caine.' And to her own astonishment, she found herself stooping to peck the old lady gently on her powdery cheek.

They walked slowly back to the car, and Shanti navigated the narrow streets towards Swanpool Beach.

'So what have we learned, Caine?'

'Marlene cared for Art as a child and was deeply in love with Callum although she never rogered him . . .'

'. . . and Art has a kinder side to him. But did you notice how flustered Marlene got when I asked if her godson helped anyone else with their recreational needs?'

'Yes, and I know what you're thinking, Shanti. You're planning to pay Art a surprise visit, aren't you?'

'Maybe you really are telepathic. Yes, that's exactly what I'm planning. I'd say we've got more than enough to obtain a warrant. Listen, Caine, between you and me, I couldn't give a damn what Art sticks up his nose. I'm on the hunt for a murderer here. What I want to know is why he was so cagey about his activities in the hours before the murder. And I think the threat of a stiff sentence for dealing might focus his mind.'

Once they had parked, Shanti and Caine removed their socks and shoes. Then they wandered amongst the happy families on the beach – a dad building elaborate sandcastles with his baby daughter; a noisy family playing beach cricket; a row of pensioners slumped in deckchairs, one with a large pink belly, another with a magazine over her face – until they spotted Amma and Paul close to the water's edge.

'Caine, Caine, come and swim with me!' shouted Paul with a dripping ice cream in his hand.

'Try and stop me,' said Caine, wrapping a towel around his waist and wriggling into swimming trunks.

Feeling more than a little self-conscious, Shanti changed into a white costume that she hadn't worn since she took Paul to Turtle Tots at Parliament Hill Lido. While Amma laid out the picnic, she made a call to Benno, asking him to organise a search warrant for Art's weekend place in Charmouth.

'That shouldn't be a problem, boss. How many do you want in the team? Will you need dogs?'

'Let's keep it simple, Benno. Just you and me and Caine. I'm not expecting much aggro from Art. Could you sort it for first light on Wednesday? I'm looking forward to giving him a wake-up call.'

After they had eaten, Shanti lay on the hot sand and closed her eyes. Above the lazy rush of waves, she could hear the muffled shouts of Paul and Caine playing football, and her mind returned to the riddle of the floating artist.

Her primary suspect was still Art Havfruen, because of the festering resentment towards his mother and his irrefutable link with ketamine. If he turned out to be a dealer, that wouldn't prove he was a killer, but it might force him to answer the questions he'd been so deftly avoiding up until now. Then there was Art's old school buddy, spider man Spencer, whose kudos in the art world, not to mention his personal wealth, had expanded like a web since Kristal's death. She thought too about Oliver Sweetman, the round-headed ginger colossus who had given most of his life to serve his idol. He had the practical skills and certainly the physical strength required, but he seemed too gentle to carry out such a complex and dastardly deed. Then of course there was Callum Oak, the tragic widower, who had been undermined and emasculated by Kristal throughout his life. And last on her list was Marlene Moss, as frail as a fledgling, but thwarted in love by Kristal, who had diverted her protégé from his artistic path.

These were the suspects in the front line, but behind them stood an army of possibilities: the nearly two hundred guests who had been present at the fatal private view; numerous employees at the Meat Hook Gallery; the couriers from MasterMoves; not to mention the scattered Havfruen and Rasmussen family from Denmark. Fortunately Shanti could be sure that Benno and his team were painstakingly following up each of these possibilities.

But at the heart of it all was the mystery of the CCTV footage, which clearly put Kristal and Art together in the very room where she was later found dead. And yet the tank had remained sealed from the moment it arrived to the moment her body was discovered.

Before her head burst with the pressure of the puzzle, Shanti hauled herself to her feet and wandered down to the sea, where Caine was now patiently teaching Paul to swim.

'Look at me, Mum!'

'Wow! That's proper front crawl. Don't go too deep now.'

At first the water felt shockingly cold around her ankles. Then surprisingly cool and refreshing around her waist. Then ecstatically warm and delightful as she submerged herself in the waves.

She kicked onto her back and remembered how as a child she had been a semi-aquatic creature. Diving down through the looking-glass surface, she entered a secret world – an amniotic realm of spangled beauty in which she floated with the weightlessness and solitude of an unborn child.

And when, twenty minutes later, she lay drying out on the powdery sand, she found that her bloodstream was cascading with endorphins, as if her whole being had been restored to factory settings.

The sun, the sea and the exercise had had the same therapeutic effect on Paul, she could tell. He seemed happier and more invigorated than he had been since ... since when? Since forever.

Amma was watching her grandson too.

'Look at those two, Shanti, just like—'

'Do not say "like father and son"!'

'No, but I like your Vincent Caine. He's lovely with Paul, and oh my goodness, what a body! He reminds me of your father when we first met, God rest his soul.'

'Mum, I beg you not to keep on about this. You know better than anyone how my marriage ended. I am off men for a long time. Possibly forever. Besides, I don't know anything about Caine. He's very secretive, you know. Maybe he has a partner. Maybe he's gay. And you know what? I don't care either way. Life is simpler without men.'

'It's only because I love you, Shanti. I want to see you happy.'

'And I love you too, Mum. Now please, help me pack everything away. It's a long drive home, and look at the sky – I think there's a storm brewing.'

Chapter 17

The Naked Fugitive

Vincent Caine floated upside down in his black raincoat, high above the moon. Somewhere in the darkness below his inverted head, the illuminated face of the clock tower stood at 4.55 a.m.

This was the sight that met Benno as he rolled his battered Ford Focus through the sodium-lit streets towards the sea. The peculiar image was a reflection in a gigantic puddle in the Cobb Gate car park, the result of a biblical quantity of rain in the night.

Benno steered the car gently through the floodwaters around the clock tower in an effort to avoid drenching the waiting cop, whose damp hair hung in rat's tails around his shoulders.

'Rough night,' said Benno, pushing open the passenger door. 'You haven't just walked through the Undercliff, have you?'

Caine climbed inside the steamy interior and the two men clasped hands.

'No. I stayed in town with Zeb. He always has a spare room.'

Benno accelerated gently out of the sleeping town, past the

Marine Theatre and up Church Street, the engine groaning and
grumbling with the ascent.

'You look tired, Vince.'

'I haven't been sleeping well. It's not like me.'

'To be honest, I'm amazed you agreed to get involved with
this case.'

'Shanti is very persuasive. How is she settling in at the nick,
by the way?'

'Well, she's acquiring what you might call grudging respect.
A bit like you, mate. You know how hard it is to impress that lot.
I actually think some of them would like to see her take a nose-
dive on the Havfruen case. But they recognise she's running a
tight investigation, and she's almost obsessive about record-
keeping.'

At the crown of the A3052, by Timber Hill, the insipid pros-
pect of morning seeped through the melancholy air.

'I've brought the bosher,' said Benno, waving his thumb
towards the back seat. 'Does it make me a bad person that I'm
itching to use it? It's that arrogance I can't stand. To be honest, I
can't wait to give young Art his early alarm call.'

Caine glanced over his shoulder. The bosher, also known as a
battering ram or the big red key, was lying across the seat like
a pet dog.

He nodded without enthusiasm, but his mind was elsewhere.
The day after the Falmouth trip, something had happened that
had thrown him off centre, so that the benefits of the retreat
seemed a distant memory. It was nothing dramatic. A rare letter
from his father, which Zeb had delivered to the cabin. But even
the sight of the familiar lettering on the envelope was enough to
stir a viper's nest of anxiety in Caine's stomach.

He had propped the unopened letter on the table, yet its very presence in the cabin disturbed his morning routine to such an extent that he rose from the meditation cushion and ripped open the envelope. He skimmed the contents briefly, then stuffed the page into the stove.

It was nothing really. Just brief news of his younger step-sister, always on her travels; and something about a new office block being built opposite the terraced house where Caine and his brother had spent their childhood, and where the old man now lived alone. There wasn't anything remotely disconcerting in the letter, and yet ever since it arrived, he had been restless and unable to clear his mind. Every time he closed his eyes, foul memories disgorged themselves like effluent from a broken pipe.

He had thought back to his time in Thailand – that whole venture a bid to distance himself from his father. A younger version of Caine had sought counsel from his first Buddhist teacher, and the old man had reminded him of the allegory 'Holding on to anger is like grasping a hot coal with the intention of throwing it at another. You are the one who gets burned.'

How true that was. And in that precious time at the forest monastery, Caine had been taught the most valuable practice of all – to simply let go. *Let it go. Let it go. Let it go.*

Yet here he was all those years later, and all it took was the sight of his father's handwriting to remind him of the hot coal that still seared his hand.

It was easy to blame his father, but there were other complicated emotions that had destabilised him and diverted him from his spiritual practice. An image of a woman in a white swimming costume, moving like a dolphin through the sea. When she turned to wave at him and the boy, her face had been radiant. As if the sea had carried away her worries and cares.

Let it go. Let it go. Let it go.

At the A35 roundabout, Benno swung off towards Charmouth, and soon they were rolling along the village's main street, between large comfortable houses with curtains closed like timorous eyelids. A grey streak in the headlamps caused Benno to brake rapidly as a cat scuttled over a wall.

At the bottom of the hill, he turned right and followed a rutted lane past a spectral school playground. At the end of the lane was a gravelled car park by the beach, and here Shanti was waiting in her Saab, studying documents by the light of her phone as dogged wipers dismissed the rain.

Caine stepped outside and took a punch from a gust of unseasonably cold air. The dawn felt damp enough that you could wring it out like a dishcloth.

Benno lifted the bosher from the back of the car and they climbed into the Saab for a briefing.

'Morning, Benno. What's up, Caine? You seem a bit distracted. Are you up for this?'

'Of course. I'm fine. I'm on it.'

'Good. That's Art's property up there.' She pointed to a bungalow on the edge of the village near the shore. A street light illuminated the building, which, in contrast to its neighbours, appeared to have been given a stylish makeover. Instead of dreary pebble-dash, an architect had cladded the facade with cool grey timbers, while poky UPVC window frames had been replaced by expanses of tinted glass.

'I'm assuming our boy is fast asleep right now, so it may take a while to rouse him. But equally I don't want to give him time to flush away his gear. So from the first knock, I'm giving him exactly two minutes, then we go in.'

Benno caressed the bosher.

'Caine, you come in with me. Benno, outside the front door until we've apprehended Art. Then a detailed interior search, please.'

The two men nodded.

'Right. It's 5.21. Let's do this . . .'

The car park was littered with driftwood, plastic bottles and tangled fishing nets, thrown up by the careless fingers of the sea. In the half-light, the village came into focus: gleaming rooftops on a gentle hillside, where a sad donkey grazed. To their left, the huge slabs of grey blue lias cliffs slid like melting chocolate towards the sea.

Outside Art's bungalow, a bright red Alfa Romeo Spider sat haughtily. There was no gate, but at the top of a driveway, a set of steps constructed of railway sleepers ascended a sloping low-maintenance garden of white shingle, pampas grass and spiky palms. Creeping steadily forward, Shanti nudged Caine and pointed out a curtained French window, which opened onto a balcony above the garden at the side of the property.

'Maybe the bedroom,' she whispered.

The front door was a smooth grey slab. Benno rolled his shoulders, as if limbering up for a forced entry. But Caine raised a finger as a signal to pause. Then he bent down and began lifting pots and stones around the door.

'What the fuck are you doing?' hissed Shanti.

'Give me a moment,' said Caine.

Eventually he rose, with a smile on his face and a Yale key between his fingers.

'How the hell . . .?'

'You wanted my local knowledge,' he whispered. 'Well, most Dorset folk keep a spare key in a wellie boot or under a garden ornament. Sorry, Benno, I know you were looking forward to that.'

Benno gave him a good-natured smile.

'Ready?' said Shanti.

Nods all round. She stepped forward and raised the hooded skull doorknocker. Then she rapped loudly several times.

They waited in the cold rain as Benno examined his watch.

'That's two minutes, boss. Not a murmur.'

'Probably fast asleep, but possibly up to no good,' said Shanti. 'Want to try that key, Caine?'

The lock was new and the door eased open soundlessly. Benno took up his position outside, while Shanti and Caine slipped into the silent building.

They found themselves in an entrance hall with a musty odour of bodies, and a distant whiff of cannabis and stale takeaways.

'Art Havfruen! This is DI Shanti Joyce!' called Shanti. Her voice sounded shockingly loud. 'I have a warrant to search your property. I'd like to do this with your full cooperation.'

No response. They moved into a room on the right, a large lounge dotted with Mies van der Rohe furniture, slender tubes of metal fused with rectangular slabs of black leather. A glass coffee table was cluttered with magazines, beer bottles, a TV remote, an untidy pile of banknotes and coins, a well-used glass bong and a clutter of head shop paraphernalia. Resting against one wall was a large framed poster – the distinctive tilted bowler and smirking wink from *A Clockwork Orange*.

They returned to the hallway and crept past a sleek but messy bathroom. At the end of the corridor, they came to a closed door. Shanti paused and placed her ear against it, then she turned the handle and pushed it gently open.

Amongst the shadows they made out a large bed where two figures lay beneath a black duvet. One was a girl, although all that could be seen was a mass of golden hair spilling onto the black satin pillow. The other was Art Havfruen, who sat up quickly, exposing his startlingly white chest and a ruffled confusion of fair hair.

'What the fuck . . .?'

'Art Havfruen, we have a warrant to—'

But Art was up and out of bed, a pale streak of bare limbs. In one bound he dived through the curtains, turned a handle and disappeared through the French windows.

The girl sat up too, and Shanti immediately moved to stop her following her lover. She was about to call out to Benno to alert him to the full-frontal fugitive, but Caine was already gone.

Caine chased Art onto the balcony just in time to see the naked young man clambering awkwardly over the side and landing with a groan on the shingle below.

In one elegant movement, he vaulted after him, his coat open wide like the spread wings of a raven. He landed neatly on the pebbles with knees bent, but Art was well ahead of him, tearing down the garden towards the lane to the beach.

Out of the corner of his eye, Caine saw Benno moving to join the chase.

'I've got him, Benno! You stay with Shanti!'

Then he was off on the trail of the desperate ivory man.

'Art!' he bellowed. 'There's no point in running!'

For someone who'd only woken moments before and whose diet was mainly chemical, Art moved like a bullet from a gun – a ghost sprinter cutting through the stormy morning. Was it the reawakening of a schoolboy athlete, or a core of fear that drove him on?

Near a closed fossil shop and café by the seafront, Caine thought he had him. He dived forward to grab a skinny arm, but at that moment Art jerked suddenly sideways and Caine's hands found nothing but air. His heart was hammering in his chest. He had a sickening feeling that Art meant to harm himself – to run into the sea and obliterate the despair that he chose to bury beneath blankets of cocaine and ketamine.

By the time Caine rounded the corner, his boots skidding on the wet surface, Art had already bounded over the sea wall, his pale form half limping, half sprinting across the stony beach. A wave crashed against the concrete seafront, sending a plume of froth over Caine's head. Down below, Art leapt from rock to rock like an albino rat, his snowy skin slick with spume.

Through the mizzle, Caine could tell that the tide was rising fast, so that Art's escape route narrowed to a dead end, the beach tapering to a point from which there were only two escape routes: the deadly blue lias cliffs to his right, or the churning vortex of waves to his left.

But Art was a man possessed, all flailing arms and slithering legs. Several times he fell and hauled himself upright, with Caine bounding behind. As Caine drew close, he noticed with horror that Art's bare feet were gashed and slashed by the jagged rocks.

Why was he so determined to escape? Caine wondered if the best tactic was simply to stop and wait. Surely there was nowhere for the runaway to go? He watched Art lurch from side to side as if choosing between the killer cliffs and the suicide of the sea. Eventually he ran towards the crashing waves, then changed his mind, wheeled about and began clambering over heaps of flotsam and jetsam at the base of the cliffs.

Caine knew only too well that these were not ordinary cliffs that might be scaled by an experienced climber. These cliffs were nature's slag heaps. A vast blue-black edifice of oozing clay, crammed with flints and fossils from two hundred million years before man.

Glancing back to see where Caine was standing, Art chose a place where the cliff was less steep – a messy spillage of flaky rock created by a recent fall – and began to scramble on all fours like a pale crab up the gluey landslip.

'Stop! Stop, Art!' shouted Caine. 'It's too dangerous. You could trigger another slip, or get trapped!' But his words were stolen by the wind and hurled into the sea.

Oblivious to the danger, Art clambered onto the mud mountain, which had been further softened and destabilised by a night of torrential rain. As Caine watched helplessly, he scrambled up the incline, hands and feet plunging deep into the foul substance, even as the rain and wind buffeted his already ungainly progress. Caine could see that Art's bloodied legs were sinking to their knees into the clay, and now the pale man reached out frantically, but there was nothing solid to cling to. As Caine reached the foot of the landslip, Art appeared to be swallowed up by the earth itself, disappearing into a void between two huge mounds of clay, ton upon ton of oozing blue lias pressing against him.

Above the crashing waves, Caine heard a low rumble – or rather, he felt the sensation in his feet. It was as if a vast Jurassic creature had awoken. High above his head, small pieces of flint began to leap and fall, and he realised with a surge of terror that the landslip that Art had stumbled into was only a prelude to the main event, and the whole section of cliff was about to give way.

With lumps of mud raining from above, he struggled towards the sinking boy. At last he lay flat on the clay, but not too close to the hole into which Art had fallen. He could see the whiteness of Art's body below, almost submerged in the cloying compound. In the grey soup of mud and salt water, what Caine fixed on was a pair of blazing eyes – the desperate, terrified eyes of A Boy Named Art.

And what he felt more powerfully than fear, more powerfully even than self-protection, was an overwhelming sense of pity for another human being. He leaned into the dark fissure as far as he could and reached towards the flailing hands. Art's arms were slippery with mud, and he was fighting so frantically, it seemed impossible to get a grip. For a brief moment, Caine had a vision of the young man being swallowed forever by the hungry earth.

'Calm yourself, Art!' he shouted powerlessly. 'Stop fighting. Just give me your hands and push slowly against the clay!'

A huge missile of earth tumbled from the sky and slammed painfully against Caine's shoulder. He feared that they were caught in a perfect storm – if they weren't crushed by the impending rock fall, they would be drowned by the incoming tide.

But with head down, he managed at last to get a firm grip around Art's bloodied wrists. At first, it was like wrenching a stubborn cork from a bottle. But slowly Art began to rise from the mire. First came the pale chest, then the stomach, then his mud-caked genitals. Now, as Caine tumbled backwards, Art's writhing legs emerged, and finally – like a baby being pulled from its mother – the clay released him from its hold.

The cliff gave out another vast groan, and as Caine and his broken captive stumbled and tumbled onto the beach, an avalanche of rock and clay spewed from land to ocean, missing them by half a body's length.

Caine hauled the young man a few metres away and laid him on his back. As he fought to regain his breath, he looked back and saw the astonishing spectacle of a full-grown hawthorn tree, with a length of barbed-wire fence trailing from it, drifting absolutely upright down the cliff towards the sea.

When the rumbling had ceased, Caine examined Art for serious injuries. The boy resembled an ancient bog man, but he was alive, and although his feet were badly lacerated, no bones seemed to be broken.

Caine knew there was no time to rest. The incoming tide was fast cutting off their escape route. He peeled off his own coat and wrapped it around Art's shivering shoulders, then, with considerable difficulty, he hauled the exhausted boy up onto his back and waded through the rising surf towards the concrete steps.

The young man was a dead weight – all the fight had left him – and it was a relief to finally set him down. When he had recovered his breath, Caine helped Art to his feet and, supporting his limping, wilting body, hauled him towards the car park, where the first dog walkers of the day were pulling on wellingtons and clipping leads to collars. They stared wide-eyed at the half-drowned barefoot boy, swathed in a filthy coat, leaning heavily against the bedraggled black-haired man.

'Morning,' said Caine. 'I think it's blowing over now.'

Chapter 18

The Ghostly Girl

'Haven't I seen you before?' said Shanti.

The girl sat up in the black sheets and pushed the mass of golden hair from her thin shoulders.

'Don't think so.'

'Well I think I have. What's your name, sweetheart?'

'Do I have to say?'

'I'm afraid you do.'

'Tess.'

'Tess what?'

'Tess Strawbridge.'

'Right, Tess, do you want to put on some clothes? Then we can have a nice cup of tea and a chat.'

Shanti looked around the room. A bundle of Art's things had been dumped on the floor – a tangled suit wrapped around some pointy boots. The girl's clothes were folded neatly on a chair.

'How old are you, Tess?' asked Shanti, tossing some underwear across.

'Eighteen.'

'No you're not.'

'I am. How do you know?'

'Because this is a school uniform, darling.'

'Yeah, well I'm in the sixth form.'

'You know what? At my local comp, the sixth-formers don't wear a uniform.'

'Are you going to arrest me?'

'I don't think so, love,' said Shanti in a soothing voice. 'Not if you're helpful, anyway.'

As they passed the living room, the girl said, 'Why's he poking about in there? Art will go apeshit.'

'This is Sergeant Bennett. It's his job to gather evidence and it looks like it's his lucky day.'

'I'll have one if you're making one,' called Benno. 'Two sugars, please.'

They sat on tall stools in the halogen-lit kitchen. In her navy blazer, skirt and white cotton shirt, Tess Strawbridge appeared exactly what she was – a nervy schoolgirl. Shanti placed her phone on the counter top.

'Tess, I'd like to record our chat, if that's OK?'

'No, it's not OK. How would you like it if I recorded you?'

'You can do that if you want, but I have to tell you that if you won't answer my questions on record, we'll have to take a drive to the police station and do it there.'

The girl gave the faintest nod of acceptance and Shanti tapped the red button on the screen.

'So, you're Art's girlfriend.'

The girl shrugged.

'Where do you live, Tess?'

'Charmouth. Sort of.'

'And I'm going to ask again how old you are . . . ?'

Tears streamed down her pretty face like pearls. She raised her hand to her mouth and mumbled something.

'I can't hear you, Tess.'

Her face reappeared, looking suddenly defiant. 'All right, I'm fifteen. Get over it.'

'Does your mum know that you stay here?'

'My mum doesn't give a shit.'

'What about your dad? Does he know?'

'Never met him.'

'OK, darling. You're doing really well. Listen, I shouldn't do this, but I'll tell you a secret – I'm not blaming you for anything. It's Art we're interested in. Can you tell me how you first met?'

Tess wiped her eyes with the back of her hand. 'I go to school in Lyme and get the bus back to Charmouth. I was walking home one day when he came out of a shop – dead cool – and we literally bumped into each other. He said I was the spit of some-one he knew. Then he asked where I lived. I told him up Stonebarrow way. He offered me a lift, 'cos it's a long walk. I wasn't going to accept – stranger danger and that – but then I saw his car! I felt like a movie star and all my mates were well jel. I gave him my number and, you know, things went on from there.'

'Does he give you drugs?'

'No. I don't take that shit . . . well, a bit of green sometimes.'

'Does he give you money?'

'Art is loaded. He doesn't care. He leaves like stashes of cash all over the place. If I need something, he just says help yourself.'

'Tess, I want to ask you some personal questions now – is

that OK? Does Art like you to wear your school uniform? Some men get a kick from that, don't they?'

'Nah, he's not into that. He likes me to wear the stuff in the wardrobe.'

'Right, I'm pausing the interview for a moment . . .'

Shanti went out of the kitchen into the living room, where Benno, in latex gloves, was bagging and tagging. A quick nod towards the kitchen meant *Keep an eye on her, we don't want another runner.*

She went back into the bedroom and switched on the light. There was a small fitted wardrobe on one wall. Although she half knew what she might find, it was still a shock when she opened the door. Several loose threads of the investigation began to knot neatly together.

Tess hadn't moved from the tall stool in the kitchen, but she looked paler and more vulnerable than ever.

'Right, I'm recording again. Interview with Tess Strawbridge, part two. So, Tess, you told me that Art liked you to wear the clothes I've just seen in the wardrobe in his bedroom – that is, a short white lacy dress and a pair of red Doc Marten boots. Is that correct?'

'It turned him on.'

'So he asked you to wear these clothes around the flat?'

'Yeah. With loads of smeary lipstick.'

'And where else? In bed?'

'Not the boots, obvs.'

'And how about outside the house – did you ever wear the outfit in public?'

'A couple of times, but it always caused a hassle. I wore it at his mum's show – she was, like, a famous artist. Art didn't invite

me, he said it was going to be boring. But I wanted to go especially when I heard there would be TV people and that. He went
on his own but I got fed up sitting here, so I thought I'd give him
a nice surprise. I called Matt Scabs—'

'Hang on. Who is Matt Scabs?'

'Soz. He's a cab driver. Him and his brother Bob Scars.'

'Matt Scabs and Bob Scars? You're making this up!'

'It's like a joke – Matt's Cabs and Bob's Cars. Everyone
knows that.'

'OK, so you called Matt Scabs and he drove you to the Meat
Hook Gallery. That's quite a journey; how did you pay for it?
You know I will follow up everything you tell me.'

The girl hesitated.

'Tell me the truth, Tess.'

'Like I say, Art leaves cash all over the place. He lets me take
what I need.'

'So you arrived at the gallery. Did the cab wait for you?'

'Yeah, Matt went for coffee in Bruton and I said I'd call him
when I was ready. I saw a big swanky crowd heading out of the
car park and up through the gardens towards this weird building
like a massive bollock on stilts. I texted Art and he came rushing
back. I thought he would be happy to see me with all his fave
clothes and everything. But he went mental. He was horrible.
He shoved me in this huge dark room and said I was a fucking
embarrassment. He made me cry, so I ran outside and called
Matt. Then I nipped onto the lane through a hole in the hedge.
There were lots of cars passing with posh guests inside, so I hid
out of sight until Matt arrived. Then I went home.'

Shanti felt exhilaration coursing through her veins. This was
what a breakthrough felt like. At last she had cracked that piece

of the puzzle – the CCTV footage that had foxed them all. How could Kristal Havfruen have been arguing with her son and yet be found hours later in a tank in the same room? A tank that had not once been tampered with? The answer was that the woman arguing with Art was not Kristal at all. It was Tess.

'You said you wore the clothes in public a couple of times. Can you tell me about the second occasion?'

'It was at her funeral . . . his mum. She died in a mental way. You probably heard about it.'

'Yes, I heard about it.'

'After she died, Art and me started arguing like 24/7. He was no fun any more – doing loads of gear and getting really psycho. He said there was no way I could come to the funeral. The actual words he said were, "It wouldn't be appropriate." I'm, like, "Appropriate never stopped you shagging me, did it?" Anyhow, he stormed off and left me and then I decided to really fuck him off and turn up at the church in the dress and boots and the make-up and everything.'

Thank you, God! thought Shanti. I'm not insane.

'Did Matt Scabs take you to the funeral, Tess? Remember, I will be checking all of this.'

'It was Bob Scars that time.'

'And what did Art do when he saw you?'

'Oh, he spotted me hiding in the churchyard and lost it big time. Dragged me by my hair and said I was insane to come there. Accused me of trying to ruin the saddest day of his life.'

'What did you do?'

Tess sniffed. 'Backed off, didn't I? I'm not a total bitch. I could see he was upset. I feel like that about my dad sometimes. But Art wasn't making it any easier by snorting like a ton of nose candy.'

She glanced furtively at Shanti, as if she knew she was saying too much.

'It's OK, Tess. We know about Art's habits.'

'Yeah, he doesn't exactly hide it, does he?'

'I saw you sitting in the churchyard, didn't I?'

Tess's eyes widened. 'That was never you! Christ! You were well gorge in that black dress. But you scared the shit out of me. I thought you were a fucking ghost or something. Ended up hiding in these spooky woods crapping myself.'

Shanti found herself actually laughing with relief. 'I think we scared each other good and proper. OK, Tess. You're being more helpful than you know. Listen, I want you to go back to the day of the private view at the art gallery. Think about this very carefully before you answer. Were you with Art all afternoon before the show?'

Tess nodded. 'Yeah. It was Saturday, wasn't it? I stayed over Friday night. We slept really late and spent the day together here. Art watched the footie, then he left for the gallery around four thirty.'

'But you thought you'd surprise him.'

'Honest, I thought he'd like it, but it went down like a cup of cold vom.'

So there it is, thought Shanti. The alibi Art had been so reluctant to provide. And now she knew why. Art Havfruen was having a relationship with an underage girl. And if that wasn't bad enough, he persuaded that girl to dress as his mother. Perhaps that revelation was even more awkward than being accused of her murder.

As Shanti finished the interview, she heard Caine's voice outside. The front door opened and a pair of outlandish figures appeared, like extras from an apocalyptic horror movie.

'Jesus, Caine!' said Shanti. 'What the hell happened to you?'

'Let's just say the cliffs around here are a reminder of impermanence.'

They were both coated from head to foot in cracking grey clay, and where they emerged from the mud-caked coat, Art's face and spindly legs were smeared with blood.

'Oh, Art! Are you all right, babes?' said Tess, rushing to his side.

As Benno steered Art towards the shower, Shanti led Tess back to the kitchen and sat her down in front of a bowl of cereal.

'Now what am I supposed to do?' wailed Tess. 'I know Art's a bit mental, but I love him. He can be dead kind and funny. I wish I hadn't told you all that stuff now. Art always says you can never trust the feds.'

'Listen, Tess,' said Shanti. 'A good friend of mine is a child welfare officer, OK? She's a lovely person. She's on her way now, and if you agree, she'll have a chat with you and maybe with your mum too. She can help sort things out at school. I want to make sure you're getting all the support you need.'

When Art emerged in his crumpled suit, looking alarmingly pale, Benno clipped on the handcuffs and read him his rights: 'Art Havfruen, I'm arresting you for possession of Class A substances, and on suspicion of indecent activity with a minor as defined in Section 9 of the Sexual Offences Act 2003. You do not have to say anything, but it may harm your defence . . .'

For the first time since Shanti had met him, the Boy Named Art was silent. As Benno led him from the bungalow, he glanced back sadly at Tess Strawbridge, the under-parented child in her school uniform, eating Coco Pops and watching cartoons on the sofa.

In the kitchen, Caine replayed the interview with Tess, which Shanti had shown him on her phone. As he listened, he slowly scrubbed his hands with a nailbrush at the sink – that blue lias stuck to the skin as if it was mixed with glue. Even after he had dried himself, his hands were coated in a film of grey silt.

Out in the living room, the welfare officer had arrived and Caine heard the muffled sound of soothing voices below the whoops and whistles of the TV. He discovered a kettle behind the Italian coffee machine and began to make tea, even borrowing a teaspoon of Art's honey in return for his exertions.

At last someone switched off the TV, and he heard voices receding and a car leaving the bungalow. Then Shanti entered the kitchen with a wry smile on her face.

'Jesus, Caine. Have you seen yourself? You look a fright!'

Caine glanced at a tinted glass cupboard door. A man stared back at him – an ancient, haggard man with a grey mane and parchment skin. It was a horrible apparition of his future self.

He slumped onto a stool and stirred his tea.

'You look absolutely done in, Caine. But listen, you did well today. No way would I have caught Art on my own. And I think Benno's sprinting days are over.'

'But there's so much fallout, Shanti! Not just Art, but that poor girl too.'

'Maybe she'll get the care she needs now. Benno took a preliminary tongue swab, and thank God it seems there's nothing in her system except a trace of cannabis. Which means Art didn't coerce her with anything stronger. That's the good news; the bad news is that she refuses to press charges against him. She says she really loved him and everything was consensual.'

'But she's underage . . .'

'Unfortunately, if she refuses to testify, Art will probably get away with nothing more than a fine for possession, or more likely just a caution. I hate the law sometimes.'

She fumbled in a cupboard and found a jar of instant coffee. 'But listen, Caine, I have to admit that you were right and I was wrong. Art has a cast-iron alibi for the day of the murder. He was innocent all along.'

'Innocent?' Caine shook his grey head. 'I wonder if humans are capable of innocence.'

'Well, the lad needs some therapy . . . and a course of multi-vitamins.'

Caine exhaled deeply. 'It's the same story every time – it all comes back to early parenting. Children are like plants, Shanti . . . or seedlings, rather. I've been thinking about this a lot lately. If they are watered with love and encouragement, then they blossom. But if they are disparaged, or denied that love . . . it's like weedkiller.'

'And you were doing so well . . . we've had a whole morning without philosophy. You know, Action Caine is so much more impressive than Philosopher Caine. I loved the way you dived through that window.'

Caine sipped his tea in gloomy silence, reflecting on the teaching that all actions had consequences – the way that weed-killer parenting had wilted Art. And Tess. And Paul . . . And maybe himself as well.

And then, in the empty bungalow, something glorious

happened. It was as if Shanti was responding to the sadness in his heart. She looked at him kindly and said:

'You know what, Caine? We should get you cleaned up and back on your feet. I need you on this case.'

She sat him on a stool by the sink and began patiently to sponge his face and hair with warm water.

It took a long time, and Caine gave himself up to the experience. It was as if Shanti was washing away his worries, and the silt spiralling down the plughole was the pain rinsing from his heart . . .

Let it go. Let it go. Let it go.

And although Shanti kept talking relentlessly about the case, it didn't diminish the tenderness he felt in her fingertips.

'You know what's creepy, Caine? The way Tess resembles a young Kristal – did you notice that? Just lean over a bit more, we don't want to mess up Art's expensive kitchen . . . I guess that's what attracted him in the first place – talk about Freudian. OK, close your eyes, you've got that damned clay in every pore . . . Anyway, you can see why I was fooled by the CCTV footage and the apparition in the graveyard, too . . . Just wait there a moment . . .'

She ran out of the kitchen and returned with a small glass bottle. 'Strictly against regs to borrow shampoo from a suspect, but it's Art who got you into this state. Mmm, nice – Tea Tree Oil for Men.'

Caine barely heard a word. As Shanti massaged the shampoo into his hair, he was transported into a mindful world of bliss, in which every nerve of his scalp was being caressed.

'Anyway, this changes everything. I'm going to officially eliminate Art as a murder suspect, and I'm shifting to the theory that Kristal was murdered at Mangrove House, where the tank and formaldehyde were delivered earlier in the day. We can be pretty certain that she was transported – already dead – inside that tank to the gallery. Art failed to notice that the figure in the tank was an actual body because he was off his face as usual, and also distracted by a guest appearance from Tess. In any case, the lights in the master gallery were dimmed, which is presumably why the guys from MasterMoves didn't notice anything either … I suppose the same goes for Ollie Sweetman when he polished the tank and placed the boots on top.'

Shanti reached for a towel and sighed. 'Trouble is, it feels like one step forward and five steps back. That damned eternal question remains – who killed Kristal? I don't know about you, but I'm coming full circle to Callum Oak. I've never trusted the guy. He had plenty of motive, as well as the brawn and brain to do it. What do you think, Caine? Don't tell me to embrace uncertainty, or I will throttle you with this towel.'

As she dried his hair, Caine felt like a warm cat lying sleepily on his mistress's lap. It was all he could do not to purr.

'Caine. I asked you a question …'

Shanti stood up and began to clean the sink, and Caine emerged from his blissful stupor.

'I know this is a little outside your radar, Shanti, but there are moments in every case when the best thing to do is pause and reflect on the situation. I think we need to spend time in the forest.'

'Oh, that's very helpful, Caine. Why didn't I think of that? We should go and have a chat with a tree. In fact, let's ask all your favourite trees to take a vote on who killed Kristal.'

'I'm being serious. I feel that we have all the clues and information in our hands. It's amazing how often answers come to me in nature. In fact I've just remembered something . . .'

'Jesus, Caine. Make sure it's a helpful thing.'

'It's a line from a poem . . . Wordsworth, I think . . . "One impulse from a vernal wood may teach you more of man, of moral evil and of good, than all the sages can."'

Chapter 19

A Sinister Symbiosis

Everything was going nicely until the call from Paul's school.

Shanti and Caine had locked the bungalow and replaced the key beneath the pot where Caine had found it, and as they walked towards the car park, the sun lit up the sea like a bright future.

Then Shanti's phone vibrated and there seemed to be an urgency in its tone.

'Hello? Is that Shantala?'

'Who is this?'

'Yvonne Khan, Paul's head teacher. Is this a convenient moment?'

'Oh, Yvonne ... Yes, of course. Paul's not in trouble again, is he? I thought he seemed more settled lately ...'

'I don't want to blow this out of proportion, Shantala, but I've decided to exclude Paul for a short time. I'm really sorry.'

'Exclude him from school? But he's only eight years old.'

'I know that, but I have to put the well-being of my staff first.

I hope you understand. Is there someone who can collect him right away?'

With trembling hands, Shanti called Amma. She told her to collect Paul as soon as she could and that she would be home in less than an hour.

Caine listened quietly as Shanti explained what had happened. Then, without hesitation, he reassured her that he was there for her and Paul, and he would gladly accompany her to Yeovil.

On the drive, with concern etched across her face, Shanti described the ways in which Paul's behaviour had deteriorated since the divorce, to the point where he sometimes raged at her and Amma. And lately she had noted something in her son's eyes that terrified her. It was a glint of pleasure at the effect his behaviour had on others. A first understanding that he had power. The reason it terrified Shanti was because it was the exact same look – in embryonic form – that she had witnessed on the face of her ex-husband, who was an unreconstructed emotional bully.

And now Paul had unleashed that aggression in the classroom, and when the teachers had intervened, it was they who had received a torrent of expletives and abuse.

'Listen, Shantala, we all love Paul to bits,' Ms Khan had reassured her. 'This exclusion is only for a few days. I just want to give him a chance to reflect. All the staff appreciate the pressures of your job – especially this Havfruen case. But I think you and I need to have a proper conversation as soon as possible. I want to know if everything is OK. Perhaps I can help in some way . . .'

So Shanti drove – a little too fast – across the Marshwood Vale, through Crewkerne and West Coker towards Yeovil, and when they arrived in her quiet cul-de-sac, the thing that swayed her towards Caine's invitation to come to the cabin with Paul was the almost mesmeric effect her colleague had on the boy. To Shanti's astonishment, Paul stepped calmly out of the house and took the tall man's hand. It was as if the confusion and anger evaporated when he saw Caine.

On the drive to Lyme and on the long, slow walk through the woods, Shanti realised that for once, the best thing was to step back and let Caine and Paul sort things out in their own mysterious, masculine way.

The way Caine did it was to take the boy outside himself. He showed him nests hidden in coppices. A green and red woodpecker drilling for bugs. With a sharp penknife, they made a spear from a length of hazel.

And at one point she heard Paul say, 'Look at the bees, Caine!'

'Yes, they're busy this year. It's a good sign because it means the meadow is healthy. You know the way it works, Paul? Bees and flowers are friends. They work together. It's called a symbiotic relationship.'

'Is that like you and Mum? Are you sinbotic?'

'Symbiotic? Ha, you'd better ask her! But everything works better with cooperation. Teachers and pupils can be symbiotic too.'

When they finally reached the Lost Chimney and climbed the steep track to the cabin, Shanti watched as Paul pulled off his shoes and placed them neatly alongside Caine's. He parked the spear next to Caine's surfboards. Then he wandered around the unfamiliar environment in an almost reverential way.

Shanti had to give it to him – Caine was a natural with the boy. He didn't try too hard, or pester the lad with questions;

instead he busied himself with tasks that would intrigue any eight-year-old, and soon the two of them were outside gathering firewood.

Caine told Shanti to make herself at home – there were books inside, or she was welcome to rest on his bed, or on the chair on the deck. She roamed around the cabin, which still felt foreign to her: the domain of a man, and an unusual man at that. There was that shrine, with sticks of incense, a candle, a small vase of wild flowers and a tiny animal skull. Beside the bronze Buddha she noticed something unusual – a small framed photograph placed face down. Glancing over her shoulder to make sure Caine and Paul were out of sight, she lifted it and studied the faded photo of an elderly man. His hair was almost white, but there was something familiar about the unusually high cheekbones. And when she looked at the oil-well eyes, she had no doubt that this was Caine's father. So why was the image here on the shrine? And why was it face down?

She replaced the photo exactly where she had found it, walked to the bookshelf, grabbed the slimmest novel she could find and stepped outside, where Caine was teaching Paul to split kindling with a hatchet.

There was something about this place that was out of time – out of everything. Now Caine and the boy nursed the fire into life within a ring of stones. Such simple, primal activities, but she realised that her ex had never been a hands-on dad, and besides, he hated the countryside.

When the meal was ready, she even restrained herself from fussing about Paul's filthy hands. And although the food was vegetarian, Paul tucked in as if he hadn't eaten for a month, chewing a corn on the cob, dripping with butter, straight off a blade. When they had finished, Caine slung a hammock across the porch and showed Paul how to climb inside. Within five minutes, the boy was asleep.

'He hasn't done that for years,' said Shanti. 'I mean, fallen asleep in the day. Thanks, Caine. You really seem to get him, and he's so angry with me these days.'

'Oh, I get him all right,' said Caine, pouring tea into two mugs and settling at her feet on the deck. 'I've had a little experience with random fathers.'

The slogan on Shanti's mug said: *Keep Calm and Meditate.*

The slogan on Caine's mug said: *This too shall pass. (It might pass like a kidney stone, but it will pass.)*

'I guess I was lucky,' said Shanti. 'You've met my mum – she drives me nuts, but she was always behind me. Dad, too. I was in my early teens when he died, and I never thought I'd get over it. The grief didn't go away, but it changed, and now the sadness has turned to love.'

'That's beautiful, Shanti. Although Paul may forget it sometimes, you are a wonderful mother to him. In the meantime, how nice is this? To sit here and watch the sun set over the sea.'

The sunset? With a surge of anxiety, Shanti realised that she hadn't even thought about the investigation for hours. What had happened to the day? And there was no phone signal out here! Supposing someone needed to contact her urgently?

Sod it. Let Benno take the reins for a while.

'So, tell me about this Buddhist thing, Caine. I mean what's it all about? I don't want a six-hour lecture … tell me in three words.'

'Compassion. Equanimity. Love.'

'A little more … though not too much.'

209

'Buddhism is about treading lightly. Living life to the full without hurting others. Accepting the dappled quality of life. Being the master of your own mind. Letting go. Being free.'

'OK, I'd like some of that. But I mean, there are lots of different sects, no? What kind of Buddhist are you?'

'I don't know. I guess I'm a free-range Buddhist.'

'Is that like being a free-range cop?'

'Maybe. I take whatever works for me. The Buddha says we shouldn't believe anything we read or hear – even what he says – unless it concurs with our common sense and is conducive to the good of all.'

'Like pick and mix.'

'If you want to know what I really think, I believe there's something like a golden thread that runs through all great religions, and all great art, and all great literature, and through nature too – especially through nature. It doesn't really matter where you grab a hold of it.'

'Hmm ... that is either unbelievably profound or the most pretentious bullshit I've ever heard in my life. I'll think about it and let you know.'

They sat for a long time watching the trees slow-waltzing in the breeze.

'Shanti, would you excuse me for a while? I usually wander down to the sea at this time of day. Just to sit, you know.'

'Sure,' said Shanti. 'Look, I've got a book.'

'*Siddhartha* by Hermann Hesse. That's a great choice. It's a magical story. You'll love it.'

As he wandered down the track towards the little bay, Caine felt a complex brew of emotions. Something like tenderness towards this little family, the unexpected visitors in the guest house of his life, but hanging over it an anxiety that he thought he had laid to rest long ago, but that was now resurfacing. Would he ever be free of what had happened? And the turbulence of the police work didn't help. So much agitation.

There was a flat patch of grass on a clifftop where he liked to sit gazing over the sea. The graceful arm of an oak shaded his head. As he settled cross-legged between the mossy roots, a memory came to him of his old teacher, whose name was Tu, addressing the young monks. He had held up a glass of water in his skinny brown hand. 'The water is our mind,' he had told them, with merriment twinkling in his eyes. 'Watch when I shake the glass ...' The water trembled. 'This is the agitated mind. The water becomes cloudy and obscure. So how can I make it clear again?' 'Stop agitating!' they had called. So Tu ceased shaking, and like magic, the water fell calm. 'When worry and desire cease, the mind becomes clear. Equilibrium is the natural state. And when there is clarity, we are able to see into the depths. This is insight.'

And Caine had a powerful feeling that if he could still his mind, the solution to the Havfruen case would fall upon him as naturally as autumn fell over the forest.

When he opened his eyes an hour or so later, Paul was standing barefoot at his side holding the spear. Just watching his meditation. Caine smiled and rose slowly to his feet. He took the boy's hand and they turned towards the cabin.

'What's that, Caine?' said Paul, pointing with his spear towards the base of the ancient tree.

'Oh, that's a fungus called chanterelle. You can eat it when it's cooked.'

'It looks like disgusting custard.'

'You know what, Paul? This is another example of symbiosis ... like the bees working with the flowers, the chanterelle and the oak work together like friends.'

'How can a tree and a fungus be friends?'

'Well, if I remember, the fungus has little threads that twist around the roots. The threads help the tree get good things from the soil, like nutrients and water, and protect the tree from nasty diseases. In return, the tree gives the chanterelle sugars, which make it tasty to eat.'

'That's cool. Disgusting but cool.'

As they climbed the track, Caine became aware of an unusual tingling at the bottom of his spine. The feeling ran slowly upwards, vertebra by vertebra, until it tickled the base of his neck. Then it exploded in his head.

Of course! This was the insight he had been waiting for! Like Wordsworth's impulse from a vernal wood.

'Paul, you are something of a genius, boy!'

'Am I?'

'You don't know it, but you are. I think you've just hit the symbiotic nail on its symbiotic head.'

'I don't get it.'

'It doesn't matter. Your mum will. Just run up to the cabin and say "symbiotic"! Tell her you've solved the case.'

Shanti was relaxing in the old chair on the deck, trying to make sense of Caine's novel.

'Hello. Did you find Caine?'

'Symbiotic!' said Paul.

'You what?'

'Symbiotic, Mum. Caine says I solved the case.'

'Oh, there you are, Caine. Do you have any idea what my son is talking about?'

'I think he may be right. Paul and I were talking about symbiosis – you know, the way two things in nature help each other out?'

'Like the birds that clean the crocodile's teeth?'

'Exactly. Well, listen. Whoever killed Kristal needed two qualities, right?'

'Caine, I never thought I would say this, but could you slow down a little?'

'I think we've been approaching this investigation from the wrong angle.'

'We should be interviewing crocodiles?'

'No. I mean maybe we should be looking at partnerships.'

'OK...'

'Specifically partnerships in which two people have complementary skills they could bring to the crime.'

Shanti closed the book and sat forward. 'So you're saying the crime might have been committed by two people?'

'Exactly. Brawn and brain.'

'One person with the intellect to plan it, and another with the physical strength to place Kristal in the tank.'

Shanti was on her feet in seconds, stuffing various items into her shoulder bag. 'Paul, I need you to stay here with Caine. I have a job to do.'

'Yay! What shall we do, Caine?'

'Shanti, you shouldn't go alone!' cautioned Caine.

'Look after Paul, please. I can handle this.'

And with that, she set off, sprinting down the narrow track

from the cabin towards the coast path. As she ran, she noted with some satisfaction that she was infinitely fitter than the first time she had struggled this way.

'Did I crack the case?' asked Paul when she had gone.

'I think you did, Paul,' said Caine, with an anxious hand on the boy's shoulder. 'Or maybe we did it together.'

'Symbiotic?' said Paul.

'Symbiotic,' said Caine.

Chapter 20

Tea for the Killerman

The daylight was fading as she arrived at Paradise Park. In the log cabin reception room, Colin Leggit was rearranging a display of leaflets advertising local attractions.

'Be with you in a minute,' he told her over his shoulder. 'Just putting these in order. Otherwise you're looking for Monkey World and you end up in Wookey Hole.'

'I need to speak to you immediately, Mr Leggit.'

The neatly bearded man turned round.

'Oh, it's you again. Haven't you caught that killer yet?'

'Is Oliver here?'

'He is. But he won't want to be disturbed at this time of day. I told you before, he's very particular about his timetable.'

'Frankly, Mr Leggit, I couldn't care less about timetables.'

'No need to be rude, young lady. Now if you'll give me a minute, I'll point out his chalet—'

'Shangri-La, I know. Near the dovecote.'

'I was going to tell you that he's got company, just so you

know. Everyone's talking about it. He's got a girlfriend. I've seen her myself through the curtains. And that's all the more reason why he won't want to be disturbed. It's teatime for Ollie . . .'

Shanti left Leggit with his hands full of Cheddar Gorge leaflets. She made her way along the immaculate drive between the pastel-coloured static homes, from which cooking smells wafted and TVs flickered. The presence of a guest in Sweetman's chalet might complicate things. She'd have to send the woman packing.

Shanti knew perfectly well that she should call Benno, but she burned to do this alone.

Shangri-La was set in an isolated spot on the western side of the park, near a stream. In front of her, an elaborate dovecote sat on top of a post. Within numerous doorways the beautiful creatures crooned and groomed each other like bridesmaids. As Shanti approached, she realised that Leggit had been correct. Sweetman was not alone.

She jumped up and down a few times in order to get a better view. There was definite movement behind the lace curtains – the unmistakable hulk of Oliver Sweetman carrying plates and cutlery. And a second figure: the outline of a woman seated at the table. Was Sweetman serving tea for his guest?

Shanti crept forward and crouched below a slightly opened window. She could hear Oliver's gentle Cornish tones, as soothing as a child at a dolls' tea party.

'Now we won't have our cake till we've had our soup. I made tomato 'cos that's your favourite, and look, I grated cheese on top for a treat . . .'

Shanti slipped around to the front, where plastic steps led to the entrance. She took a deep breath and rapped firmly on the flimsy door.

'Now then, whoever can that be?' said Sweetman from inside. 'We don't usually get visitors, do we? Perhaps Mr Leggit has come to pay a call. Let's hope there's nothing wrong with the doves.'

The static home swayed and creaked as he lumbered towards the door.

Shanti heard the lock being turned, and the door swung outwards, almost knocking her off the step. Above her head, framed by the interior lights, stood the mountainous hulk of Oliver Sweetman.

'Oh, it's Shanti Joyce,' he said. 'But it's not golf time now.' And he began to close the door.

'This won't take a moment, Oliver,' she said, grabbing the edge and pulling firmly. 'I'm not here to play mini golf. Just a little chat, if that's OK?'

His freckled face peered around the door. 'Well, see, I've got company, and we're having tea if you don't mind . . .'

Shanti hauled against him. The man was as strong as a bison.

'Oliver, you may have forgotten that I'm a police detective. I'd like to ask you a few questions.'

'You come back tomorrow, Shanti Joyce. I'll call Mr Leggit.'

'Mr Leggit said it was all right. He said you wouldn't mind, because this is important.'

She could feel him hesitating and considering the irregular request.

'Well, I can't pretend I like it, but I suppose you'd better come in if that's what Mr Leggit says. But I'm telling you now, Shanti Joyce, there's not enough soup for three.'

The smell was the first thing Shanti noticed. Tomato soup, yes; but another smell, like pickled onions. As she followed his huge back, it occurred to her that she'd smelt that stench before.

With that realisation came a stab of fear in her chest. She reached into her shoulder bag and her fingers found the canister of pepper spray.

There was a small doorway that opened into the living and dining area. In order to squeeze through, Sweetman had to constrict his massive arms and bunch up his shoulders. Shanti followed into a long, narrow room where a table stood in front of an L-shaped settee. It was covered with a red and white checked tablecloth and set with an elaborate meal.

Sitting on the settee, with her back to the window, was Kristal Havfruen.

As Sweetman returned to his place beside her, Shanti's heart belted like a traction engine.

'Better budge up, Kristal,' he said. 'Seems we've got a visitor.'

Kristal's impassive face was smeared with red lipstick and her green eyes stared coldly into the steaming bowl of soup.

Shanti blinked, unable to process what she was seeing. Then the whole thing came together – the whiff of formaldehyde, the frozen posture. This was the unspeakably lifelike effigy that Kristal had created for her happening.

'Well, don't stand on ceremony,' said Sweetman. 'There's not enough soup, but I suppose you can have some tea and cake if you behave nicely.'

His voice betrayed his annoyance. As far as Oliver was concerned, Shanti had disturbed a cosy evening with his lover.

'Hello, Kristal,' she stammered. Whatever reality Sweetman lived in, it was best to play along.

'That smell, Oliver – isn't that formaldehyde?'

'It is! We took lots of showers, didn't we, Kristal? But it won't wash away.'

Shanti nodded as if it all made perfect sense.

'In any case,' continued Sweetman, leaning across to nuzzle the side of the effigy's neck, 'the smell grows on you after a while, doesn't it, dear?'

Kristal said nothing in return.

Oliver tucked a napkin into his collar and adjusted Kristal's napkin too.

'She barely eats a thing. That's why she's so skinny.'

With a faint air of desperation, he began spooning the red gunk into Kristal's unsmiling mouth. It splattered down her lacy dress and onto the table.

'Hurry up and sit down, Shanti Joyce. You're making her uncomfortable.'

Almost in a trance, Shanti took a seat on the orange and purple settee beside Kristal.

'Oh please, Kristal,' said Sweetman. 'Just a few mouthfuls for me. Here . . . you watch Ollie . . .'

And he began ladling spoonfuls of soup between his own slurping lips.

Shanti felt as paralysed as her blonde-headed neighbour.

Eventually she managed, 'Oliver? Can I ask you something?'

'S'pose so.'

'Ollie. This isn't really Kristal, is it?'

He stared at her with horror and disbelief.

'Don't know what you're talking about.'

'Sorry. I shouldn't have said that. I mean that this is quiet Kristal, isn't it? The one who's nice to you. Not the one who used to tell you off and slap your hand.'

Sweetman scrunched his eyes tightly, as if trying to shut out the world. 'I don't know. I don't know nothing.'

'You were at the funeral, remember? You saw the other Kristal in the glass coffin. I'm wondering whether you helped to swap them over. Did you help to give Kristal an injection in her studio that sent her to sleep?'

The twitching eyelids remained closed. The shaky spoon hovered.

'Did you lift this nice, quiet Kristal out of the tank and put sleepy Kristal inside?'

'It's a secret,' he whispered.

'And who asked you to keep that secret?'

'If I tell, it won't be a secret, silly.'

'Was it Callum, Ollie? Was it Callum Oak?'

'Not listening. Can't hear . . .'

'Did Callum ask you to keep it secret?'

'Tra-la-la . . . I got my pointy things in my heary holes.'

'Oliver, please. I need to know the truth.'

He pushed himself upright and raised the humanoid from her seat. Then he tenderly wiped her smeared lips with a napkin.

'It's past bedtime, as a matter of fact. Pyjamas on, Kristal. Pyjamas on, Shanti Joyce. It's time to lock the door.'

He bumbled across the room and through the narrow doorway. Alone with Kristal, Shanti heard the lock turn, and a moment later Oliver returned, pushing a key into his shirt pocket.

'It's too late to leave now, Shanti Joyce. You'll have to sleep with Kristal and me. Although we don't sleep all the time, do we, dear?'

Shanti's fingers tightened around the pepper spray.

'Oliver Sweetman. Did you murder Kristal Havfruen at

Mangrove House on the afternoon of the twenty-second of July?'

His flame-coloured head twitched with confusion.

'Now you've done it, Shanti Joyce ... Now you made me kill you too.'

'Ollie, if you do that, you will go to prison, and then who will look after Kristal?'

His face was puffy and red. His eyes blinked rapidly as he approached her, arms outstretched, fingers opening and closing in the air.

Shanti retreated to the back of the room and grabbed the mannequin by the arm. It was heavier than she'd expected – not hollow like a shop dummy, but a dense mass of resin and silicone. She managed to yank it from its seat and drag it towards her, carrying the tablecloth with it and sending Kristal's bowl tumbling to the carpet, where soup splattered like a massacre.

Oliver was shaking. 'Don't you touch her, Shanti Joyce! She ain't done nothing to you.'

'She's not real, Oliver! She's made of plastic! Look!' She pinched Kristal's cold cheeks. Poked her in the ribs. 'She doesn't make a sound, does she? That's *because she's not real!*'

Suddenly Sweetman towered over her. 'You're frightening her. She doesn't like that. Ollie don't like it neither. Put her down now. Otherwise you know what I'll do ...'

Shanti snatched the canister from her bag and pointed it at him. 'Stop right there, Oliver, or I'll spray this in your eyes. It will hurt.'

'Don't care! Want Kristal.'

He drew closer. Shanti aimed the canister at his spherical

face and pressed hard with her forefinger. Nothing except a weedy hiss. The damned thing was empty!

As Sweetman circled the chaotic table, she scanned the surface for a weapon. In desperation, she seized a small knife beside the sponge cake.

'That little knife won't hurt me,' sniggered Oliver. 'I'm not a cake.'

'It's not for you, Ollie.' And in one swift movement she brought the knife to the mannequin's neck. With her other hand, she pulled at Kristal's hair so the polymer neck was exposed. 'Stay right where you are, Oliver Sweetman, or I will cut her throat.'

Sweetman froze.

'I'm going to go now and you are not going to follow me. If I hear you behind me, I swear I will kill her.'

Sweetman slumped onto the settee and buried his face in his hands. 'Don't! Don't! She didn't do nothing to you!'

'Hand me the keys from your pocket, Oliver.'

He dumped them sulkily on the table like a schoolboy relinquishing contraband. With the cake knife held tightly to the mannequin's throat, Shanti backed out of the lounge and along the corridor towards the door. Sweetman sat motionless, his lower lip trembling. Fumbling behind her, Shanti unlocked the door and kicked it open with her heel. Then she stepped backwards down the steps.

As she retreated from the chalet, she dropped the cake knife and let the dummy swing by its arm at her side. Using her free hand, she pulled her phone from her pocket. She was about to call for backup when she heard an inhuman howl, and pivoted to see Sweetman lunging at her, arms outstretched, face crimson, like a hysterical child. 'Give her back to me!' he bawled, tugging at Kristal's legs.

Shanti hauled in the other direction, and to her dismay, Kristal's right arm came away in her hand. Sweetman stared aghast, then carefully laid the dismembered body on the ground and lunged at her.

Rotating the resin arm above her head, Shanti swung it hard and made contact with Sweetman's head with a thud. The big man emitted a groan and then tumbled backwards, cracking his skull against the base of the dovecote, from which a cooing flock exploded into the night.

In seconds, she was upon him. By the time she had handcuffed his wrists behind his back, many curtains were twitching along the avenues of Paradise Park.

As Sweetman groaned and stirred, Shanti heard the sound of a fast-approaching vehicle, the throaty roar of an engine from somewhere behind the chalets, and suddenly a red Vauxhall Astra came hurtling towards her.

It whirled around the dovecote and skidded to a halt in a burst of squealing tyres and scorching brakes.

Chapter 21

The Arm of the Law

As Caine leapt from the driving seat, the glare of his headlamps illuminated Shanti in the act of hauling a dazed and handcuffed Oliver Sweetman into a sitting position against the column of the dovecote. At her side was a disembodied arm.

A little further away, near the steps of the static home, lay a one-armed corpse, its white mini dress splattered with red.

'Shanti! Shanti! Are you OK?'

She rose to her feet and stared at him intently.

'OK, I'm going to ask you one question, Vincent Caine, and I want an answer right away.'

'All right,' said Caine. 'I'll try.'

'Where is Paul? If you tell me that you have left my son on his own in the middle of a forest, I will have you prosecuted for neglect.'

'Hold on, Shanti. Of course I didn't.'

'So where—'

'Paul is with Zeb.'

'Zeb? Who the actual fuck is Zeb? He's a voice on the phone. I've never met him. And neither has Paul. Does he even exist?'

'Relax, Shanti. Paul is one hundred per cent safe, I guarantee it. Zeb is the local youth leader and has four kids of his own. I left Paul playing snooker.'

'You had so better be right.'

'Trust me, Shanti. I would put my life in Zeb's hands. I couldn't just let you handle this on your own.'

'I handled it, Caine.' She pointed a foot in the direction of Sweetman, who was groaning softly.

'I can see that. But why didn't you call for backup?'

'I did. Eventually. Benno's on his way now.'

'Was he violent, Shanti? Did he attack you?'

'Wait a minute, Caine. I haven't finished *my* questions yet. How did you do that? The squealie car thing? You don't own a car. You can't even drive a car.'

'I never said that. I said I don't *like* to drive. This is Zeb's car.'

'I need to speak to Paul.'

'Of course. You've got Zeb's number.'

'Keep an eye on him,' she said, nodding towards Sweetman. 'He's a bloody maniac.'

As Shanti wandered off to make her call, the doves hovered and descended like migrants returning to their homeland.

In the distance, Caine heard the faint wail of sirens. And from all around, in the glow of Victorian street lamps, the bemused residents of Paradise began to emerge nervously from their static homes, in dressing gowns and nightwear and string vests and underwear.

'Can you keep back, please?' he called to the gawping crowd. 'This is a murder inquiry.'

There was an audible intake of breath.

'Not our Ollie.'

'Like a big dove, he is.'

'Soft as a feather.'

A bald gentleman wearing nothing but a bath towel and round spectacles stepped forward and tugged Caine's sleeve. 'I don't want to teach you your job, young fellow, but that body over there with the missing arm? I don't think it's real. That's tomato soup, not blood. Ollie wouldn't kill a real person.'

'Thanks,' said Caine. 'It's a bit complicated . . .'

The night was split with sirens and pulsing lights as Benno's Ford Focus led a patrol car and an ambulance rapidly along the drive towards them.

Shanti returned looking happier.

'Everything OK, Shanti?' asked a blinking blue Caine.

'He potted the black. And there's a nice girl looking after him.'

'One of Zeb's daughters. She's a sweetheart.'

'I'm sorry, Caine.'

'No problem. You have good reason to be protective.'

'I was in such a hurry. It felt like everything rested on this. My life, my career, my reputation.'

'Hey. It's OK. You did well.' He rubbed her shoulder gently.

She smiled at him. 'I like that you broke your holy oath of non-driving to rescue me.'

'Shanti, I've never known anyone in less need of rescuing.'

'Sweetman killed Kristal. He more or less admitted it. In any case, the mannequin puts him at the scene. It still reeks of formaldehyde. He's been living with her, Caine – as man and wife.'

'Poor Ollie.'

'Poor Shanti. He was all set for a *ménage à trois*.'

When the paramedics who had been examining Sweetman were satisfied, Benno hauled the big man to his feet.

'Do you want to do this, boss?' he asked.

'Oliver Sweetman, I am arresting you for the murder of Kristal Havfruen, at Mangrove House, Devon, on the twenty-second of July. You do not have to say anything. But it may harm your defence if you do not mention when questioned something which you later rely on in court. Anything you do say may be given in evidence.'

'No, you killed her . . . you killed my Kristal!' sobbed Sweetman.

'Shall we take him to the station, boss?' asked Benno.

'I don't want to go on no train,' Sweetman wailed.

'He's very confused,' said Shanti. 'I don't think we'll get much out of him here, poor man. But there is one person I'd like to talk to.'

She pointed towards the diminutive figure of the park's proprietor amongst the crowd. He was immaculately dressed in striped pyjamas, dressing gown and slippers.

'Mr Leggit, we'd like a word, please.'

As the neon convoy retreated, Shanti, Caine and Leggit sat on a bench beneath an ornate lamp post, looking across at Shangri-La, which had been sealed off in preparation for the crime scene investigation team. The bench appeared to be another Sweetman creation, artfully constructed from interwoven driftwood, with a cat on one arm.

'I can't believe Ollie would be involved in this,' said Leggit, shaking his head in disbelief. 'Paradise will never be the same again.'

'Mr Leggit,' said Shanti, 'I'm going to ask you to cast your mind back to Saturday the twenty-second of July.'

'I'm sorry, but I can't remember back that far.'

'It was the day of Kristal Havfruen's murder ... Mr Leggit, please, I need you to concentrate.'

'I didn't know anything about that murder until the following day, when my wife saw it on the news. Saturday is changeover day, you see. It's the busiest day of the week in Paradise.'

'How about we approach it another way, Mr Leggit?' suggested Caine. 'Have you ever noticed any unusual visitors on those Saturdays? People who don't arrive with luggage, perhaps, or who don't check in with you?'

'Now you've put me in a tizzy. You see, my wife and I have to clean the short-let chalets on Saturdays. Most people don't realise how much work is involved in running a place like this, but there are folk coming and going all day long. As for unusual ... well, I remember a naturist family who turned up one Saturday, and that needed some careful handling. We sometimes have a clown from Chard for a children's tea party. He was unusual too – blue and yellow hair. But he made the children cry so we sent him away. People don't like clowns any more and I'm not sure why.'

'Anyone else? We're thinking of people who might have visited Oliver.'

'Ah! Well you said unusual. Mr Oak often comes on a Saturday to collect Ollie. He drives a silver estate ... a Volvo, I think.'

'Busted!' muttered Shanti.

'But there's nothing unusual about that. Ollie sometimes worked over there at the weekend, so I would certainly have seen him in July, quite possibly on the day you mention.'

'Back of the net!' whispered Shanti.

'That's helpful,' said Caine. 'How about anyone else? Did Ollie have other visitors?'

'Ollie has lived here for years and years. I know him extremely well and he's the kindest gentleman you could ever meet. I simply can't believe he would hurt anyone. You should see him with his doves. They're more like homing pigeons – they follow him wherever he goes and literally eat out of his hands. I always think that you can tell a lot about people by the way animals respond to them.'

'That's very true,' said Caine. 'But you see, we think someone might have made Oliver do something terrible without him realising it. That's why our questions are important. What other friends did he have?'

'Everyone! Everyone was Oliver's friend.'

'Visitors from outside the park?'

'A little old lady in a small car like a Golf. She came several times over the years. I remember because she was a heavy smoker, and we don't allow smoking in Paradise.'

'Ah! Can you tell us more?'

'I encourage people to leave their cars at the top car park and walk. Safer for children and animals, you see. But she was partially disabled so she used to drive down to Shangri-La, then Ollie would help her into a wheelchair and push her around, showing off his handiwork. I remember this clearly because it seemed odd to see a lady in a wheelchair with a cigarette in her hand. I pointed out the No Smoking sign, but she responded with such a sweet smile that I let it go.'

'And why did she visit Oliver?' asked Shanti.

'I think they were old friends. She would sometimes take him out for the day in her car.'

'Could you put a date on any of these visits? That Saturday in July?'

'Oh dear . . . possibly. I don't monitor Ollie's movements, you know.'

'Hang on,' said Shanti. 'I saw a security camera in the reception lodge . . .'

'Yes, we have several on site.'

'That's wonderful. So you can retrieve footage?'

'I'll trust you to keep this to yourself, but they are all dummy cameras. As I said, we never had crime in Paradise until you lot came along.'

'Thank you, Mr Leggit,' said Caine. 'That's been most helpful. Will you promise to call if you think of any other details? No matter how trivial.'

'I will. And will you promise that Ollie will be well looked after? In many ways he's a genius, but in other ways he's a child. He'll be terribly disorientated and anxious about his birds.'

'You have my word,' said Caine. 'I'll keep an eye on him myself.'

Shanti's Saab and Zeb's Astra drove in tandem back to Lyme, where Shanti had to prise Paul away from the older girls who were making a fuss of him.

'It's late, darling,' she said. 'Amma will be worried. Say thank you to Zeb and goodbye to Caine.'

Paul hugged Caine and climbed peacefully into the passenger seat of Shanti's car, where he promptly fell asleep.

'He's exhausted, poor lamb.'

'That was a long walk he did earlier.'

'Oh yes, I'd forgotten. And then he must have walked all the way back to Lyme with you.'

'Well, he rode on my shoulders most of the way.'

'You're very good with him, Caine.'

They stood beside the Saab, high above the twinkling lights of Lyme.

'So,' said Caine. 'What are you thinking?'

'It pains me to say it, but you were bang on. It's exactly what you said – a symbiotic crime. It's too late tonight, but tomorrow morning I'm going to arrest the person who planned Kristal's murder and coerced Oliver into killing her.'

'And that person is . . . ?'

'Caine, you know who it is.'

'Marlene.'

'Oak.'

'Did you say Marlene, Caine?'

'Did you say Oak, Shanti?'

'Jesus, and I thought you were a professional. Let me spell this out for you. Oliver is on the payroll, right? He is completely malleable and does exactly what Oak tells him. On top of that, Oak has a big, *big* motive – Kristal humiliated him for decades: deprived him of sex, mocked his painting, et cetera et cetera. He was also skint. By murdering Kristal, he gets rid of the woman he hates and solves his financial difficulties by inheriting a fat stack of Danish krone . . . Wait a minute, I haven't finished. Oak also had the perfect opportunity. He had keys to Kristal's studio and not a single soul saw his movements. His alibi doesn't stack up, Caine. On the afternoon of the twenty-second, when he claims he was walking the dogs on the beach, he could have been anywhere. I reckon those stinky dogs pooed in the garden while their master bullied poor old Ollie into stuffing his wife in a glass tank.'

'Woo!' said Caine. 'That is a very impressive list. And it would be completely convincing except for one thing . . .'

'Which is?'

'Which is that you're wrong. I think you're forgetting how symbiosis works. Listen, Oak and Sweetman aren't complementary. Oak is a strong man too. He could have carried this out on his own, so why would he enlist Sweetman to help?'

'I don't know . . . Maybe he didn't have the guts to do it himself. Maybe he wanted to finger Sweetman. Balls to symbiosis, Caine. Tomorrow morning we are heading to Mangrove House, where I will take the greatest pleasure in bringing that pious bugger to justice. I bet you a jar of honey I'm right.'

'Organic?'

'Organic.'

Chapter 22

Doughnuts at the Deathbed

On the way to Mangrove House the following morning, the discussion resumed as if it had never ceased.

'So I was talking to Paul about your symbiosis theory,' said Shanti at the wheel.

'You're coming round to it?' asked Caine, drawing cryptic symbols in his notebook.

'Jesus, Caine, you really haven't thought this through.'

'How so?'

'OK, think about this – Paul said you came up with all this superstitious jiggery-pokery when you noticed some kind of fungus growing against a tree.'

'That's true.'

'And what kind of tree was it?'

'An oak tree.'

'Exactly. An oak tree. Get it? Oak! The universe is speaking to you and you're not listening. Now, if you remember, I supplied you with a long and credible list of motives that make Oak the killer. Can you give me even one decent reason why you think he's innocent?'

'I looked into his eyes.'

'You looked into his eyes! And tell me, what did you see in there?'

'Shanti, Callum is a deeply moral man and a sensitive artist. That's why Kristal was able to walk all over him.'

'And what about Sweetman? Everyone described him as gentle too. He keeps doves and plays mini golf and has cake for tea. But he is a twisted killer, as I nearly experienced myself. He also has sex with dummies.'

'It's not the same.'

'Detective work is about motive. What was Marlene's motive?'

'She was in love with Callum.'

'But that was years ago. She fell out of love with him, remember? Trust me, Oak is our man.'

'I do trust you, Shanti. But my intuition tells me that you're making a mistake.'

'And what is that based on? Your third eye? This is a murder investigation, DI Caine. Not a men's workshop in the sweat lodge.'

'Ah, maybe you're right. This is why I'll never make a good cop. To be honest, I find the whole thing deeply upsetting.'

'What are you upset about? Tissues in the glove compartment, by the way.'

'I'm upset about all of it – Ollie, Art, Tess ... Police work destabilises me. It knocks me off centre.'

'Listen, I don't give out compliments easily, but you *are* a good cop. But you need to leave feelings out of it. Feelings are

great in families and, you know … relationships. But solving a
crime requires cold, hard logic. Cops are scientists, Caine. Ask
me about my emotions.'

'OK, what are your emotions?'

'Right now, I am pumped for action. Like an Amazon war-
rior. I think today is going to be massive. Right … We're here
now, so leave your notebook and your feelings in the car.'

They climbed out and walked towards the high sunbeam
gates of Mangrove House. They were closed and locked, with
weeds growing around the stone gateposts. Even from here, they
could see that there were no vehicles near the house.

'It doesn't look like Mr Oak is home,' Shanti muttered. 'How
very convenient.'

'He's probably shopping. Or in church.'

'Church, my arse. He's done a runner. He'll have heard about
Sweetman by now and he's shitting his corduroy breeches.'

Caine pulled off his coat and bundled it through the car window. 'I'll take a look around,' he said.

Shanti watched as he swiftly scaled the gates and dropped to
the other side, as fluid as a jaguar, then jogged briskly up the
drive. He circled the house; checked a shed or two; nipped up
the spiral staircase by the garage, from where he scanned the
gardens and peered into Oak's studio.

In five minutes, he was back at her side. 'You're right, there's
no one home. The dogs are indoors, but Callum has laid newspaper on the floor and piled their bowls with food. It's as if he's
away overnight.'

What Shanti thought was: You agile bastard. You're not even
out breath!

What she said was, 'Benno, get me an ANPR on Oak's

vehicle. Got the details? Silver Volvo estate: Golf One Five Sierra Alpha Juliette Yankee. Super-fast. Over.'

Then she paced restlessly about the Saab, waiting for a response. 'Are you ready for this, Caine? I'm Shanti Schwarzenegger today. I'm on an Oak hunt.'

Caine seemed more relaxed. 'How's Paul?' he asked.

'He's better. He's with my mum. But he's calmer. He wants to learn how to meditate.'

The phone buzzed in her pocket.

'Benno, that was quick . . . He what? . . . Is he now? OK, great work . . . No, we won't need backup. We've got this covered. You know what Caine's like when he's after a scalp – a bloody animal.'

She fired up the engine and the vehicle was moving before Caine was fully inside. As he fastened his seat belt, Shanti gunned up the lane, gravel spitting from beneath the tyres.

'The ANPR cameras picked him up on the A30, heading west towards Bodmin. Benno will get back to us with more up-to-date sightings.'

'What are you thinking?'

'I'm thinking that Callous Callum the Killer is a desperate man. I'm thinking that he's heading straight for Falmouth. That's the place he knows best . . . It's where all the anger began.'

'Shanti, can I make a suggestion? Why don't you simply call Callum and ask him where he's going?'

'Oh, Caine, you really are the sweetest cop in the force. I bet villains feel warm all over when DI Caine nabs them.'

They hurtled past the outskirts of Exeter, pushing 110 mph over the long flank of Dartmoor. Shanti adjusted a dial until she found Radio Devon.

'Ooh, I used to love this one!' she said, cranking up the volume. '*You gotta search for the hero inside yourself*... What kind of music do you like, Caine ... ? Pink Floyd? Björk? Manfred Mann?'

'All kinds of stuff. I'm a big Philip Glass fan. I like Brian Eno, too, especially the early stuff like *Music for Airports*.'

'Don't know that one. I'm a soul girl really – anything you can dance to ...'

'You're really enjoying this, aren't you?' said Caine with a wry smile.

'Don't tell me you didn't get a kick out of that drive last night. All the squealie-wheelie stuff.'

'To be honest, I prefer a spiritual journey.'

'Guess where he is now?' called Benno from inside the dashboard. Shanti dipped the music.

'Um ... heading towards Falmouth?' she suggested.

'How did you know that, boss? Yes, he's an hour ahead of you. Let me intercept him before someone gets hurt. We've got three units within twenty miles. Over.'

'Do you ever watch cricket, Benno? You know what happens when too many players run for the same ball? This is my catch. Over and out.'

To Caine she said, 'Learn from me, Caine. You have to get inside the killer's head. Like an actor, you know? Best scenario: Oak's wandering tearfully around the art school looking for his lost virginity. Worst scenario: Marlene knows that Oak has murdered his wife and he's terrified that she'll squeal. He's killed once. How much trouble is an old lady? It would take two minutes with a pillow.'

'Shanti, I really don't think Oak is a serial killer. But if he does do something silly – to himself or someone else – and you refused backup, that could terminate your career. You know that. Why take the risk?'

She said nothing. Just gritted her teeth, pushed her foot down, and stared down the asphalt towards Land's End.

As the old gold hands on the marketplace clock pointed to 10.25, they touched down in Falmouth. By 10.27, Shanti was reversing into a tiny space on Vernon Place behind Oak's silver Volvo, thirty yards from Marlene's door.

'Gotcha!' she breathed as her heels hit the pavement.

With hands cupped over eyes, she peered into the depths of Oak's car, then legged it along the row of terraced houses, built for a smaller, more peaceful age.

Thrusting her thumb against the doorbell, all she heard was the wind, and the distant wail of gulls.

Marlene's bell was deceased.

She rapped and pounded on the door. Gave it twenty seconds, then ran around the back. Caine chased after her, along a narrow cobbled alleyway where washing fluttered like families dancing upside down.

'This is the one,' said Caine, opening the latch of a knee-high gate. They stepped into an unloved yard where a brown bra hung stiffly on a line. In an ashtray beside a white plastic chair, cardboard roaches and cigarette stubs spumed like lava. The door of the small conservatory was open, and they slid into the tropical interior, as hot and heady as a hemp rainforest.

Shanti tested the handle into the house and nodded. They entered the kitchen.

'Marlene!' she called. 'Marlene!'

No answer.

Caine followed her into the art-filled sitting room. The house felt cold. No one had sat here for a while. Something about the place felt wrong.

Like a gunslinger in a Western, he pirouetted around the banister and crept up the carpeted stairs beside the Stannah stairlift. Shanti followed, treads creaking under her boots. The atmosphere was thick with nicotine and dust, like a pyramid inhabited by chain-smoking mummies.

Caine skulked along the sloping corridor, checking out an olive bathroom fitted with grab bars and hoists like a geriatric gymnasium. Another door opened into a spare room, filled with a spare bed and a lifetime's spare things. At the far end of the landing, a low pink door bore an enamelled Monet name plaque: *Marlene*.

Slow as a sloth, Shanti turned the handle and they stepped cautiously into the claustrophobic interior, where a dozen candles burned.

Marlene was laid out on the bed. Eyelids closed deep within their sockets. Cheekbones protruding like hips. Her parchment hands encircled a ceramic bowl filled with dog ends as though it was a holy icon. The room reeked of tobacco and warm urine.

Callum Oak was kneeling with his back towards them, hands raised in supplication. He wore coffee-coloured corduroys and a white grandad shirt with vermilion braces. The back of his curly head showed the first signs of balding.

In his raised hands he held aloft a stubby bible and a silver cross, which sparkled in the light of the flickering flames.

'Step away from the body,' ordered Shanti. 'Move slowly, Mr Oak, so I can see your hands.'

Callum Oak turned to face her. His palms still raised. A never-ending prayer tumbling from his lips.

'Callum Oak, I am charging you with the murder of your wife, Kristal Havfruen, and also the lady beside you, your friend Marlene Moss.'

Oak stopped praying, dropped his arms and stared at her in disbelief.

'Will this be a weekly occurrence? Accusing me of murder, I mean.'

'What did Marlene ever do to you, Callum?'

'But I never touched Marlene!'

On the bed, Marlene's thin eyelids sprang open, and she smiled. 'Someone's using my name in vain,' she said.

'Jesus! Marlene! You're alive!' said Shanti.

'Another excellent observation from the West Country constabulary.'

'But then ... then what is *he* doing here?' said Shanti, pointing at Oak.

'I've been leading us in prayer,' he said.

'Leading us into sleep more like,' said Marlene. 'It's the bible readings that send me off. We should tape it, Ms Joyce, and sell it to insomniacs. We'd make a fortune.'

'I'm sorry. I'm rather confused.'

As he rose to his full height, Oak's curls grazed the ceiling. 'Look, I don't see that this is any of your business, but Marlene phoned me to say that the illness had reached a critical stage, so I drove down to share her vigil.'

'It's true!' wailed Marlene theatrically. 'The Grim Reaper has me in his cold embrace.'

'I'm sorry, Marlene. How long have they given you, if you don't mind me asking?'

'A week. A month. The worst thing is, I just paid my car

insurance. Someone give me a drink, for Christ's sake. I'm absolutely parched.'

Callum took a glass of water from the bedside table and gently raised her fragile head. She pecked at the liquid like a pigeon in a puddle, then irritably brushed him aside.

'Do the fun bit again, dear. You were arresting Callum ...'

'Yes, um ... Callum Oak, I have reason to believe that you coerced Oliver Sweetman into murdering your wife. What do you have to say?'

'Don't just stand there, Callum,' snapped Marlene. 'Speak up for yourself for once in your life.'

'Look, I've had enough of your insinuations, Inspector Joyce. I hear you arrested poor Ollie last night, but unless you have some actual evidence against me, I'd ask you to leave the house immediately.'

'Hooray!' said Marlene, whose voice had been restored by the water. 'You tell her!'

Caine stepped forward and gently took hold of the old woman's hand. 'Marlene, perhaps the best thing would be if you told us the whole story from beginning to end. I'd like to know exactly what happened on the day of the private view. Here, let me sit you up a little.'

He plumped the pillows against the bedstead and raised her feather-light body.

'Ooh, such strong hands!' sighed Marlene. 'Now there's a real man! Razor-sharp detective skills, too. I spotted that intellect the moment I saw him. Get out the cuffs, DI Caine, and bear me away.'

'We've been through this, Marlene,' said Shanti. 'I'm trying to arrest a murderer, not someone who's been growing wacky baccy in the conservatory.'

Marlene fixed Shanti with her beady eyes. A wicked smile flickered across her emaciated face. 'You underestimate me, Inspector Joyce. If you will allow me to misquote Elizabeth I, "I may have the body of a weak and feeble woman, but I have the heart and stomach of a cold-blooded serial killer."'

Every eye in the room was fixed on the weeny woman half submerged in a cumulus of pillows.

'Ah ha! Just look at you all! You don't know whether to believe me or not. Well, if I was handing out the gongs at the police ball, I'd give a big shiny one to handsome Mr Caine. I'd make him wear a uniform, though.'

'Is this for real?' gasped Shanti.

'I don't know why you're all so shocked. That bitch had it coming for years.'

A hand shot to Oak's mouth, and he backed away from the bed as if the old woman had the plague.

'So tell me, Marlene,' said Shanti suspiciously. 'How did you carry out this offence?'

'Shall I tell her, or shall I take it to my grave? That's the question . . . I know, let's make a deal – if Callum pops downstairs and makes us all a nice cup of tea, then Marlene will reveal all. Does that sound fair?'

'I . . . I will do no such thing!' gasped Callum Oak. 'Marlene . . . I always thought of you as my dearest friend. Now you tell me that you killed my wife. Am I to believe you? Someone tell me – what am I supposed to do?'

Marlene sighed and lit a cigarette. 'Callum, I honestly don't care what you do. All I ask is that you run along and make the tea. I wouldn't swear to it, but I think there may be a bag of jam doughnuts in the larder. I'm sure Mr Caine would enjoy a doughnut.'

Oak backed towards the door with an expression of utter bewilderment plastered across his boyish face.

'You'd better hurry, Callum,' called Marlene. 'Otherwise I might be dead.'

Chapter 23

All the Deadly Details

Callum Oak's footsteps thundered down the stairs. They heard him gasping and puffing in dismay as he leapt four steps at a time.

Almost submerged in the bed, the emaciated old lady pulled deeply on her cigarette, a mischievous grin on her elfin face.

'Such a weak man,' she sighed. 'Handsome, but spineless. But look at me! I'm so spoiled. It's such a treat to have all these lovely visitors in my bedroom. Now it is rather a long story, so we may as well get comfy. There are folding chairs in the spare room, Mr Caine. And Ms Joyce, would you be so kind as to empty the potty? It's a bit whiffy, isn't it?'

When Oak returned with a tray, he was gasping with emotion. There were no clear surfaces amongst the numerous candles in the tiny bedroom, so he placed everything on the floor – plates, doughnuts, a teapot, four cups, teaspoons, milk and sugar. Caine thought of honey.

'Now gather round, children,' began the aged raconteur, smoke streaming from each nostril. 'It's story time!'

Shanti found her phone and furtively hit Record.

'To be honest, I would have gladly murdered Kristal the moment I laid eyes on her. I'm sorry, Callum, but that girl was so full of herself, with her little tits poking out like this and her little arse poking out like that. But it wasn't until years later, when I was diagnosed with this death thing, that the plot began to fully form into its magnificent shape. What did I have to lose, Inspector Joyce? Bugger all is the answer to that. All those hours I spent waiting in hospital corridors, reading my Agatha Christies, until eventually I thought: if not now, then it will never happen. By a stroke of fortune, I had already begun to squirrel away the odd bit of ketamine each time I visited Mangrove House. Art was always careless with his powders, and the original plan was to give myself a happy exit to the hereafter if life became a bore. But with the help of Milly, Molly and Mandy, I was able to control the pain ... and by the way, Inspector Caine, I was quite wrong – all the plants *are* girls. Isn't that marvellous! Milly was just a slow developer, but she has a lovely head of bud now ...'

Oak, who had been uncomfortably perched on the end of the bed, rose to his feet. 'Sorry, would anyone mind if I opened the window? I feel rather queasy.'

He jiggled the sash until it burst open. A smoky weather front departed the room and a blast of salty ozone burst in.

'On the day Art delivered the flowerpots, he told me about the ghastly show that his mother was planning with that silly man Spencer at the Meat Hook Gallery. All that pretentious nonsense and the absolutely puerile "happening" in the final gallery with the melodramatic music and spotlights and the

ridiculous pretend Kristal floating in the glass tank … as if
Damien Hirst hadn't done the same thing thirty years ago. Pah!
I know Hirst and even he would have laughed. And as for the
masters … Turner would have spat in her eye! Frida would have
smacked her silly bottom. After Art had gone, I sat in my living
room smoking my little spliffs, ruminating on your painting,
Callum Oak. Suddenly, it was as if the Muse herself had waltzed
into the living room. A moment of pure artistic genius! It came
to me that there was a far more creative application for my ketamine collection.'

Oak groaned and shook his head in disbelief.

'Now for a sturdy young body like Mr Caine's here, or Ms
Joyce's, there would be no difficulty in carrying out my little
scheme, but look …' She raised the sleeve of her nightie and
flexed a bicep like a sparrow's. 'Nothing wrong up here.' She
tapped her thin hairline. 'But the old bod has seen better days. It
came to me that I needed an accomplice – someone with a bit of
brawn.'

'Ollie!' mumbled Oak like a terrified child.

'Do stop whimpering, Callum. And eat your doughnut or
give it to DI Caine. If you'd had the balls to deal with her years
ago, I would never have had to do this.'

She brushed ash from the quilt and sipped her tea.

'Yes, poor dear Ollie. Such an easily manipulated man.' She
sighed deeply. 'Of course, I didn't bother him with the details
until the day. He would only have got muddled. Now, as I said,
Art had told me all about this monstrous artwork Kristal had
planned, and that it would be collected from her studio on the
day of the private view. I realised there would be a window of
opportunity.

'You know how close I've been to the family, Callum, and in all those years I've never seen you miss a holy day of obligation. As luck would have it, the twenty-second of July is the feast day of St Mary Magdalene, which is rather fitting, since she was a fallen woman like me – I bet she liked a little wacky baccy too. So I telephoned the very helpful vicar of Branscombe and asked what time the service was due to begin, and how long it was likely to go on for. We humans are creatures of habit, Ms Joyce, so I also guessed that Callum would stop at the Fountain Head for half a pint of Branoc and a crab sandwich . . . Was I correct, Callum? I also calculated that Ollie would not be at Mangrove House, given that Callum was at church. So I left Falmouth bright and early and whizzed up to Paradise Park.

'How did I feel? Elated! Delirious with excitement! It was the first time I had used my little car for ages – and the last, as it turned out. It was a golden day. The sun was shining, and I had a *mission*, Ms Joyce! I'm sure you know how that feels. In my handbag, I carried a hypodermic syringe, which I had pilfered from the nice nurse who visits me. It was pre-filled with enough ketamine to take down a mammoth. I stopped only once, at Trago Mills, to buy a large polythene sheet. As I expected, I found dear Ollie feeding his doves. At first he was reluctant to break his routine, but after a little persuasion, he warmed to the idea of a day out with Auntie Marlene.'

Oak, looking decidedly nauseous, clutched his bible and stared with increasing horror.

'On the way, he told me that Kristal had been particularly horrid lately – all spiky and agitated. On several occasions she had told him that he was stupid and useless. So I put an idea to

247

him: "Shall we help her relax, Ollie?" Oliver thought it was a splendid suggestion.

'I was delighted to find that no one was at home at Mangrove House except Kristal, tearing about in her studio like an insane poodle, barking into her phone and generally being the puffed-up prima donna we all loved to despise. "What are you doing here?" she shrieked at me. She was wearing the usual ridiculous pre-teen clothing. "You know I cannot be disturbed when I am preparing for a show." Ollie smiled that lovely innocent smile of his and, just as I had instructed, moved behind Kristal to grab her, enveloping her entire torso and arms. She started screaming. I popped open my handbag, and then—'

Callum had turned a bilious shade of green. He rushed from the room and vomited copiously into the avocado toilet bowl.

'A weak constitution,' sighed Marlene, lighting another cigarette from the stub of the old one. 'It's all that religion that does it. Where was I now . . . ah, yes. Ollie had a good grip on her, but she made such a song and dance that he began to get distressed. That's when I moved in as fast as the old pins would allow. I *plunged* the syringe deep into her jugular – decades of studying anatomy classes really paid off – and pressed it home. I must admit that my hands are rather shaky these days, so it wasn't the neatest job, but it did the trick. Within seconds, that abominable screeching subsided and Kristal went all flippety-flop in Ollie's arms. "You see," I said to him. "She's all relaxed and happy now, Ollie. She's having a lovely, lovely sleep. Night night, Kristal!"'

Oak staggered back into the room, wiping his mouth with a handkerchief. His bloodshot eyes fixed on Marlene and his mouth opened as if he was about to speak. But no words were forthcoming.

Marlene smiled triumphantly as she continued. 'My main concern was the disposal of the body, preferably with a degree of elegance and drama. Getting away with my crime ... well, that was just a bonus. But I've never been afraid of doing bird ... Is that the expression, Ms Joyce?'

'Not since the 1970s,' said Shanti.

'I'd love to pretend I had every detail planned in advance, but to be honest, it wasn't until I was standing in Kristal's studio that the Muse really came up trumps. As Ollie laid her out on a couch, I noticed a boxed object sitting on a pallet by the French doors, ready for collection. It was plastered with FRAGILE stickers and I guessed that this must be the centrepiece of Kristal's self-indulgent pageant. It was all in such poor taste, Ms Joyce, that was the thing I really objected to! Poor aesthetics would be an imprisonable offence if I had my way.

'I asked Ollie to remove the plywood packing, and inside was the glass tank with an astonishingly lifelike replica of Madame Havfruen floating within. Bingo! Bingo, Mr Caine! Bingo, Ms Joyce! Ollie is so good with his hands, it took him only moments to unscrew the lid, and oh, the stench of that formaldehyde! How it aggravates the breathing. Nonetheless, needs must. I instructed him to don rubber gloves and a mask and apron, which were readily available in the studio. Then I told him to carefully remove the effigy from the tank. He appeared a little distressed and doubtful at this stage of the proceedings, so I promised that he could keep synthetic Kristal as a reward for his labours. He cheered up quite a bit at that, and laid the vile mannequin on the polythene sheet as instructed. Then as gently as a parent bathing a newborn, he lowered the real sleeping Kristal inside the tank. It took a bit of poking about to create that nice foetal position, but he managed it in the end.

'It was perfect! I knew that Kristal would be drowning peacefully, avoiding all that disagreeable thrashing about, so she would look beautiful for her big night, just as she would have wanted . . . Oh, Callum, you're not going to vomit again . . . ?'

The bathroom door banged.

Marlene winked confidentially. 'Frankly, it was a merciful end for a woman who deserved none. Then it was plain sailing. Ollie re-boxed the tank and we sped away in my little car, giggling like infants, with synthetic Kristal tucked up in the boot. This was his prize: to keep a kind, gentle Kristal forever – a new, improved version of the woman he'd always adored. One who would never utter an unkind word. He was absolutely thrilled. And he promised, promised, promised to keep our little secret.

'Back at Shangri-La, we had tea and took it in turns to shower and dress for the private view. Although I did my best to dissuade him, I just couldn't prevent him from taking Kristal into the shower with him. Distasteful as it was, at least it washed away some of that formaldehyde.

'We arrived at the gallery in plenty of time, and it was the crowning moment of a perfect day to witness the awe with which my masterpiece was received. Huge fun! And of course I pretended to be as shocked as everyone else. Ollie was as good as gold, but to be honest, I dread to think what became of that poor mannequin when I dropped him off back at Shangri-La that night . . . All those pent-up emotions.'

There was a stunned silence. Even Caine, who had been convinced of Marlene's guilt, was slow to speak. Eventually he managed a question that had been troubling him. 'The gloves, plastic sheet and syringe. Where did you dispose of them?'

Marlene dismissed the question with a flick of her hand. 'I'm no master criminal, Mr Caine, but I've never understood why murderers dump incriminating evidence so close to the scene for the boys in blue to find in minutes. I flung the syringe over a bridge outside Axminster, where it must have plopped into the river. The sheet we discarded on a farm close to Paradise Park, one of those places covered in pools of slurry and cast-off farm equipment – the kind of spot where bad smells are par for the course. As for the gloves, Ollie shoved them in a bin outside Sainsbury's in Chard.'

'So you killed Kristal because she was a prima donna and a bully?' asked Shanti, with a note of hostility in her voice. 'Or was it because she thwarted you in love so many years ago?'

'Oh no, dear. I mean, all of those reasons are perfectly valid. But my motive was infinitely grander. I killed Kristal to save Art.'

'Art, your godson?'

'No, silly girl, not A Boy Named Art – I'm talking about *Art*, the lifeblood of humanity! When Kristal came to Falmouth as a student with that horrible, licentious sex show, she turned my beloved school upside down. Many people claimed that she was good for the place – look at the Havfruen Building and all the money that flowed in. But over the years, I had lovingly, *painstakingly* created a hothouse of creativity, where the heirs to Velázquez, Rembrandt, Ingres, Delacroix and Cézanne bloomed. Where did all that "performance art" and "conceptualism" leave my painting school? I'll tell you where! Unloved! Underfunded! Dying, Ms Joyce … as I am now. Kristal had the audacity to claim that she gave birth to Art, but as far as I was concerned, she murdered Art itself. And for that . . . I killed her.'

The wind had left Marlene's sails. She slumped into the pillows like a deflating balloon.

'Can I say it now?' asked Shanti.

'All right by me,' said Caine.

'Marlene Moss, I am arresting you for the murder of Kristal Havfruen. You do not have to say anything, but it may harm your defence if you do not mention when questioned something which you later rely on in court. Anything you do say may be given in evidence.'

Marlene rallied a little and her cloudy eyes sparkled. 'Oh, how utterly marvellous! You've no idea how long I've waited to hear those words. Will I get the flashing lights? And the big burly constables? And the sirens? Don't forget the sirens, I beg you.'

'First we'll need to verify everything you've told us,' said Shanti. 'But if it turns out to be true, I'm afraid you'll be in no position to demand anything.'

'But I will go to prison? Surely I will. I demand a life sentence.'

'I hate to disappoint you, Marlene,' said Caine, 'but given your health, it's more likely that you will be cared for in a secure hospital.'

'Oh really! That doesn't seem fair at all. This was premeditated murder, Mr Caine.'

'Marlene, I honestly don't think prison is the place for you.'

'Well, look, supposing we add a few more offences?'

'What sort of offences?'

'Oh, all kinds of things. For example, do you remember Ratty, the painting tutor I mentioned who committed suicide by flinging himself off a cliff? He took me out to paint the hills and sky, but it turned out the only hills Ratty had in mind were these.' She lifted her breasts like empty paper bags.

Shanti and Caine stared in disbelief.

'We were working side by side on the clifftop and he kept coming over and pawing me, so I used my easel to give him a little shove. I didn't mean to send him to his doom, but it was rather satisfying. I spread a rumour that he had been driven insane by Kristal's happening – you know, *Preconception*. I couldn't believe how easily I got away with it. Then murder became a habit, Mr Caine, and I've always had a problem with habits.'

The tiny bedroom fell silent. All eyes were on the old lady sucking the last breath of nicotine from the stub of her cigarette.

'Murder is like smoking,' explained Marlene Moss. 'It's just so moreish!'

Chapter 24

The Motel on the Moor

The final departure from Vernon Place was not what Marlene had hoped for – horizontal in an ambulance rather than hand-cuffed in a wailing patrol car.

By the time Shanti had released Callum Oak, debriefed the SOCO squad and overseen a full search of Marlene's house, it was after 9 p.m. She called home and spoke to Paul.

'Sweetheart, I'm sorry. I thought I'd be back hours ago . . . but guess what?'

'What?'

'You were right about symbiosis. We cracked the case. I'll tell you all about it when I see you.'

'Tonight?'

'No. Not tonight. I'm still in Cornwall. I won't be home until very late, or tomorrow. But Amma will look after you, and listen, Paul . . . I've got some holiday coming up. We're going to spend lots of time together. What would you like to do?'

'Go to Caine's place. Sleep in a hammock.'

***

Plump raindrops tumbled onto the windscreen, and following an hour stuck in roadworks outside Truro, it was after 11 p.m. by the time they reached the lonesome wilderness of Bodmin Moor.

The satisfaction of concluding the case had crumpled into sheer exhaustion. Shanti realised they wouldn't arrive in Lyme Regis until the small hours, and then Caine would have an hour and a half's walk through the Undercliff, and she would have another hour's drive to Yeovil.

The man was annoyingly telepathic. 'There's a motel up here on the moor. It's a bit of a dive, but we can get a meal and a shower and a bed.'

'Two beds.'

'Of course that's what I mean. Pull in over there and we'll see what it's like.'

The Blisland Motel was quite possibly the most depressing place Shanti had ever seen – a drab single-storey building within rumbling distance of the A30, fronted by a potholed car park full of heavy goods vehicles. But she was freezing now and it was an effort to keep her eyes open.

In the motel reception, a bowl of ancient potpourri on the untidy desk battled with the odour of overcooked vegetables. Above a filing cabinet, a faded picture of a wild Bodmin pony was draped with a lonely strand of tinsel from a long-forgotten Christmas. The pony looked as weary as Shanti felt. She pinged a bell on the desk. It was a full ten minutes before a large woman in a nightie appeared.

'We're closed.'

'We were hoping to get two rooms.'

'Fell out with your chap, did you?'

'He's not my chap. We're work colleagues.'

'None of my business, I'm sure. But there's only one twin room and I haven't made the beds.'

'Is there another hotel around here? Or a B and B?'

'Ha! Not for miles. It's a nice room. Views across the moor. We've got a star, you know.'

'What do you mean, you've got a star?'

'Some places don't have no stars. We got a star and we do a nice breakfast.' She leaned across and whispered, 'I wouldn't mind getting cosy if he was *my* colleague.'

'For God's sake. Can you get us some sheets? And I want a discount too, or you won't have that star for much longer.'

The room was large, with two single beds. Shanti had brought no nightclothes and not even a toothbrush. But that wasn't the worst thing. To her utter dismay, she noticed that the bathroom had been constructed behind nothing more than a glass screen at the end of the room. With a cautious finger she slid back the door and took in an array of hideous details: algae around the shower, stray pubic hairs, crescent nail clippings by a half-full bin, a mottled mirror, and a commune of watching spiders.

'Caine, I need a shower. And I need to get to bed. So bugger off and meditate or walk on the moor or something and don't come back till I'm in the land of the fairies. Is that OK?'

He grinned at her. 'Do you want me to sleep in the car? That would be fine.'

'Yes. No. Shit. Just give me half an hour, OK. And here ... make your sodding bed.'

She hurled a set of nylon sheets and pillowcases in his direction.

***

Despite the rumbling traffic, Shanti plunged into a bottomless sleep. She dreamed that she was still driving while the incessant rain hammered on the windscreen. In the passenger seat beside her sat the skeletal form of Marlene Moss. 'Marlene?' Shanti asked. 'Was it really you? How could you do that? How could you kill Kristal?' The old lady turned to tell her something of great significance, but when she opened her mouth, her face was that of Munch's *Scream*.

She struggled to wake, and when she did, she found that a sickly dawn was breaking outside the worn curtains, and the relentless sound was not the rain on the windscreen but water pounding on the glass screen, behind which her work colleague, Vincent Caine, was soaping his athletic body.

Shanti lay motionless beneath the viscous sheets and found she could do nothing but feign sleep and watch. Well, she could have closed her eyes or turned to face the other way, but that would have been sort of . . . wasteful. Still in her dreamy stupor, the sight of Vincent Caine appeared to her as a bronzed vision, his toned torso formed an elongated triangle from wide shoulders to lean waist. For a full ten minutes she was obliged to spy through her fingers as Caine raised his face in ecstasy to the streaming water. She contemplated the sparkling rivulets cascading down the furrow of his spine, the chiselled dimples of his buttocks and it was without doubt the most unsettling thing she had ever seen.

How much easier it would be if Caine had some obvious defect – a sagging beer paunch; a dense coat of ape-like hair; a tiny gerbil's penis. She would never mention his shortcoming, but she would always know that her colleague was not quite as perfect as he pretended to be. But as he worked shampoo through his long tresses, and she took advantage of his tightly closed eyes to fully scrutinise his anatomy, it became evident that none of these things were true. Caine was as faultless a physical specimen as ever walked the earth. His abdomen was as honed as a peppermill; his golden skin was smooth but for a silky black trail connecting navel to pubic hair. And his penis was shockingly long and sleepily beautiful.

Supposing they teamed up on another case? How could she work with him now? How could she delete this data from her hard drive? She lay rigidly unmoving as Caine dried himself carefully, dressed and slipped from the room. And later, as they sat opposite each other in the Blisland Breakfast Bar, cautiously prodding their one-star breakfast – tinned pineapple and a soft-boiled egg for him, the Full Cornish for her – her mind returned again and again to the steaming spectacle of Caine's muscular waterfall body, which had nothing – absolutely nothing – to do with the case in hand and the pressing business of the day.

They drove silently through the morning, lost in their own thoughts. Near the clock tower in Lyme Regis, Caine climbed out of the car. He slung his bag over his shoulder, waved once and began to walk away.

Shanti wound down her window and called to him.

'Caine ... come here a moment.'

He returned to her window and smiled. For the first time, she acknowledged that maybe Dawn Knightly had been right. There was something strangely attractive about the man.

'Listen ... I should say thanks and everything.'

'You're welcome.' Jesus, his teeth were white.

'And I was wondering ... maybe this is a bit much to ask, but

Paul has developed a bit of a thing about sleeping in a hammock. I'll have to wind things down at the station, which could take a week or two, but if you're free and it's not too much trouble, I guess we'll need a debrief, if you know what I mean. There are still a few loose threads that need tying up . . .'

'Let's do that, Shanti. Let's tie up those loose threads.'

Caine stood watching the Saab heading up Broad Street. When she had gone, he turned up the collar of his coat and set off in the direction of the Undercliff.

The silence of the forest was like a tonic. How he longed for the solitude of his cabin. Life was so much simpler on your own.

And yet she talked about threads. Against all his instincts, a slender thread seemed to run from his heart back towards the town, up Broad Street and all the way along the winding West Country roads and lanes to the strong, brown-eyed woman in the retreating Saab.

She had called it a debrief, but Caine sensed something beyond the call of duty from this unexpected visitor in his life.

As she neared Yeovil, the brown-eyed woman was experiencing something that she hadn't felt for a long time. It was such an unfamiliar sensation that she had trouble naming it . . . Happiness, that was what it was. She cranked up the dial on the radio, singing loudly all the way.

On the industrial outskirts of town, she ran into heavy traffic, and as she accelerated in slow fits and starts, her eyes wandered to a huge billboard advertising, of all things, meat-free soya sausages. Below the words *TENDER AND SATISFYING*, a vast glistening sausage was impaled on a fork.

She found herself blushing, and then laughing out loud. What the hell was wrong with her? Too much time on her own.

She drove into the silent cul-de-sac that was her new home, and when she saw the apple-faced boy with the football, her own face lit up with joy.

Chapter 25

The Wings of a Dove

Caine showed his ID to the guard at the barrier. He was pleased to notice that beyond the high mesh fences, the many windows of the secure hospital overlooked fields and woodland.

He was directed towards a reception desk in the main building, where a male nurse and a female doctor assured him that patient C193 Oliver Sweetman had settled in nicely and was in good spirits – his ready smile and obliging ways had already made him friends on the ward.

'So long as he can get into the gardens, he seems perfectly happy,' said the doctor. 'I'll take you to find him if you want.'

Caine followed her along a maze of magnolia corridors and through a TV lounge where the troubled souls of society sat out their days. Along the way she talked about the many challenges of balancing care with custody.

'The public have a right to feel safe, and our service users, as we call them, need to have their mental health issues treated humanely and effectively.'

'And none of that comes cheap,' said Caine.

'Everyone here is considered a danger to themselves or to others,' said the doctor, as she tapped a code into an airlock security door. 'I know about Oliver's culpability in the Havfruen case, but a man like that wouldn't last a week in a mainstream prison.'

'I agree,' said Caine. 'Thankfully his lawyer did a good job. He successfully argued that Ollie couldn't be charged because he didn't have the capacity to form a criminal intent.'

They stepped into the gardens, where men of various ages wandered around the gravelled paths with visitors or nurses.

Caine spotted Oliver on a bench, his orange hair in shocking contrast to the green rhododendron leaves.

'Hello, Ollie. Remember me?'

'Hello, Vincent Caine. You want to see what I made?'

'I certainly do.'

Caine and the doctor followed the big man along a neatly edged path towards a tidy grassed area surrounded by trees and brick buildings bristling with security cameras.

In the centre of the lawn stood an extraordinarily elaborate structure on a thick wooden post. It was a dovecote, but infinitely more elaborate than the one at Paradise Park. This was a veritable palace for doves, with dozens of arched doorways, staircases, delicate crenellations, spires and turrets.

'It's astonishing, Ollie!' said Caine. 'I'd love to know where it all comes from.'

'From the workshop over there,' Oliver said.

'We heard that Ollie liked making things,' explained the doctor. 'So we gave him access to the workshops. Then he built this incredible thing, and one of the gardeners helped him to instal it.'

Oliver seemed to be in a dream, a distant smile on his face. He was staring through the high fence at the countryside and the pale sky beyond.

'I think he's a kind of a genius really,' said Caine. 'It's a shame he doesn't have his birds any more.'

'That's what I was going to tell you,' said the doctor. 'It was like magic. One day we saw him standing here, staring up at the sky, just as he is now. We couldn't work out what he was doing, and then ... well, you'll see for yourself.'

Oliver's hands were raised in front of him like Francis of Assisi, and from out of the heavens, first one, then two and then three white birds descended.

As Caine and the doctor looked on, an entire flock of doves appeared like angels. They settled all over the dovecote palace and on Oliver's arms and shoulders and the top of his flaming head.

'They must have followed him from Paradise Park,' said Caine. 'Just like homing pigeons.'

'There's my girls,' said Ollie happily. 'There's my beauties. Fly free, my lovelies ... fly free ...'

Chapter 26

I Cannot Put You Down

'I know what you're thinking, Caine.'

'I wasn't thinking anything.'

'Jesus, Caine, it's not even possible not to think.'

'That's what you think, Shanti.'

There was a long pause. But out here at Caine's cove, those silences felt as easy as the lull between waves.

Behind them, at the edge of the forest, Paul slept soundly in a hammock cocoon slung between two trees.

Caine watched the smoke from the campfire. Eventually he said:

'So what do you think I was thinking?'

'That you were right and I was wrong.'

'See, Shanti, this was always my problem as a cop. I actually don't believe in right and wrong, or good and bad. The Buddha didn't either. He reckoned that there is skilful action and unskilful action. Skilful action is what benefits you and other beings. And unskilful action is what impedes the journey.'

'Well I don't know how that would work in a court of law. Anyway, look, I've got something for you . . .'

She rummaged in her bag, and passed him a jar in a paper bag.

'Organic honey, like I promised. Now we're square. You did good. I did good. I don't want to hear another word about it.'

Caine smiled and thanked her. He shoved another piece of driftwood onto the flames, sending a surge of sparks towards the stars. The summer was at an end. A sprinkle of gold had tumbled over the Undercliff.

'So I guess that's it, Caine. The Havfruen case is closed. Marlene will go to trial in a few months – if she lasts that long. Then the press will go crazy for a few days and the whole thing will settle down.'

The kettle began to boil and Caine wrapped a towel around one hand and removed it carefully from the fire. Slowly and methodically, he made tea.

The slogan on Caine's mug said: *Born-again Buddhist (and again and again and again . . .).* The slogan on Shanti's mug said: *I can't believe it's not Buddha.*

'You deserve some time out, Shanti. Relax. Do stuff with Paul. You are always welcome here, you know that.'

'Thanks, Caine, that's exactly what I'm going to do. I feel I've proved something to the Yeovil crew, and I've proved something to myself as well. But you know what else this case has proved, don't you?'

'What's that?'

'It proves that you are no longer sick. The Super is most impressed with your efforts. He says he can't wait to welcome you back to the team.'

'I can't go back into that station, Shanti.'

'Not even to work with me?'

Maybe he imagined it, but it seemed that Shanti had shifted a fraction closer on the sand. He unfolded a blanket and wrapped it around her shoulders.

'The thing is, DI Caine, although you're a bit of a freak, we're almost like mates, aren't we?'

'Almost. Now, you said there were some loose threads?'

'There are a couple of things. I wondered if you ever heard from the Danes?'

'Of course. I meant to tell you. This is unbelievably bizarre! You're not going to believe it . . .'

'You know what, Caine? My credulity has been stretched so far since I met you . . . It's like giving birth – you think you can't stretch any further, but somehow you do.'

'I got a message from Aksel. Remember him?'

'Rasmussen's nephew.'

'Right. Him and brother Carl are setting up an art museum in Copenhagen. It seems there's been a huge resurgence of interest in Kristal's work since her death, so the Rasmussen family have invested a small fortune in a permanent Havfruen collection, taking up an entire floor.'

'I won't be visiting.'

'They already have the body casts. And Spencer persuaded Callum to sell them *Preconception2*, the steel sculpture in his garden. I expect he was glad to see the back of it. But here's the thing . . . it seems that Spencer finally pulled off a deal on that unique and priceless Havfruen artwork he was talking about.'

'Do I want to know this?'

'The church authorities wouldn't allow Kristal's glass coffin to be buried at Branscombe, so . . .'

'Oh no!'

'That's right. Kristal's coffin was filled with formaldehyde and resealed. She will be gazed upon forever.'

'That's obscene! Is it even legal?'

'It's what she would have wanted.'

High above Shanti's head, the indigo sky was pricked with inestimable pinholes, a reminder of how tiny and insignificant her troubles were.

'Is that everything, Shanti? Is that all the loose threads?'

'You know it isn't.'

'I'm sorry, I don't understand.'

'Listen, Caine. I've been honest with you, haven't I? You know everything about me. You've met my mum. I've talked about my dad. Paul thinks you're his best mate. And I've even told you about my divorce.'

'It's true. You are incredibly open.'

'But this is it. I don't know anything about you. Not one thing. You are an enigma. A man of mystery.'

'There's nothing to tell.'

'You're such a liar, Caine. You call yourself a Buddhist . . .'

'A Buddhist is just someone walking a path. I never claimed to be enlightened.'

She glared fiercely with those big brown eyes.

'Let me know when that happens, Vincent Caine! In the meantime, maybe this is a bad idea – you know, you and me and Paul on the beach.'

'Mum! Be quiet!' called a voice from the cocoon.

'Oh, I'm sorry, Paul. It's just that Caine is—'

'I mean, why don't you be quiet and listen to Caine?'

'Jesus. OK. Right, go back to sleep, sweetheart. I won't shout any more.'

She lowered her voice. 'OK, I'll be straight with you, Caine. I probably shouldn't have done this, but last time I visited the cabin, I noticed a photograph face down on the ... what do you call it?'

'The shrine.'

'Right. On the shrine. That's Papa Caine, isn't it?'

There was another pause. But this one was awkward. Uneasy. Tense.

'Thing is, Caine, in a normal house – my house, for example – there are photos everywhere. I mean, we literally have an entire wall in the kitchen covered with pictures of the family. There are even a few of my ex, you know, for Paul's sake. But as far as I can tell, that weird little photo, face down on the ...'

'On the shrine.'

'Yeah, the shrine. Well, that's the only image you have of your family ... So it does kinda make a girl wonder ...'

Caine said nothing. He sipped his tea and stared into the embers.

A long time passed. And then Shanti said, 'You know what? Forget it. I was beginning to think that you were different from other men. I thought you were all about honesty and openness and being in touch with your feelings.'

'I'm sorry, Shanti. It's hard. Can I just say that some stuff happened? A long time ago. It's like a shadow in my life. I am trying to deal with it, but it's something I have to do alone.'

'What are you saying? Are you telling me that you were a bent cop or something?'

'No, of course not! Nothing like that. All of this happened when I was practically a kid. I was a victim – just like Ollie and Tess and even Art. It's the reason I left home and went travelling. That's how I ended up in the forest monastery in Thailand, and it was the best thing that ever happened to me. One thing they taught us is that actions have consequences, and the consequences of what happened in my family were huge. That's all I can say right now. I know you want to tie up all the loose threads, but life isn't always that simple. One day I will tell you everything. I promise I will.'

'You know these mugs, Caine?'

'What mugs?'

'Your mug collection.'

'OK.'

'Did you take them into work when you were based in Yeovil?'

'I don't know. Maybe.'

'You see, this is why people laugh at you. It's time someone told you the truth – these mugs are just terrible. In fact, Vincent Caine, your mug collection is the shittiest mug collection in the West Country. Maybe the whole world.'

'That seems a bit harsh. You haven't seen them all.'

'*Seen them all?* You're trying to tell me that you have a mug that will change my mind?'

'I'm sorry, Shanti. I'm sorry about the mugs and I'm sorry I can't be more open with you. I hope you will forgive me some day. But I will tell you something . . .'

'Go on.'

A flame danced in each eye.

'Remember that first morning, when you walked into the cabin?'

'How can I forget?'

'It was like a ray of sunshine entering my life.'

She felt herself melting. It was hard to be angry with a soft man on the soft sand.

'OK. Maybe I was a bit unfair about the shitty mugs. They're *your* shitty mugs after all. You know what? Let's forget all about it. Let's forget about Kristal Havfruen. Let's forget about your dark and sordid past. It's very beautiful out here. It's good for Paul, too. Tell me one of your stories, Vincent Caine. A nice story.'

She shuffled a little closer, and the heat of their bodies was warmer than fire.

'A story, eh? Well, after I left home, I went wandering. I visited many places and eventually I was drawn to the monastery in Thailand. You know the saying? "When the student is ready, the teacher shall appear."'

'I think I read that on a shitty mug.'

'That's possible. Anyway, I stayed in the forest for nearly three years. We meditated for hours each day and studied the Dharma, which is the fundamental teaching of Buddhism—'

'Hold on – did you shave your head and wear robes?'

'The whole thing. At night, I slept in a dormitory with ten other students from all over the world. We became close friends, and every evening our old teacher, Tu, would tell us stories – you know, Buddhist tales thousands of years old. Some of them were really funny, and some were very wise.'

'Go on. Tell me one.' She lay on her back at his side.

'Let me think ... OK, well an old Zen master and a young monk are walking in the mountains. After many miles, they come to a river and meet a young woman trying to cross to the other side. She's a guest at a wedding and she doesn't want to spoil her beautiful clothes. Without a thought, the old master bows, lifts her in his arms, carries her across the river and sets her gently on the other side. When she is gone, the master and the student walk on in silence.

'After a few hours, the old man realises that the young monk is kind of seething. "What's the matter, son?" he says. "You seem troubled." The young one replies, "Master, I can't believe what you did back there!" The old man isn't aware that he's done anything lately except sort of *be*. "What did I do?" he asks. "What? You know perfectly well what you did! Remember that young woman – the outrageously beautiful young woman by the river with the golden nose ring and the long fingernails ... Well, you literally picked her up and you literally carried her across that river. And we are *so* banned from touching women!" The old monk smiles, and then he says, "Listen, my son, I literally left her on the riverbank. But you, it seems, are still carrying her."'

'Is this another of your sexist folk tales, Caine? About the predatory powers of women?'

'It's thousands of years old and it's kind of a sweet story.'

'But what's it got to do with you? Or with me?'

'This is the problem, Shanti. I'm that young monk. And I literally cannot put you down.'

'Jesus, Caine!'

'Would you do one thing for me?'

'Possibly.'

'We've known each other a little while, and I wonder if there's any chance you could call me Vincent? You know, instead of Jesus Caine.'

She laughed and said she'd think about it.

They watched the smoke rise to the stars, and for the first

time in her life, Shanti truly heard the silence. So deep, it was like noise. Without realising it, she found she was resting her head in his lap, and she felt peace settle in every cell of her body.

'Sometimes ... not very often ... I'd quite like to kiss you, Vincent Caine.'

'That's OK. I could live with that.'

'But then I remember I'm a professional and you are my work colleague.'

'There's no harm in a kiss.'

'But the trouble with kissing is it's a gateway drug.'

'What does that mean?'

'You start with kissing, and before you know it, you've moved onto the hard stuff.'

'And the soft stuff, Shanti ... Don't forget the soft stuff ...'

Chapter 27

Six Months Later

The swarm of journalists around the main doors of Yeovil police HQ buzzed like an agitated wasps' nest.

From her elevated position on the top step, Shanti looked down at a churning sea of TV crews, flashing cameras, waggling woolly microphones and numerous vehicles bristling with aerials and antennae and satellite dishes.

'DI Joyce? DI Joyce! Can you give us a statement?'

'One at a time, please,' said Benno at her side.

Shanti waited for calm. Then she began to speak.

'Now that the trial has concluded, I am able to make a final statement about this unusual and distressing case. In August of last year, we made two significant arrests. One of the accused, Oliver Sweetman, was deemed unfit to stand trial and is now receiving psychiatric care. We have reason to believe that Mr Sweetman, an otherwise gentle and talented man, was coerced into this brutal act by a devious and manipulative woman who had killed on previous occasions.'

'Was that Marlene Moss, Inspector?'

'Yes, the person I am referring to is an eighty-four-year-old retired art teacher from Falmouth named Marlene Moss. However ...'

She paused for the buzzing to abate.

'However, I am sorry to say that earlier this week, as a result of a long-term illness, Ms Moss passed away before the judge was able to pronounce sentence, thereby evading justice. There are no winners in a case like this – simply a number of victims who have lost a great deal. I want to pass on my sincere condolences to the families concerned, and in particular, I'd like to take the opportunity to offer my apologies to the victim's husband, Callum Oak, who suffered a double misfortune. Not only did he have to cope with the sudden loss of his wife; in addition, he had to put up with the media ... and with me and my team, who were in a hurry to solve this case as rapidly as possible. Thanks for bearing with us, sir, and I would like to convey my warmest wishes to you and your family.'

It was as if a stick had been poked in the nest. 'Inspector ... Inspector Joyce, did you have a partner on this case?'

'Thank you. I'd like to acknowledge the dedicated work of the whole team, led by Sergeant Bennett to my left. But yes, there were two detectives leading this inquiry. I worked hand in glove with DI Vincent Caine.'

'Is that the man they call Veggie Cop?'

'Hasn't Caine retired from police work?'

'What was the nature of your working relationship?'

'Inspector Caine has previously taken time out on leave, but he was fully invested in this case and it is doubtful it would have been solved so smoothly and effectively without his contribution. It was a pleasure to work with someone of his calibre. In fact, it has been noted that DI Caine and I have complementary skills – you could almost call it a symbiotic relationship.'

'DI Joyce, people are describing you and Vincent Caine as the West Country's new crime-fighting duo. Can you say something about that?'

'Will you be working together on future cases?'

'Ha, well I don't know about that. You'll have to ask DI Caine himself. DI Caine? Is he here? He was here earlier . . .'

In a light rain shower at Swanvale cemetery in Falmouth, a modest burial ceremony was drawing to an end.

Apart from the impassive undertaker and his entourage, there were only two mourners at the funeral of Marlene Moss. In the damp shadows at the back of the graveyard, a tall, long-haired man in a black coat brushed a tear from his eye. Some distance away, a younger man in a rumpled suit and pointy boots stood silently in the mizzle that drifted in from the sea.

When the perfunctory ceremony had reached a conclusion and the coffin had been lowered into the grave, Caine walked over and shook Art's hand.

'It was good of you to come.'

'She was my godmother. I knew her all my life. At least I thought I knew her.'

'Perhaps we never fully know anyone. Least of all ourselves. I thought perhaps your father would come . . .'

'Don't go there. Dad practically had a meltdown trying to choose between doing his Christian duty by coming to the funeral, and the fact that Marlene turned out to be the devil incarnate. In the end, he decided to battle it out on canvas.'

'Good decision.'

'Yeah. I'm trying to persuade him to take over Mum's studio and sleep in the big bedroom, but he says he's happy where he is.'

'These things take time, Art. But I'm glad to hear he's painting. Callum has a huge talent, as you know.'

'Yeah, his work is changing. Like he's beginning to find himself again. Saul went over to Mangrove to take a look and he was well impressed. Don't say anything, mate, but there's a chance of a Callum Oak show at the Meat Hook next year.'

'And what about you, Art?'

'I'm OK. I'm getting my shit together. Maybe I'll go travelling or something. I haven't touched so much as a spliff in weeks.'

'Not even a little snifter this morning?'

'Christ ... yeah, all right, I had a toot before the burial, but after today ...'

'It's your choice, Art. In the end, everything is our own choice. A teacher once said that drugs are spiritual baby food.'

'Fuck, that's deep! I'll have to think about that one.'

'You squeaked through this by the skin of your teeth. But now you're free. If you make wise choices, you will have an amazing life.'

'Yeah, thanks, Caine. All cops are bastards, but you're better than most. You saved my life, you know that?'

'It's good of you to see it that way. I suppose you wouldn't have been halfway up a cliff if we hadn't visited so early in the morning. Listen, I won't pretend I approved of that relationship with Tess. You know it's only because she refused to cooperate that you didn't go before a judge.'

'That's because she loves me.'

They had been strolling along a narrow pathway between the

graves. Now they paused at an intersection where the path divided. Caine could see the red Alfa Romeo below.

'That's my car down there. You want a ride back to Lyme?'

'Thanks, but I have a return ticket to Axminster and a book to read. But come and see me any time if you need support.'

'Yeah. I might do that. That's decent of you.'

'Have you noticed? We're standing at a crossroads. From here, the path divides. Make a choice, Art. Walk towards the light.'

'For a cop, you talk in weird riddles.'

'I don't think I am a cop.'

'Well if you're not a cop, what the fuck are you?'

'I'm a human being, just like you. So while I'm at it, I'd like to pass on one more piece of advice. The fun stuff is just that. It's fun. Then it's gone. But it's actually the hard times that teach us. Times like this – times of adversity – are an opportunity to awaken and grow. Sit with the suffering, don't try to dull the pain. Here, borrow this. I've read it anyway . . . Catch!'

'What's this?'

'Poems by Rumi. My favourite is called "The Guest House".'

'Cheers. I'll check it out. Like I say, you're a weird one, Vincent Caine – cop or no cop. But I'm kind of glad I met you.'

They shook hands and went their separate ways.

The man in the black coat. And the boy named Art.

This being human is a guest house.
Every morning a new arrival.

A joy, a depression, a meanness,
some momentary awareness comes
as an unexpected visitor.

Welcome and entertain them all!
Even if they're a crowd of sorrows,
who violently sweep your house
empty of its furniture,
still, treat each guest honourably.
He may be clearing you out
for some new delight.

The dark thought, the shame, the malice,
meet them at the door laughing,
and invite them in.

Be grateful for whoever comes,
because each has been sent
as a guide from beyond.

Jalal ad-Din Rumi, reproduced with the kind
permission of the translator, Coleman Barks

Acknowledgements

I am beyond fortunate to be represented by British Book Award Agent of the Year Madeleine Milburn, and her dynamic team, who provided rock solid support in the creation of this series.

Huge thanks to Publishing Director Krystyna Green, and her creative crew, for welcoming Shanti and Caine to the illustrious Constable family of crime.

Blessings and all good things to my talented friend, author and psychologist, Paddy Magrane, who inspired, supported and contributed so much to this book. May your path shine.

Thanks to serving police officer Mike Harper and bestselling author and former police officer Rebecca Bradley for insights into investigative procedure.

Alayasri and Suddhacitta for precious Buddhist teachings.

Coleman Barks, renowned interpreter of Rumi's works, for kind permission to reproduce 'The Guest House'.

Hugs to my shockingly brilliant friend Paul Blow, who created the stunning original cover art.

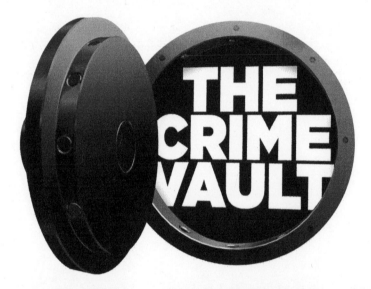